Just a Train Ride

By

Elizabeth Wehman

Summit Street Publishing

JUST A TRAIN RIDE

Published by Summit Street Publishing
131 West Grand River
Owosso, Michigan 48867

ISBN 978-0-9905580-4-0

ISBN 978-0-9905580-5-7

Publishing in the United States by Summit Street Publishing, Owosso, Michigan

Library of Congress Catloging-in-Publication data
Wehman, Elizabeth
Just a Train Ride/Elizabeth Wehman-1st ed.

20179112329

Printed in the United States of America
2017

10 9 8 7 6 5 4 3 2 1

Cover Photo: Emily E. Lawson Photography

Cover Art: Kristina Sweers

I would like to dedicate "Just a Train Ride" to all my family who have strived to be faithful in their marriages. They include my maternal great-grandparents David and Sarah Gray, grandparents Pearl and Wilbur Schnepp and Edward and Pearl Habermehl, my parents Jeanette and Floyd Habermehl. But most importantly, to my husband of 31 years, David Andrew Wehman.

"Many claim to have unfailing love, but a faithful person who can find? The righteous lead blameless lives; blessed are their children after them."
Proverbs 20:6-7

Acknowledgements

It's hard to believe that this is my third novel. I'm so thankful for all those who help me along the way with either encouragement, suggestions, and their expertise.

I'm always grateful to a husband and children who see the value in my work. They're often daily encouragers. Sometimes they give up "wife" or "mom" time so I can plug along in the process of this business. They pick me up when I'm down. They don't let me stop this crazy thing called, being an author. I love them deeply.

I'm also thankful to my family. Each and every one of them, either living or now gone, have played a part in this writing process. Their stories, their legacies, their willingness to keep going in life, even when life gets rough are incredible blessings to me. Thanks for letting me share those memories.

To all of my readers. You are amazing followers. You encourage me each and every single day with your well-wishes and questions like "is it done yet" or "where can I get my hands on a copy." Each and every comment encourages me to keep going. To keep striving to do better.

I'm thankful to my daughter, Emily, who is always patient with my writing endeavors, and this time used her amazing photography skills to capture exactly what was in my mind for this book cover. And to my sweet model, Liberty Schmidt, and her willingness to wear a heavy coat on a hot day in July to get my amazing cover photo.

I'm excited for you all to read this latest labor of love. I hope it encourages you. Inspires you to faithfulness in every endeavor you achieve in life. May this virtue never fade.

Elizabeth Wehman

Psalm 34:8

Chapter 1

Had it been a mistake to come? As Camilla Reynolds, Callie to close friends, struggled to keep up with her grandson, she shook her head in disgust. Out of breath, tired, and heart pounding like a freight train, this visit only proved one thing. This would be her last trip to Chicago alone.

She'd tell herself for weeks before traveling that she didn't need to make the trip. Her grandson was fine. He didn't need her anymore. Yet her longing to see him, especially on their annual visit just before Christmas, would win over her doubts. She'd strike out with as much enthusiasm as a woman in her eighties could muster. Convincing her heart she could do it like a woman in her fifties was easy, prodding her old body through Chicago's Union Station felt like a triathlon.

Callie felt her purse strap slip from her left shoulder. Why couldn't she remember to clean out her purse before traveling? The weight caused her elbow to ache, but even that was no match for the pressure and pain growing in her chest. They'd better find a seat in the depot soon, or she'd collapse from exhaustion.

Her grandson looked at her over his shoulder. Mason carried the rest of Callie's heavy bags. One suitcase was on wheels, which he pulled behind him. She needed to learn to pack lighter. Tighter. Except, what if

Callie needed a sweater in Mason's chilly apartment? And who liked running around on less-than-clean floors without slippers?

"Comin', Nana?" He stopped and turned around. "Gonna make it?"

She hoped he didn't see the moisture she now felt forming on her forehead, "Are we close to the sitting room?"

He nodded and held up his elbow with her backpack on it. "Yup, just up here. Not far. We're nearly to the stairs." He continued walking, heading in the direction he'd indicated to her. At the top of the stairs he turned again, "Why don't you wait here? I'll find a spot for you and then come back up to get you."

Callie nodded and stopped, "Thank you, honey." Grateful for a chance to breathe, she placed her duffle bag on the floor beside her, watching her grandson disappear down the staircase. Her head throbbed, her breath came in short puffs, the pressure in her chest subsided while she waited.

A man brushed past her. Then a young woman on a phone skirted around her. She realized she must have stopped directly in other passenger's ways. She turned just in time to see a whole family approach her. A man pushing a stroller, with three children gripping the bars on each side, looked at her as if she were as wide as the marble-floored aisle. Picking up her duffle bag; only made her arm ache more. Placing it back on the floor, she drug the bag backward, until she could lean against a wall. The family zipped past her.

People living in Chicago never failed to dumbfound her. Each going in a purposeful direction, oblivious to those around them. Common courtesy, like opening doors for older women, didn't seem to be necessary. If people were on the sidewalk, many were on their phones. Even standing on a street corner waiting to cross the street, people made no eye contact with anyone around them. It wasn't like back home where everyone chirped a greeting at whomever they met, whether they knew them or not. Callie would never understand city-dwellers.

Mason was such a sweet host when Callie came to visit. He always met her at the station with wide smiles and excitement. He seemed to love showing her around the place he called home. For a man of twenty-four, he didn't seem to fit into the mentality and temperament of the impetuous crowds around him. Callie felt sure she was a burden to him when she'd visit, but if she were, Mason never let on. Always a gentleman, his manners were impeccable.

Rarely home during the day, he would bring her dinner every night after work. It would usually be plenty for her to have leftovers for lunch the next day. She'd beg him to allow her to cook him dinner, and sometimes he'd give in and let her, but then he'd have to go out and purchase the ingredients she needed, which took up more of his limited time. Bringing home meals was nice. She liked to cook, but she enjoyed the many ethnic treats big-city cuisine had to offer.

It was almost Christmas, and a few blocks from his apartment was an authentic German market. He'd taken her there on one of her annual pre-Christmas visits. Shopping for anything was almost impossible due to the crowds, especially in the middle of the day, but the aromas of the German food made up for the discomfort. Partially German herself, she loved how many of the baked goods they found to purchase reminded her of recipes passed down from generations of grandmothers.

Some of those delicious baked goods had been packed in her duffle bag, now setting at her feet. Mason topped the stairs in a hurry, "Come on. I'd hate for someone to steal those cute fuzzy slippers of yours." He laughed, moaning as he picked up her duffle bag.

"It's not that heavy, is it, Mason?"

He winked at her, "Naw, it's just fun to give you a hard time."

Callie smiled at him as he grabbed her elbow to help her descend the staircase.

Callie held the railing with her left hand and Mason clutched her other arm. He'd found a bench close to the stairs. They could see her belongings clearly from the stairs. As soon as Callie reached the bottom step, she stopped to look around the majestic waiting room of Union Station.

The massive room echoed with the click of women's heels, the murmurs of waiting travelers, and even laughter. Giant wreaths hung above doorways. An assortment of decorated pine trees glowed in each corner. The only thing Callie wanted to do was take it all in. Mason held her arm but now urged her closer to a bench, and her belongings. As soon as she sat down, she looked up to see the two statues adorning an archway which took her back to a moment over seventy years before.

"Mason?"

Mason was placing her duffle bag at her feet, pushing her luggage closer to her. "Yeah, Nana?"

"This station brings back so many memories for me."

Mason smiled, "I know." He sat down beside her, pulling his cell phone out of his coat pocket, glancing at it. He needed to get to work soon.

"Your great-grandma and I sat right here. Although, it was much darker. They'd boarded up the ceiling windows because of the war. A building like this was considered a prime target for a bomb drop."

Mason nodded, "You sat right here," he pointed to the bench, "waiting to board a train for California. To see Grandpa."

Callie smiled and patted her grandson's hand. "I'm a boring old woman with lots of tales." She could finally relax enough to catch her breath, "I repeat too much."

Mason sat back against the bench and smiled, "It's a cool old building. I love coming here." Mason leaned into her, "Especially with you."

Callie couldn't get over how much Mason reminded her of Miles at times. How she wished he were here to see what a fine young man he'd become.

"I still like hearing your stories. This building always seems untouched by the smog of Chicago." He grasped her hand. "Thanks for coming. I love your visits. Sorry I'm so busy," He leaned closer and kissed her cheek, "I wish you lived closer."

Mason was such a sweet boy to lug her from and to the train station for her visits, entertain her while in town, and putting up with her incessant chatter without any complaints. She loved her grandson.

"So, you'd better get moving. I don't want you to be late." The handsome boy with the dark hair and blue eyes grinned at her. Every time he did, Callie melted. Even his dimple took her back to sweeter days. "I love you, Nana."

Callie leaned forward with pursed lips. He bent closer and she kissed his cheek. "I love you, too, kid. When I come back next time, I expect you to have found a beautiful girl to share your life with."

Mason laughed and stood, "Why would I need one of those, when I already have a beautiful woman like you?"

"You're such a good catch. These Chicago women don't know that because they rarely talk to one another." Callie motioned as if to include those seated around them.

Mason glanced again at his phone, "Are you sure you'll be okay here?" Then he mumbled, "I should have taken time off work this morning."

"I'm fine." Callie tried to sound determined.

Mason looked around as if he were trying to find someone to take over for him.

"Mason?"

"Hmmm?" He looked down at her.

"I'm fine." She shooed him away with her hand. "Get yourself to work."

"You'll manage this suitcase?"

"I managed to get it here. I'll manage to get it back on the train again. Anyway, look around; there's plenty of people to help me."

Mason looked down at his phone again. "I'm so sorry. I have to run."

"I love you."

Mason's eyes grew moist. "I love you, too, Nana." Walking away he called over his shoulder before going up the staircase, "Call me when you get home."

Callie watched the young man leave her. She worried about him in this big city. All alone. She had to remind herself that he was a grown man. Not that sweet little boy who used to visit her each summer. She wished he could find a sweet, young girl to love him, share his life with, especially so he didn't have to have takeout every night.

She breathed a silent prayer for him, asking God to follow him with His protection and grace. And then muttered, "You could find him a good wife." Callie chided herself for trying to tell God how to take care of her family. Young people seem lost until they find someone to share their life. Callie shook her head, realizing she was trying to justify her telling God what to do. Would she ever learn?

Callie took in her surroundings. A surge of memories filled her thoughts. She cherished each time she could sit and take it all in. People scurrying to catch a train or climb staircases. Everyone in such a hurry to get to their destinations. She loved sitting. God made old people lame and stiff so for once they would stop, listen, to see others. Everyone had a story, on a mission, enduring a life challenge, or missing someone they love.

Always drawn to people, Callie loved places filled with activity. Whenever she could sit and watch, she'd imagine what was happening to each person. She loved watching families teach their children how to sit still and quiet in a restaurant, trying not to grimace when it didn't seem important. She loved wondering where that middle-aged woman was traveling to and if she bought that bright-red purse while shopping in Chicago. Her imagination ran wild with endless possibilities.

Glancing down at her wristwatch, Callie noted the time. She hoped she didn't fall asleep on this bench and miss her train. That would be her. She'd have to call Mason and have him come down after work to retrieve her. Then she'd end up staying another night and they'd have to make this same trudge to the station again in the morning. She breathed a silent prayer that God would keep her awake.

The room was chilly from the freezing temperatures just outside the station doors. She pulled her coat up higher on her shoulders and zipped it to her chin. Then she smiled. God was answering her prayer. She rarely fell asleep when cold.

A lady across from her bench was talking to herself. Callie looked closer and noticed one of those clip-on phones attached to her ear. This world was seldom disconnected from electronic devices. Did people realize how silly they looked talking into the air? Once she had to stop herself from answering a question someone asked in the grocery aisle one day, realizing they were asking someone else.

Callie sighed. She missed Mason already. She thought about his parents, so far away. She wished they could all be together for Christmas, but Africa was too far away. Callie knew what she'd be telling Amy in her next letter about Mason. She also knew she'd brag him up at the ladies' meeting at church next week. Most of them had given Callie an earful when she had told them Mason was returning from the mission field to live in Chicago. Alone.

Even though Callie worried about Mason on a daily basis, she remembered how his mother had done on her first missionary adventure to a foreign country. She'd been all alone. Soon she found another to share her desire to minister to the African people and on her next furlough had married Mason's father.

Perhaps she'd get out a piece of paper and write a few ideas down of what she could tell her. She began looking through her purse for a pen and scrap piece of paper. As she was digging, finding neither, she heard shouting coming from the top of the staircase. Callie looked up to see a young couple making their way down the stairway.

"What do you mean?" A young man, about Mason's age, came after a girl carrying her luggage, backpack straps hugging her shoulders.

"You know what I mean." The girl stopped mid-way down the stairs and turned to the man, "It's simple. The answer is no."

"No, now?" The young man, hair bobbing too long on top and nothing on the sides, came down, crossed his arms, and stood in front of her. "Or never?"

'*What would possess him to look that ridiculous?*' Callie thought.

The girl shook her head. "No, now." She skirted around him and down the rest of the stairs.

The boy turned, cocking his head like he wasn't sure of her reply and added, "But why?"

Without turning back, the girl hollered back, "You're causing a scene."

She plodded over to the bench where Callie was sitting and sat down beside her. The young man looked exasperated, whipped off his glasses, slipping one bow of them under the top of his shirt, and stood in front of her.

"So, what do you want?"

The girl pulled her phone out of her pocket. "I need to think about it."

The young man sat down beside her. "Think about what?"

The girl poked at her phone. "I don't want to talk about this anymore. I'm going home for Christmas. Stop pressuring me." She never looked up at him, "I'll give you my answer when I get back."

The man folded his arms. "You drive me crazy."

The girl set down her phone. "See? Why would you want to do this. If I drive you crazy?"

"That's not what I meant."

"Well," the girl looked back at her phone, "that's what I heard."

The young man leaned close to her, looking as if he wanted to kiss her, but the girl shifted and ignored his advances. This seemed to make him even more angry. "I gotta go. You make no sense. The guys are waiting for me at the gym."

The girl ignored him, but kept pressing the buttons on her phone. Callie looked away, but it was hard not to overhear the heated conversation.

"Blaine. Look at me. Who are you texting?"

Callie couldn't help herself; she looked over again. The girl ignored him, set her phone down, and picked up her purse. She began rummaging as Callie had done just moments before.

The boy shook his head and stood. "Blaine?"

She stopped, but didn't look at the boy. "I'll see you in a few days."

As the young man walked away she called after him, "Have a great workout." It sounded as if she wanted to say something else, her tone less than encouraging.

Callie felt like she was intruding, even though she was just sitting there. That's when she heard the girl mutter quietly, "I hope you break a leg."

Pulling out an emery board, the girl began to file her nail. Callie watched the young man go up the staircase and not turn around. When he was out of sight, Callie decided to glance over at the girl. She was watching him. When he was completely out of sight, she put down her file and stared at her feet. She sighed heavily, sat back up, and fumbled through her purse. She was soon wiping her eyes with the back of her hand.

And that's when it happened. The weight of the conversation must have caused her more grief than Callie even knew because the young woman began to sob. Her shoulders shook, her moans audible to many around her, but in complete Chicago style everyone but Callie ignored her.

Chapter 2

Callie retrieved her purse and dug through it again. She'd thrown some of the leftover Danish from the German marketplace in this bag. Her ticket was close to the top, but her checkbook, wallet, expired coupons, and sales receipts impeded her search to find a tissue. She kept digging. Finally, at the bottom, was a rumpled, but clean tissue. She took it out of her purse, inched closer to the young woman, and handed it to her. The girl was doing another swipe with the back of her hand.

The girl gave her a disgusted look.

"It's not used. Just rumpled," Callie smiled. "I'm an old woman be thankful I didn't hand you a real handkerchief."

The girl took the tissue, muttering a, "Thanks." After one last hiccup of air, she blew her nose.

"You okay?"

The girl shook her head, "Men are stupid."

"Yes, they can be."

The young woman, placed her phone down beside her, leaned forward with her elbows on her knees, and rubbed her forehead.

Callie couldn’t help herself. "But...they can also be strong comforts. Handy to have around. Often times supportive and encouraging."

"What man do you know?" The girl gave her a 'are you stupid' stare.

"I had one." Callie sighed and stared down into her lap. "Once."

"Yeah. Well, I can't seem to find one like that."

Callie looked up. "Sometimes, we look in the wrong places."

The girl looked disgusted. "Probably." Her phone rang. She picked it up, glanced at the screen, and set it down unanswered.

The phone kept ringing. Callie glanced around the room. No one seemed bothered by it. Only a couple of people glanced up. But after the third ring, the girl picked it up again and pressed the screen. It stopped ringing.

Callie wanted to speak. Say something more, but she also knew, after encounters like this, it was better to allow God to control the conversation. If He needed her to speak, He would make it clear.

The girl glanced around the room. She turned around completely and looked behind her.

"Are you looking for someone?"

"I'm starving. No breakfast."

"There's food services through there, but you have to walk quite a ways."

The girl sighed. "I don't want to walk. I've done enough of that this morning."

"Hey," Callie dug back into her purse and brought out the carefully wrapped packet, "Danish?"

"What kind?" The girl gave her an odd, scowling look.

"It's delicious. My grandson bought it for me last night. To take home. It's apple."

"I guess." The girl nodded. "Are you sure?"

"Of course." Callie unwrapped the bundle and held it out for the girl to take her own piece. "It's from the German marketplace here in town. Their baked goods are delicious. Do you like almonds?"

The girl took a large bite, announcing as she chewed, "I haven't eaten anything this good in months." She took another bite. "Is that cinnamon?"

Callie dug into her purse one more time. Thank goodness Mason had loaded her up before going home. The girl seemed ravenous. She pulled out the pretty wrapped bag of almonds and pulled off the red ribbon holding the bag together at the top. She wanted to save it for Christmas morning, but sometimes other things are more important.

The girl ate all the Danish like she hadn't had food for a week. If she were going to eat Callie's treats, the least she could do was talk to her. Get this whole conversation rolling. Callie held out her hand. "My name's Callie. What's yours?"

The girl had flakes of Danish on her cheek and as she brushed it off she looked at the woman and shook Callie's outstretched hand. "Blaine."

"Nice to meet you, Blaine."

"Thanks for the food." She licked each finger clean.

Callie smiled. "Sure. It will look better on you than me."

Blaine smirked as she took a few almonds and popped them, one at a time, into her mouth.

* * *

Blaine wasn't sure how to take this old woman sitting next to her on the hard, wooden bench. The treats from her purse were good. She was starving. She could never eat like this in front of Kyle. His looks always made her feel unhealthy. Fat. She knew she had to be careful, as the only option while with him was starving herself.

"Where you headed?"

Callie smiled. "Home. Lapeer." She had the sweetest smile. "Michigan."

"Close to me. I'm going..." Blaine had to think fast. "Port Huron."

"I love Port Huron."

"Me, too." She hoped she liked it.

"Is that home?"

"Sure." Blaine took another few almonds from the bag now sitting between her and Callie. She thought quick. "It's where most of my family lives. Two brothers, two sisters'-in-law, and a new nephew. His name is Kayden." Blaine picked up her phone and scrolled through the photos she'd recently received in her messages. Quickly, she found the photo she wanted and held out the phone to Callie. "He's just three weeks old, born on Thanksgiving."

Callie took her phone and looked at the photo. "What a big boy."

"Ten pounds. Well, actually, nine pounds. And like, ten ounces." What else could she add? "His father is six-foot-two. So, he'll probably be big like him."

"He's adorable."

"I haven't seen him yet. I get only a few days off at Christmas. I can't wait to hold him." That sounded fairly honest. The food helped her to think quick.

"Well if you're going to Port Huron and me to Lapeer, we must be on the same train out of here."

Blaine placed her phone on the bench again. "Must be."

The old woman glanced around the room again. "I just love this old place."

Blaine nodded. "I saw on the news last night that children from the local schools were having concerts here the last few weeks. They do that during the Christmas season."

"That sounds wonderful."

Blaine added, "If you're around to hear it."

"What do you do, Blaine?"

She wouldn't have to think so hard for this one. "I'm a waitress. I use my tips to travel." Then added, "or go home for Christmas." Sounded nostalgic.

"That's a hard job." Callie said, adding, "I had a bookkeeping job once. Worked long hours and my pay really wasn't anything to write home about."

Blaine mumbled through a mouthful of food, "Did you like it?"

"The man I worked for was picky, all business."

"Aren't they all?"

An announcement broadcasted through the room, interrupting their conversation, "Amtrak train to Des Moines, Iowa will be leaving soon from Gate Four. All passengers with tickets may head to the gate now for boarding. Again, Amtrak passengers headed to..."

"Well, that's not us."

Blaine shook her head. "How long have you been in Chicago, Callie?"

"A few weeks. I often visit around Thanksgiving. My grandson lives here. There are so many wonderful things to see during the holiday season. The animated, beautiful store windows, and of course, the German marketplace full of beautiful decorations and treats." The old woman's face wrinkled as if she were in pain. "Although, every year it seems to get harder and harder for me to get around." She looked down at her lap.

"You should call an Uber."

She looked up, her face a bit brighter. "Oh, Mason was telling me about that. You call them from your phone or something and they come to get you? Like a taxi?"

"Yeah, they're great. I'm kinda scared doing it by myself, but when Kyle's around, that's the only way we get around town. We hate driving around Chicago, especially during Christmas. Too many tourists."

"Prices aren't really an issue with Mason; we just usually take a taxi."

Blaine worried she'd have enough money for a ticket. Thinking past that thought was daunting. She decided to use the money she'd save for Kyle's Christmas present on a one-way ticket. He didn't deserve a gift anyway.

"Are you finished with these almonds? I think I'll put them away now."

"Oh, sure. Thanks for sharing. I'm feeling a little better now."

"Didn't you eat breakfast?"

Blaine shook her head. "It's complicated. I don't feel so lightheaded anymore."

"You need to eat breakfast." Callie laughed. "Listen to me. I sound like an old mother hen. I'm sorry."

Blaine shrugged off the comment. This strange, old woman had cared more for her in the last few minutes than anyone had done in a long time.

***

Callie grew weary with worry. She wanted to be on the train. Blaine was busy looking at something on her phone.

Callie looked down at her luggage, again agonizing over the daunting task before her. Next time, she'd have to time her departure on one of Mason's days off, then he could stay to help her. Another reason for this to be her last time.

Whenever pressure would put Callie into worrying mode, she knew only one thing that would help. After eighty-four years of being on the earth, she had only one thing to do to put her mind at ease. She murmured a prayer to the One she knew would help her in any situation.

Looking up from her silent prayer, she saw a couple come down the staircase. He was tall, broad, and dressed in Marine blues. She had on a pretty red dress and shiny black boots. Her arm was wrapped in his, and they seemed as if the world was turning without them.

Callie looked on and remembered. The years floated away like balloons on a windy day. Everyone dissolved around her, and she couldn't take her eyes off the couple now sitting down across the aisle from her.

That first-found love. The moment when you look someone in the eye and know that, without a doubt, he or she is the one. In your eyes, they can do nothing wrong. At a single moment in time they cross your path, yet live in your heart forever. Each story about that encounter is different and unique. But for most, it's a moment a woman never forgets.

It's funny she would remember this moment, here and now. She had never been with Miles at Chicago's Union Station. While sitting in almost this exact same spot, it was only a promise of seeing him.

"Callie?"

She answered, "What?" Her eyes continued watching the couple across the way.

"Callie?" Someone touched her arm, which startled her back to the present.

"Are you okay?"

Callie nodded and smiled at Blaine. "I'm sorry. That couple over there, they just took me away for a few moments."

"Sickening, isn't it?"

Callie came fully back. "What? Sickening?"

"Yeah, look at her drool over him. Wait until reality sets in. Wait until he tells her she's fat or won't stop calling her while she's trying to balance a whole tray of plates, hot with food."

"What?"

Blaine picked up her phone and punched in another message to someone. "Makes me want to lash out irrationally."

Funny how a single moment can be looked at in such a different way.

"You seem to be into them."

"Who?"

Blaine looked at her as if she weren't listening to anything she was saying. "Them." Blaine pointed with her phone. "You seemed a million miles away."

Callie looked back at the couple, now exchanging whispers and a kiss on the cheek. "I just remember my time."

"Your time?" Blaine put down her phone and looked at her.

"It doesn't seem as though it was that long ago, but we were just like them. Everything he said was magical. Everything he did was perfect."

"Oh, please. That doesn't happen anymore."

"Well, it should." Callie looked right at Blaine. As soon as it left her mouth, Callie knew she'd been too outspoken. It was one of her worst habits.

Blaine put up her hand. "Um, sorry. Didn't mean to say something wrong."

Callie shook her head. "No. I'm sorry. Not all of it was like that, but in the beginning..."

"Yeah, everyone's stupid in the beginning."

Callie laughed. "Yes, I guess we are."

"Who did that one couple remind you of?"

Callie looked over at her new friend. "Well, it was a long time ago. Many years, in fact." She looked down at her hand and noticed again the wrinkled skin and the age spots. "Longer ago than I care to admit, but I was here. On this very bench. Well, not really at this spot, but down there." Callie pointed to the other side of the room. "Closer to the main aisle, and I was with my soon-to-be mother-in-law. Her name was Gertie and she was a sweet woman."

"What were you doing here?"

"We were headed to California. My boyfriend, Miles, was being shipped out on the next boat and we wanted to be together. One last time. Although," Callie recalled, "we prayed that it wasn't our last time. Back then you prepared yourself. We really weren't sure if he would come back. Or even home. But we hoped.

"We'd left Durand that morning and had spent most of the early morning getting to Chicago. It was snowing. Badly. Gertie-wasn't sure she wanted to go. She was a worrier. Never able to give things to God and trust Him for the outcome. But there we were. Mother Gertie, short for Gertrude, was in her fifties and I was only nineteen. Back then, you didn't go to visit a boyfriend without a chaperone. But Miles was her son. The baby of the family. She wanted to see him off, too, so the situation worked out well for both of us.

"We sat in this very station waiting for our train to Iowa. Headed straight out west. I'd never been that far away from home. I was glad Mile's mother was with me, especially when we arrived in Chicago. The windows above us here," Callie pointed up, "were all boarded up. It was wartime and it was the first sign to me that our country was engaged in battle. It was much darker in here and I knew that if the windows were boarded up, that must mean this may be a target for the enemy.

"Upon seeing it, I remembered Pearl Harbor just two short years before. I knew what could happen. On that day the world was awakened from their slumber. From their thoughts that nothing bad like this could happen here in the States. Oh, how wrong we were to not believe it."

"Like September 11th," Blaine added.

Callie agreed. "Yes, it was much like that. Pearl Harbor plunged us into a World War. And none of us was prepared to have to deal with it or send our boys overseas to fight it. Yet, soon they went. A neighbor boy, the young man who ushered at church, the father of the small children next door. Soon food was rationed. Tires were scarce. Men weren't there anymore to run the farms or the factories. Women had to step up."

"And they did, whoo-hoo!" Blaine pumped her fist in the air.

Callie smiled. "Yes, many did. The rest of us just sat home by the radio, and prayed. Prayed for everyone involved which was often our fathers, brothers, cousins, and neighbors. Kids we'd grown up with in school. When a familiar face would no longer be seen around town, we'd know he enlisted, too."

Another announcement over the speaker echoed through the Grand Hall, startling Callie from her story. "Passengers heading to Port Huron on Amtrak #6345 need to head to Gate Six. Passengers with tickets into Michigan with stops in Battle Creek, Kalamazoo, East Lansing, Durand, Lapeer, and Port Huron need to board. Gate Six, please."

Callie stopped talking long enough to look down at her bags. All of them. She sighed and whispered, "God help me." Callie glanced up to see if Blaine had overheard her muttered prayer.

Blaine had stood up and began pulling the straps of her backpack onto her shoulders. She grabbed her suitcase, flipping open the handle. "It's been nice talking to you, Callie. Thanks again for the food." Off she went toward the train's boarding docks.

Callie nodded and stood. She picked up her bags, but dropped her duffle bag trying to get the handle open on her suitcase. She started to panic. As she bent down to grab the duffle bag, she felt someone touch her shoulder. Looking up, she saw the young Marine.

"Can I help you?" He bent down and set it on the bench beside Callie. Then he flipped open the handle for Callie to grab. "Here, does that help?"

Callie smiled. "Thank you, young man. God bless you."

He picked up her duffle bag, taking the handle and settling it on Callie's shoulder. "How's that?"

Callie nodded. "Perfect. Thanks so much." He was so handsome in his uniform. But now Callie knew there was goodness inside that uniform as well.

"Got it all?" The young man smiled at Callie and patted her back. Callie nodded.

"Well God, here I go." She hadn't gone ten feet and knew getting to the train would be her greatest challenge of the day. Year even. What if she missed it? Mason would come for her, but not until after work. Could she sit in the waiting room for another nine hours?

She struggled to get another ten feet. Winded and achy, she thought about sitting in the chair just outside the grand room, but stopped herself. She had to get to the train. Her seat. Home.

Chapter 3

Blaine found the perfect window seat on the train. She'd wanted to bring Kyle's Kindle but didn't quite know how she'd get it back to him. As several passengers boarded, she hoped no one wanted to sit by her. Not knowing why, she looked around for the old woman. You rarely find someone so generous in Chicago. What was taking her so long? Surely, she'd be on the same car as her, heading almost to the last stop in Michigan.

Perhaps she should go back and find out. Callie was booked for the same train. Many passengers began taking up all the seats around her. Perhaps she should save her a seat. Blaine turned again in her seat to see if she'd boarded behind her. There was no sign of her.

Frustrated with her thoughts, Blaine grew tired of worrying about the stranger. What did it matter to her? Yet she continued turning in her seat to see if she was there. Would the train wait? How would they know the old woman was making her way to the train? Could she encourage the conductor to wait for her? At that moment, Blaine began to think of her grandmother. She used to grow so frustrated waiting on her. At the checkout counter at the grocery store while her shaky fingers wrote out a check, getting her hair done every Friday afternoon which always took longer than the scheduled hour, trying to deposit her pension check at the bank. Everything she did took her five to ten minutes longer than everyone else. Blaine lacked patience for it.

And then one day she was gone. This time it wasn't just a few months in Florida, and she wasn't going to the grocery store for more ice cream. She passed away. Never to return. Blaine bit her lip. She pressed her phone button to reveal the time. She stood up and looked out one of the windows closest to the boarding dock outside the train. There was no sign of the old woman.

Blaine shook her head, and spouted a swear word. Should she take her things or leave them there? If she didn't take the chance, she'd lose her seat. Obviously, she wouldn't be able to pull Callie's luggage and handle her things, too. She'd packed nearly everything she had. Glancing up, she saw a middle-aged woman in the seat opposite her seat. "Would you do me huge favor?" Before the woman could answer, Blaine scurried down the train aisle and got off the train.

A conductor tried to stop her, "Um Miss, where are you going? We're just about ready to leave."

She waved him off. "I'll be right back. Can you wait?"

The man, holding a clipboard, shouted out to her, "That's not how this works!"

What was she doing? For some reason, there was this unexplainable pull to go help this old woman. She wasn't sure where it was coming from. Blaine often viewed herself as selfish; living with Kyle for the past few months made her more so. She hated when other people pried into her business, but this was different. This was an old woman who'd been so kind to her, it was the least she could do for another human being.

Maybe it was because she had shared her food. She didn't have to do that. Perhaps it was the story she'd begun about her past. Blaine loved history and often asked her grandmother what it had been like to live through a world war. What caused people to go off and fight for a country in the prime of their life?

Whatever the pull, Blaine couldn't help herself. It wasn't her grandmother, but it was someone's, and at that moment...that was enough.

* * *

Callie longed for her seat. Once on the train, surely there'd be someone to help her. Another ten feet. She was outside the grand room now, facing a ramp going downhill. She was close to the boarding sidewalk. The downward slope helped ease her breathing.

She'd made it to the ramp, stopping to catch her breath. Almost there, if not halfway. The pressure she'd been feeling in her chest the last few months grew strong. Her breathing labored. Pain began to radiate down one of her arms. This wasn't good.

Callie grasped the cold, steel railing, leaning up against a nearby cement wall. The coolness brought some relief to her aching arm. Bowing her head she asked again for help. "Please, God. Don't let me have a heart attack waiting for an answer."

Callie opened her eyes to find Blaine hurrying toward her. She smiled. "Callie, can I help you to the train? We'll probably be on the same car anyway."

Callie smiled again. "Thank you, Blaine. That's so kind." Blaine took her duffle bag, her backpack, and grabbed the handle of her suitcase. Callie pulled her purse straps back onto her shoulder. It didn't bring much relief to her arm, but it helped.

"I could take your purse, too. If you'd be comfortable with me doing that?"

Callie struggle for a breath. "I have to carry something."

Callie learned long ago that trusting God didn't always mean instant answers. Again, she scolded herself for coming to the train station alone. It always took her longer to learn lessons, but God knew that about her.

According to the conductor, they'd reached the train just in time. Blaine helped Callie load her luggage in the overhead compartments. The older woman worried Blaine. Her face was flushed, her hair damp surrounding her face, her breathing slow and labored. She hoped her kind gesture wouldn't require her to perform CPR on the woman now slumping into the seat just moments before she had been enjoying herself.

She sat down in the seat beside Callie. "Did you happen to bring any water in that handbag of yours?" It wasn't she who needed the water, but if she approached the woman this way perhaps she could help her keep her dignity. Callie nodded, and rummaged through the bag now resting on her lap.

"I'm sorry, Blaine, I only have one bottle."

Blaine shook her head. "No biggie. You drink it. I'll get my own as soon as the train starts." She smiled as she watched Callie guzzle a few mouthfuls. Her breathing was slowing now, color returning to her wrinkled cheeks as she rested her head on the headrest of the seat.

"I'm," Callie wiped her mouth with the back of her hand, "glad we're able to sit together." She took another gulp. "Thanks so much for coming back. God bless you."

Blaine smiled. "I should have helped you from the beginning. Sometimes..." she could feel her face blush, "I forget that it isn't always about me."

Callie smiled. "Don't we all."

Blaine relaxed a little more as Callie's breathing gradually returned to normal. Callie pulled a beautiful compact out of her purse, dabbing at her cheeks with powder to remove the sweaty glow. She pushed up under her gold-rimmed glasses, then patted her forehead. Blaine was always amazed at how older women's curls stayed in place, even on the windy streets of Chicago. She always wondered if it was the old-fashioned curlers they still used, or was it their number five, stiff, never shifting, hairspray? Despite her morning, Callie's white hair hadn't shifted.

As the conductor made his way down the aisle to assist the final loading of luggage, Blaine began to consider what she'd just done. Surely, a good deed would not be overlooked, but the old woman would probably not shut up for the whole ride. Blaine needed to think. What was going to be her next step? Did she really want an old woman yakking her ear off? She glanced over at the old woman now sighing heavily. Worse yet, what if she were to pass away in the seat right next to her? That would be just Blaine's luck.

***

Callie looked over to see Blaine resting. Despite a scowled, heavy look, she was beautiful. Her blonde-streaked hair was swept up and drawn tight into a ponytail. Her eyelashes were long and black, her makeup impeccable. Her complexion soft and pink. What she wouldn't do for a smooth, firm face like that again. Free of wrinkles, creases, sagging jowls.

She wiped her hand across her cheek. She hoped the powder hadn't caked her skin. Miles loved her skin. He didn't care if she wore makeup. When he'd kiss her cheek, he'd tell her he liked her best,*'au naturel,'* in a pitiful French accent. She'd scold him and refuse to go without moisturizer. Now she couldn't control the sweat.

It was her weight. How embarrassing it got when droplets slipped down her face like humidity on a mirror after a hot shower. She wondered if Miles would find her beautiful, even now. She'd never know.

They'd only been sitting a couple of minutes when the conductor chimed his review of the next few destinations. Michigan cities and towns recited were familiar, and Callie began to relax in her seat more. Her chest was still heavy, but the pain had subsided. She gazed out the window at the dark train station under the Chicago streets. Like a hidden world. She could barely make out the trains on the tracks beside them. Squinting, she wondered where the passengers now boarding a train next to them were headed. As she closed her eyes, she thought back to her first trip on a train in 1943.

"Callie?" Blaine grabbed her forearm. "Are you okay?" Callie blinked a bit and then looked over at her new friend. "Of course."

"I didn't mean to bother you."

"Blaine, why would you think that? If it wasn't for you, I'll still be limping my way to this train." Callie sighed. "What would I have done if I'd missed the train? I'd have had to call Mason and he's so busy. He'd have had to leave work." Callie shook her head. "No, I'm fine now. Thanks again for coming back to help me."

Blaine asked, “So, Mason is your grandson?”

Callie smiled. “That’s why I was here in Chicago. To visit him.”

“What does he do?”

“He’s a financial manager at F.P. Franklin. Have you heard of it?”

Blaine shook her head.

“I love to come visit him every chance I get.”

Callie watched Blaine settle back into her seat.

"Have you ever been on a train, Blaine?"

Blaine pulled the back of her ponytail with two hands, the sides of her hair tightening as she did. "Lots of times."

"I was just thinking about our trip to California. Remember how I told you a little about that at the train station?”

Blaine's blue eyes sparkled as she gazed at Callie, "Yes. What year was that?"

"1943. It was a long time ago."

"Where were you going again?"

"Fort Ord." Callie leaned her head back and turned toward Blaine.

"Where was your boyfriend again?"

"Miles? He was stationed there, before heading overseas."

Blaine looked over and smiled. "Were you engaged or just dating?"

"Not quite engaged, but the letters he sent home made it inevitable we'd have a future together. Then we had the attack on Pearl Harbor, and just like that," Callie sighed, "the world changed." Callie looked out her dark window and saw her own reflection. She closed her eyes. "Has that ever happened to you? Everything is going smooth until a phone call or a knock at the door changes everything in an instant. That's how it was that day. Everything was normal. I was at work and he came through the front door of the store."

Callie smiled thinking of that moment so long ago. It was a story she loved to tell.

***

Callie didn't notice him at first. She was busy with month-end receipts. It always took all her concentration. She could hear laughter at the front of the store, but that was common. Customers knew her boss well. They loved coming in for a yard of fabric or a bag of potatoes, just so they could talk to Clarence. He was the owner and Callie's boss. One messed-up number of a receipt took Callie hours and hours of time to find the misplaced or wrong digit. She hated having to go back and find a mistake, always desiring to be perfect the first time.

Clarence demanded it out of her. Quick work, but accurate was his philosophy. If she were busy with the bookwork, he had more time to stand and talk to the customers. He called it, 'masterful sales,' but Callie called it what it was 'putting his best mouth forward.'

He approached Callie's desk, a young man in tow. The young man followed him, reluctantly, yet smiling. The first thing she noticed was his ear. His left ear, limp at the top as if it had lost a battle. He was against the sun pouring in through the front store windows. A fresh snow that night had made everything glimmer in the morning sun. The sunlight surrounded him like a glow.

Taking off his hat, Callie watched as the top of his right ear drooped a bit. But when he smiled, all Callie saw were his dimples. A deep one on his right cheek. A less impressionable one on his left cheek. And that smile. That smile which made her rethink the reason why she had a pen in her hand or even the number she needed to enter in the accounts payable margin.

"Good morning." At the sound of his voice, Callie dropped the pen.

Clarence now scooted between the front counter and the display of ladies' hats. One hat almost fell off the head model as he moved in for the introductions. "Callie, this is my little brother."

Callie stood up, held out her now moist hand. She prayed he didn't notice. "How do you do?"

Miles took her hand and smiled. "Very well now, thank you."

Callie's hand lingered in his for a moment. She didn't realize it until Clarence spoke again. "Callie, this is the brother I've been telling you about."

Callie nodded. For some reason, she couldn't speak. She pulled her hand away and tucked it into the pocket of her skirt. "I've heard lots about you."

The dimples appeared again. "I'm sure you have." Miles slapped his brother on the shoulder.

Clarence leaned into his little brother. "I told you she was pretty." He smiled at Callie.

Callie must have blushed because she saw both brothers smile as she turned from them to sit back down. She'd wanted nothing more than to finish the books today and now, with this somewhat handsome man in front of her, she wasn't sure if her concentration would be the only thing null and void in this transaction. She did her best to get back to work.

Clarence showed Miles through the store. He pointed up to his display of hunting gear, what was left over from the Christmas sales the month before. Merchandise rarely went on sale, but Clarence had slashed prices in that department this month to further the clearance of it all before planting season sales began. "Got some ammo left, Miles. Check it out."

Miles went to the section just under the right store window. His back was to Callie as she took a quick glance in his direction. He looked rather nice. Just a couple of inches taller than Callie, he filled out the gray pants and suit jacket well. Again, she noticed his ear.

"Miles, you know the family discount for merchandise. If you find anything you like, let me know." Clarence pointed to the back of the store. "Some nice flannels on sale back there, too. I know how you like sales."

Miles turned and Callie dropped her gaze back to her accounting numbers now blurry on the page. Concentration was long gone. Her thoughts were going haywire. She couldn't remember why she'd put down forty-one dollars and sixty-two cents. Was it a debit or a credit? She didn't want to look up. She could feel his eyes on her as she pushed a strand of hair behind her right ear.

"Got any gum drops left from Christmas, Clarence?"

Callie smiled. There weren't any left. Clarence had taken most of the leftover candy home with him over the holidays for his children. "Donna Jean loves those things, Miles. You know that."

Callie glanced up again for just a moment to see Miles push his hands into his pants pockets and began to whistle as he made his way to the back of the store. The moment made Callie think of Jimmy Stewart. He whistled a tune played during the last New Year celebration by Bing Crosby. Callie couldn't remember the title, but it had been a radio favorite during the holiday season.

Callie tried again to concentrate on the sixty-two cents. Why would she have entered such an odd number on the page? Most of the numbers on this page had no change. Puzzled, she glanced up at Clarence. He'd returned to his job of stacking cans of corn.

"Hey, Clarence, do you have any blue socks?"

Clarence turned from his job to answer his brother. "Um, check that pile over there but, Miles, you'll get those issued once you're on base."

Callie looked up again. He looked back at the same moment and smiled, "Yeah, you're probably right." He didn't look away from her. Callie smiled back. Then it happened. Not one moment of hesitation, Miles winked at her.

She lowered her head again at the entry of sixty-two cents. She needed to concentrate. Shaking her head, she knew if Miles didn't leave the store, she'd have to return to work tomorrow and finish up the month of December sales. But for that second, she really didn't care.

Chapter 4

"So, it was love at first sight?" Blaine grinned at Callie.

"No, no, Blaine." Callie shook her head and wiped her mouth with a tissue from her purse. She was still warm from her walk to the train. "It's not really like that. I was angry with him."

"Angry?" Blaine's eyebrows furrowed. "Why? Sounds like the beginning of a beautiful relationship."

"Well, it was the beginning. That's for sure. But even a beautiful beginning has shifts, curves, and a few speed bumps."

Blaine tucked a single strand of her blonde hair back behind an ear. "Not you, too."

"Every relationship has issues. Miles and I caught each other's attention in the beginning to be sure, but soon I wasn't so sure I wanted a relationship with my boss's brother." Callie pulled the bag of almonds out of her purse. She handed the bag to Blaine. "Would you like some more? Aren't they delicious?"

Blaine nodded and took the bag. "Just a few more. I don't want to hog them."

Callie laughed, patting her belly. "Do I appear malnourished?"

Blaine took a handful of nuts. "Why is it that women have to be so careful of what they eat? It isn't the same with guys; Kyle is constantly pointing out my weight problems."

"Your boyfriend comments about your weight?"

Blaine popped a nut into her mouth. "All the time."

"Do you like it?"

"What choice do I have? He's paranoid about his weight. If he isn't at the gym, he's home on his elliptical. Last week I caught him in my laundry basket checking out my pants, probably looking at the size."

"My word." Callie couldn't believe what Blaine was telling her. "What's wrong with men these days?"

Blaine shook her head. "He's right. I've been putting pounds on since the weather has gotten cold."

Callie sat forward in her seat and looked Blaine over. "Where?"

She laughed. "So, Miles never questioned you about how much you weigh?"

"He would have had to fear for his life." Callie shook her head. "In fact, he always said I was perfect even though, he knew good and well that I wasn't."

"He did?" Blaine looked puzzled, "I don't know what I'd do if Kyle said anything like that. It'd give me a coronary."

"Honey, would you stay with a girlfriend if she pointed out to you your weight problems?"

Blaine shook her head. "Well, that's a bit different, but if they were mean about it, probably not."

"Then why would you put up with it from a boyfriend?"

"Callie, that's not real life. That never happens."

"Says who?"

Blaine shook her head. "Maybe in the movies."

The conductor's announcement interrupted their conversation. "Sorry, folks, having a bit of a hold-up pulling out of Chicago. Heavy traffic. We'll be on our way soon. Thank you for your patience."

Their train had stopped just outside the station and now was helping give Callie a perfect view of the train tracks heading into the station. Walls of buildings blocked any view of the sun coming up over the Chicago landscape. With nothing to see, and a train going to nowhere yet, Callie knew just what to talk about.

* * *

Callie really didn't appreciate a sly wink, let alone from a man. Some girls went crazy over men who did it, but not Callie. She liked men who approached her face to face. Were bold about telling them they were interested in her. Winks were for silly girls. Flirty women. Which she was not.

Clarence had told her about Miles many times. She knew it was just a matter of time before he brought him into the store to introduce them.

Callie had started as a bookkeeper just after graduation. She'd taken on the job to help her parents manage their struggling farm. The less her father had to work on people's automobiles, the more he could concentrate on the crops.

Her father would be too proud to take her hard-earned money, so she told him it was her rent. She was the eldest of three daughters, and informed her father she wanted to pay him rent. Her father had smiled and accepted it. The offer wasn't a large sum, but it did feel good to help out a bit. She earned more money in a month than her father probably saw in a year from selling produce from his garden.

The family had just moved out into the country from the big city of Flint. They'd acquired a farm, complete with several acres of land, for quite a good deal. Her father was a mechanic and he could fix not only cars, but also farm machinery and tractors to help supplement their income. Once 1940 hit, many families felt they could do better and take a bit more of a risk, yet the struggles of the 1930s were still raw. Living in the country and off the land proved even more economical for Callie's family than living in town.

Her two younger sisters were busy in high school and not prepared to go out and work yet. They helped out at the farm, acting nothing like young women, but more like field hands. Callie had graduated from high school before they left the city and knew that if she could work as a bookkeeper or secretary, she could help. She'd leave the gathering of eggs, haying, and planting up to her two younger sisters. Every day she would walk up their dirt road to catch the bus at the corner. By working, she was doing her part to help.

The walk was nice most of the year, but the winters were brutal in Michigan. She'd try to dress in her nicest clothes for work, with boots on, carrying her heels. Some days the snow was so high she could feel the wet, cold moisture saturating her feet by the time she reached the end of the road. On the bus, the snow would melt in her boots and her feet would grow even colder. It was always a relief to take them off once she got to work. She'd prop the wet boots up on a radiator at the back of the store so they'd be warm and dry before she had to leave for home at night.

Callie loved her job. She loved the challenge of making the books agree at the end of the day. Having a real job at her age made her feel proud and satisfied with herself. It wasn't quite what she wanted to do her whole life, but for now it was rewarding. She dreamed of the day she could quit her job and become a wife and mother.

Miles came into the store every other day now. Her first day of ignoring him deemed successful, but not in the way Callie had hoped. He was now adamant in his pursuit of her. Why couldn't men get the hint? Didn't they know when a girl ignored them they were trying to tell them something? Yet, for Miles, it was the exact enticement for him to continue with a fervent vengeance.

Clarence was all for it. He'd egg Miles on and often pull him aside and whisper. Miles would return with some new questions and advances.

Callie tried to be polite, smile, and thank him for his compliments, but she'd do her best to keep her nose to the ledgers. When Miles' lines weren't giving him the reaction he desired from her, he tried a new tactic. Candy. Callie loved candy and it was hard not to accept the treats he'd place on her desk while she stood around the store doing inventory. He often left her favorites. Chocolate-covered jelly sticks.

One day she stopped him. "Are you leaving these treats for me?"

Miles would smile, and say, "Of course."

"Please stop."

"Don't you like them?"

Callie never wanted to lie. She'd nod but then add, "Doesn't help a girl's figure."

Miles would flash her another large grin, his dimples showing and say, "I can watch that for you."

She'd blush and get just that much more aggravated with him. His flirting was uncalled for. She'd shake her head. Miles would laugh.

After nearly a month of these kind of exchanges, Callie knew she had to cut this man off. Free him from the burden of getting his way with her. Send him on his way. Waiting for the bus one morning, she planned it all out in her head. She knew what she was going to say and how she'd leave dimple-face wishing he'd never seen her. Determined, she entered the store reciting her retaliating words to herself.

But that day and even the next, Miles was nowhere to be seen. He stopped coming in. Each morning she recited her words of rejection. She didn't want to be harsh; Miles had been nice, but he needed to stop. Days turned into a week and soon Friday afternoon loomed. Callie hadn't seen Miles since the week before. It was odd for him not to stop by. She wanted to ask Clarence where he was, but she knew if she did, it would seem as if she was interested, which she was not.

She left work on Friday afternoon, wondering what had happened to him.

* * *

The train jerked forward after sitting on the tracks for what seemed like hours instead of minutes.

"We're never stopped this long just outside the city," Callie commented upon looking out the window.

"I've only been on a train a few times. Kyle usually drives us everywhere. Do you take the train often?"

Callie turned back. "Whenever I come to see Mason. His job keeps him pretty busy, but sometimes he'll come up to visit me in the summer, usually for my birthday in August."

"What a nice guy."

Callie laughed. "Yes, he is, but I have a feeling most grandmothers say that about their grandsons."

"I lost both of my grandparents when I was small. I don't even remember my grandfather. I was six months old when he passed away. My grandmother passed away a few years ago."

Callie sipped some more of her water. "That's too bad. I love being a part of Mason's life. His parents are missionaries in Africa, their furloughs are every four years. I'm about all the family he has here in the States."

"No brothers or sisters?"

"No, he's an only child."

"You're nice to do that for them."

"Well," Callie said, smiling, "I often wonder if it's he who is comforting me. I miss my daughter so much while she's gone. It's nice to have Mason back in the States again so I can go and at least spoil him from time to time. But..." Callie turned away to look out the window again.

"What?"

"I don't know how much longer I can do this. You saw." Callie turned back and pointed to the front of the train. "I don't get around as well as I once did. I feel more like a burden to Mason when I come now. In fact, I think this will be my last time."

Chapter 5

Callie was beginning to really take to Blaine. She seemed intrigued by her stories. A girl her age would rather talk on her phone or browse Facebook than sit and talk to an old woman. It was hard for Callie not to share stories about Miles. He'd been her whole life for nearly seventy years.

The train was now headed out of Chicago. The clicking of the rails produced a rhythmic cadence of sorts. Its whistle echoed back through the train cars as it passed through road intersections. The train yards just out of the station revealed piles and piles of coal ready to load into freighters on Lake Michigan.

The train car was full of travelers. A young family was seated just across the aisle from them. Laptops were now open and the tapping of fingers to keys filled the crowded car.

"I need something to drink, Callie. I'm going to head back to the food car. Would you like anything?"

Callie shook her head.

"I'll be right back. Can you watch my things?"

Callie smiled. "Of course."

Soon the young girl returned with what looked like a cup of coffee in hand. Callie rushed through her morning so much, she now wished she'd agreed to have a cup herself.

Blaine took a sip and winced at the hot liquid. "Hot!"

Callie added, "Be careful, dear."

"So, did he ever come back?"

"Who, dear?"

"Miles?"

"Oh him. Well, yes. By the time I saw him again, my speech to end his flirting had long disappeared." Callie laughed.

* * *

Instead of rehearsing her speech to stop Miles from flirting, she now recited over and over how she'd ask Clarence about Miles without sounding too interested. She knew if she gave Clarence the wrong impression, Miles would be told that she was interested and he'd be back with a vengeance.

One day after lunch, nearly two weeks since Callie had last seen Miles, she got up the nerve.

"So, Clarence, it's been pretty quiet around here lately."

"Yes; I think we need to order some more of those flannel shirts. We're low on sizes and I think people are going elsewhere to find them."

The shirts had sold really well at Christmas. Callie knew that if they were to keep people coming in the store, they needed to be stocked well.

"I keep dwelling on the seeds we need for spring and completely forget to order them. Although, it will take a few weeks for delivery and by then, men will be looking for short-sleeve shirts instead. But, we'll see how it goes. What we don't sell this winter, we can add to next year's inventory. Can you do that for me today, Callie?"

Callie nodded. She'd get an order out later this afternoon. She jotted herself a note. "But I wasn't talking so much about customers. Haven't seen any of your brothers in awhile." Clarence had five other brothers and a sister, so Callie felt safe in asking about all of them instead of just Miles.

"They're all busy these days. Miles joined the service last week. He had to travel to Lansing to be sworn in. I've been expecting him back any day now."

So that was it. He'd gone to Lansing to join the service. Callie wasn't surprised. Many young men were either being drafted or joining up these days, brought on by the recent attack on Pearl Harbor.

"Why?"

Callie looked up from her work to see Clarence smiling at her.

"No reason. I was just thinking I hadn't seen him lately. That's all."

Callie did her best to seem indifferent to Miles' whereabouts. But for some reason she must not have been very convincing, because Clarence burst into laughter.

"Why are you laughing at me?"

Clarence got down from his ladder and moved it closer to Callie's desk. He'd been pulling wool pants off the shelves above her head and must have wanted a different color. "I'm not laughing at you. I'm laughing at the situation. You're missing that son-of-a-gun, aren't you?"

Callie shook her head. "Of course not. I just wondered." Callie picked up a pen and tried to write herself a note, but now she couldn't seem to remember what it was supposed to be about.

Clarence smiled as he went back up the ladder, to the blue pants higher up. "He thought you weren't interested in him."

Callie needed to set this record straight and fast, "I'm not."

"Okay, then why did you just ask about him?"

"I asked about people visiting the store. Not just about Miles."

Clarence laughed. "Okay, Callie. Whatever you say."

Callie wasn't sure if she missed Miles or not. She had thought she'd only been wondering where he was, but she did miss the candy. The sweet way he looked at her when he thought she wasn't looking and the dimples. He might be a flirt, but for some reason, she missed the attention. She wanted to tell Clarence it wasn't Miles she was missing, but that wouldn't be completely true and Callie knew it.

While they were on the subject of Miles, Callie decided she probably did want to ask one more question. She forged ahead. "When does he leave?" It was concern, that's all.

Clarence pulled off three more sets of blue pants and smiled down at Callie. "We'll find out when he gets home. I don't know."

He stepped down the ladder and put the pants on Callie's desk. "Can you be sure these get priced, Callie? I must have stocked them without pricing them first."

Callie nodded and pulled the pants toward her on the desk. She wondered how long the wool supplies would last to order more pants like these. Most men's pants were uniforms now.

"And when he gets home, you can ask him yourself."

Callie stood up to get the price tags from a drawer behind her desk. "It's not a big deal. I was just wondering."

"Okay, Callie." Clarence folded up the ladder and headed to the back of the store. "Anything you say."

Men drove her crazy. She wasn't interested like a woman after a man, she really wanted to know about Miles. He was Clarence's brother. Why wouldn't she ask about him?

***

The train was picking up speed now. They'd maneuvered through the train yards just outside of the big city.

"So, you didn't like Miles right off, then?" Blaine sipped from her coffee cup, tipping it up to drink, what seemed to be tapping the last drop of it out before placing the cup on the top of her purse on the floor.

"Heavens yes." Callie smiled. "I try not to tell lies to others, but on the other hand," she laughed, "I lie to myself all the time. God's been working in my heart about that one for a long time."

"So, you did like him?"

"I began to realize that when I caught myself watching for him and primping my hair a little better each morning. It was one of my sisters who sensed it first. She asked me one morning at breakfast."

* * *

"So, what's his name?" Callie took her cup of water off the kitchen counter and brought it to the table. Her mother was busy whipping up pancake batter in a bowl on the counter.

Callie was puzzled. "What are you talking about?"

Her sister crossed her legs and smiled. "Callie, don't be pious."

Callie hated how her sisters always made her feel like a goody-two-shoes. "Why do you ask me such a thing?"

"Well, because every morning you check yourself in the mirror like twelve times. You've found these new barrettes and have one in your hair every morning before going to work. Who is he?"

Callie sat down and took a long gulp of her water. "I don't know what you're talking about." She looked up to see her mother had stopped beating the batter and was eyeing her. She laughed and shook her head. She could rarely keep a secret from her mother or lie without her knowing it.

That morning on the bus, Callie rummaged in her purse for a compact. The walk up the hill to the bus was windy. Her hair must be totally out of place, even though her scarf covered most of it. She removed the scarf, balanced the mirror in her hand, and used her other hand to plump up her hair.

As she gazed at herself, she realized her sister might be seeing something she hadn't yet told herself. Why was she primping so much for work? She stopped, pinched the compact together, and tossed it into her purse. She hated it when her sister was right. She needed to stop acting like a fourteen-year-old having a crush and just go into work and do her job, like a grown woman. The rest of the trip to Flint, she chided herself.

She came into the store with a shiver as today's weather proved to be the coldest day yet. Propping her boots up again, she slipped on her high heels, sat down at her desk and began filling out the inventory sheet she'd put away half done the day before. Entering the figures proved to get her mind off Miles.

Callie loved bookkeeping. She'd studied it in school and always had gotten good grades. More reasons for her sisters to tease her. They'd rather be out in the fields with their father or milking Percy, the milk cow. Callie only wanted to be a modern-day clerk. She loved her job.

As she entered the last of the store inventory in the register, she stood up to sharpen her pencil and nearly ran right into Miles, who was coming around the counter. He smiled as Callie stumbled right into him.

"Miles. I didn't see you."

Miles grinned and Callie saw the dimple. Flustered, she giggled. Miles laughed, too. "You were awful busy."

"How long have you been here?"

Miles crossed his arms, and that's when Callie saw him. All of him. He was in a finely pressed, brand new military uniform. He looked absolutely divine. "Oh, maybe ten minutes or so."

"Ten minutes!" Callie felt her face grow warm. Her hands began to perspire as she wrung them together.

Miles stood his ground right in front of her. He towered over her and smiled.

Callie couldn't seem to move. She went from his dimple to his pretty green eyes. He looked back at her. She wasn't sure how long they stood there gazing at each other, but she knew she needed to make the first move. "I was just..." What was she just going to do?

Miles picked up her hand. "Sharpen your pencil?"

He was being presumptuous. Her mission came back with a vengeance. "Yes, sharpen my pencil. Will you excuse me?"

"What if I say no?"

Callie backed up a bit and walked around Miles. "I'll do it anyway."

As she made her way to the pencil sharpener, Callie rubbed the back of her neck. All the way to the sharpener, Callie knew Miles was eyeing her from behind. He'd turned with her as she'd walked around him. But it was quiet behind her.

She didn't turn around as she put the pencil in the sharpener and began turning the crank to sharpen it. Suddenly, she felt a body press against her back. A shiver ran through her body like nothing she'd ever felt before. He was now directly behind her and very close. He whispered in her ear. "Will you go out with me?"

She lost all power to continue turning the crank on the sharpener. Her pencil fell out of her hand and to the floor. She stood still.

"Well?" Miles asked again.

Callie knew that if she didn't get control of herself, she might melt like an ice cream cone at a Fourth of July picnic despite it being January in Michigan. She backed up a bit and said, "I need to get my pencil." Miles didn't back up at all, and now he was even closer. She'd never been this close to a man her own age before.

Miles whispered in her ear again, "You need to answer my question."

Callie knew he probably wouldn't move for her until she did. "What if I say no?"

"I'll be devastated."

Callie could smell a mixture of shaving cream and coffee. "What will we do on this so-called date?"

Miles backed up a bit. "I'll come to your house. I'll pick you up and perhaps take you out for coffee."

"You don't know where I live."

"I'll figure it out. Beauty like yours can't be hidden."

Callie turned completely around, pushing him away with her hands. "Tomorrow is Saturday. My sisters and I were going to go ice skating. Do you know how to skate?"

Miles smiled. "Yes, I do. Let's go skating."

Callie nudged past him and back to her desk. Again, she knew, he'd turned. She could feel his presence, still smell him.

As she sat down, she heard steps approach her from behind. She felt herself nearly melt into her chair. What had she been doing? What did she need to return to doing? She looked around for a pencil.

Miles was soon standing over her desk and he placed her pencil back on it. "You forgot your pencil." He then turned around and started toward the front door of the store. "I'll be over to your house right after lunch tomorrow. Would that be okay?"

"If you insist."

Miles leaned forward to turn the knob on the front door of the store. "I do. I've gone by your house a million times in the past month. Isn't it the gray house on the north side of Old Miller Road?"

Callie again could feel herself blush. "How? When?"

Miles grinned back at her. "See you then."

Callie couldn't concentrate the rest of her work day. Miles looked fabulous in his uniform. More than fabulous. Why did he have to come into the store looking like that? It should be illegal. Although, it only proved one thing, her sister was right.

Chapter 6

Callie stooped to pick up her purse again as a female conductor announced the first stop on their train journey over the loud speaker. Talking about Miles brought back so many wonderful memories. She needed a tissue to dab her eyes.

"Next stop, New Buffalo. If you are getting off the train, please gather your luggage now and we'll be stopping in just five minutes, folks. Just five minutes."

"How beautiful." Blaine smiled at Callie. "I love your story. Almost like a dream. A fairy tale. Right out of the movies."

Callie smiled. At that moment of their relationship, it had seemed magical. Callie couldn't wait for Miles to visit the next day, even though her younger sisters would drive her crazy if she were to divulge her date. She'd never had a beau or even anyone interested in her. Enduring relentless teasing from them would ensue, but she could handle it. But what would her father do? None of his daughters had ever had a boy visit, let alone go on a date. She'd be forging the path for all of them.

"What did your sisters say?"

Callie laughed. "I didn't tell them right away, but my excitement got the best of me. I pulled my younger sister aside that evening and told her. I knew Esther could keep a secret."

"What did she say?"

Callie looked out the window of the train. "You'd have thought the next morning was Christmas."

* * *

Callie woke up the next morning as the winter sun streamed in through her bedroom window. She hadn't slept well but tossed and turned most of the night. What had she thought to allow this stranger to visit her? What would her father say? He could often get gruff and ornery around others. What would he do when a strange man came around and wanted to spend time with his eldest daughter?

Callie pulled the covers closer around her chin. Perhaps she'd pretend she didn't know anything about it. Act naive.

Upstairs in the old farmhouse, on January mornings you could breathe into the air while getting out of bed and easily see it hang in the air for a few minutes. Callie scooted her feet into her slippers by her bed, and grabbed her heavy, cotton bathrobe off the hook on her bedroom door as she huddled inside it for warmth. One of her metal curlers got stuck on the edge of her bathrobe collar, sharply pulling her hair. Callie winced as she peeled it off her collar. She'd taken such care in wrapping her hair in curlers the night before, but her restless night had caused most of them to unravel and now they hung down from her head. It would be a wonder if she had any curl. Standing in front of her mirror, she tightened each curler, hoping that through breakfast, they'd hold more spring to her otherwise-straight hair.

Rushing down into the kitchen, she hoped she could have a word with her mother before her father came in for breakfast. She hoped he was still out doing chores.

She found her mother frying bacon on the stove. Callie glanced around the room to see if she was alone. She breathed a sigh of relief to discover she was the first one up. Thankfully, her father was still out doing chores. The smell and warmth of the room penetrated her soul. She loved Saturday mornings with her mother.

"Good morning, sleepy head." Her mother turned and began cracking eggs on the edge of a bowl.

"Good morning, Mother."

"Did you sleep well?" Another egg joined the others in the bowl.

"Um, not as well as usual."

Her mother turned from the counter. "Do you feel well?"

Callie knew this was it. She needed to tell her mother. If she didn't, her father might join them soon and she'd never have another chance. Her mother could always ease her father into precarious circumstances and make the situation not so traumatic. It was imperative that Callie tell her first.

"I'm fine, but I have something to tell you."

Her mother wiped her hands on a towel. "What, dear?"

Callie went over to a drawer, pulled out a fork and began scrambling the eggs her mother had deposited in the bowl.

"What do you think Father would do if I have a visitor today?"

Her mother answered, "He has quite a few chores to do today. The weather seems to be cold today, but sunny. I think he wanted to replace some boards on the back barn that came off in the last wind storm we had." Another egg cracked and joined the others. "Why, who's coming over? Anna?" Anna and Callie had been inseparable in high school.

Callie whipped faster. "Um, no, not Anna."

"Callie?" Her mother turned to face her. "Why would your father care whether you have a friend over or not?"

Callie continued until the eggs were frothy.

Her mother grabbed her hand and took away the fork. "Scrambled honey, they aren't pie meringue."

She set the fork down on the counter. Callie couldn't look up at her mother.

"Callie, is it a male visitor we might be having?"

Callie nodded without looking up at her mother.

"Is it one of Clarence's brothers?"

Callie nodded again.

"Which one?"

"Miles." Callie looked up at her mother who she found smiling. "The youngest."

Her grin broadened. "Well, it's about time."

"What? What do you mean by that?"

"He's been driving by this house for weeks now. Your daddy has been seeing him."

Callie shook her head. "Daddy saw him?"

Her mother picked up the bowl of eggs and poured them into a hot skillet on the stove. "Of course; we don't often get traffic by the house."

"What did he say?"

"He wasn't sure which of his daughters the young man was interested in, but it's been happening more and more. This one is a new one."

"Who else has been driving by?"

"Mary's been eyeing another car as she does her chores. We were hoping," her mother swiped the pan with a spatula, "this one was interested in you. It's hard when the younger sisters have interested visitors before the oldest finds someone."

"What do you think Daddy will say?" Callie wasn't sure she wanted to hear the answer, but having an answer would help alleviate her fear.

"I think he'll be fine. He may pretend to be a little perturbed and will probably have a few questions for the young man, but he'll get over it." Her mother winked at her.

Just then the door opened and in walked Callie's father. Steam poured off him as he came into the extra warm kitchen and deposited his hat on the hook by the door. "Woo-hoo. It's a mighty cold one out there this morning. But it smells delicious in here, Pearl."

* * *

"So, how did he take it?" Blaine looked over at Callie, who seemed to be deep in thought. Blaine loved hearing about Miles. The mystery of a new relationship. What woman didn't want to hear about how it started?

"Miles?" Callie asked.

"No, Callie. Your father."

Callie smiled. "Oh, Daddy thought it funny. He laughed, but then told me that if the boy wasn't mannerly or treated me badly, he could go take a hike or he'd be sure he never stopped by the house again. He also said something about his hunting rifle, but I knew he was only teasing me.

"My sisters were the worst ones. As soon as they both found out Miles was coming over, they rushed through their morning chores faster than I've ever seen them. They wanted to be sure they were out on the ice when Miles arrived. They wanted to know all about this fellow and the only way to do that was to pretend they were out ice skating before he arrived. They drove me crazy back then."

The train lurched forward again. New passengers had boarded and seats began to fill up more around Callie and Blaine.

Blaine grew curious about Callie. Why was she intent on sharing this story with her? She was also glad Kyle wasn't with her. He'd want to dominate the conversation and would want to ignore a stranger. She'd be a bother to him. Callie's story was drawing her in. It reminded her of her own grandmother's stories. She missed hearing her reminisce.

"So, what happened, Callie?" Blaine turned more in her seat. "How was your first date?"

* * *

The morning had stretched on, and as the family sat down for lunch Callie's sisters just wouldn't leave her alone about the upcoming visit.

'What does he look like?' 'Is he handsome?''I can't wait for this to be me.' Questions spilled out of her sisters faster than the food going in. Finally Callie's mother shushed them and told them to eat their lunch.

Callie's father was silent at the other end of the table. She wasn't sure what he thought about the upcoming visit, other than what he'd told her at breakfast. He soon directed the conversation elsewhere, and Callie breathed easier. She was nervous enough about having Miles visit.

"I think I'll order a little more seed this year, Pearl. The fields did so well last year. I think I can manage to plant more."

"Are you sure? That's a lot on your plate, Wilbur."

"The girls can help me."

Both of Callie's younger sisters groaned until they looked up to see their parents staring them down. They both lowered their heads and went back to their sandwiches.

Callie always managed to stay out of the barns and outdoor chores. She was more of a help to their mother in the kitchen. She loved to cook and clean. She'd much rather darn a sock, than feed chickens. Her sisters didn't seem to mind the outdoor chores, but always teased her that she was 'too frail and dainty to be out doing the farm duties.' Then they'd pull on their boots, put on their knitted hats, and head out into the cold or hot summer day with their father. He always had something for them to do.

Callie often felt sad to think of their father not having boys to help him. He was just learning how to farm again after moving from the city and his car repair business in town. Yet he wasn't alone. Many fathers found themselves alone at home as boy after boy went off to serve their country. Callie had high school friends who had left for boot camp shortly after graduation.

And now, Miles would be joining them. What would happen to this new friendship of hers? Why did it feel like it would put a rift between them? Would he want to continue to date her while he was away? They could probably send each other letters. But would that be enough? She was thinking of this as his car pulled into the driveway. He flipped a set of skates over his shoulder as he walked up to the kitchen door. Her mother answered the door.

"Good afternoon." Callie's mother held out her hand. "I'm Callie's mother, and you are?"

Miles took off his cap and held out his hand. "Miles, ma'am."

"Nice to meet you, Miles. Why don't you come in and warm up before heading out to the pond? You kids are going skating, I imagine."

Callie walked into the kitchen. She pulled her gloves out of her coat pocket and looked up to see Miles smiling at her. The dimple was visible. Callie smiled back. "Hello, Miles."

He bowed his head to her and smiled, "Good afternoon, Callie." Callie saw another side to him. Formal, and polite. She blushed as she thought back to their closeness in the store just a day before. What would her mother think?

"You two better head out to the barn and meet your daddy before going to the pond, Callie."

Callie nodded. "Yes, Mother."

Miles backed up and opened the door again to go outside. He left it open and stood by while Callie made her way outside first. This made Callie smile. He was a gentleman, despite his earlier flirting.

Callie's mother closed the door behind them. Callie breathed a little easier now that her mother had met Miles, but she knew she would be the easy one to convince that Miles might just be a good choice, valuing her parents' opinion.

They walked silently to the barn until Callie grew brave enough to speak. "Daddy is working on the side barn today. The siding came off in that last wind storm we had just after Christmas."

"That was quite the wind storm. We had some damage at our place, too."

Michigan winters always proved the sturdiness of buildings. A winter wind could rip apart barns or easily flip over an outhouse. Farmers would often get everything repaired and then a windstorm could erase all their summer or fall hard work. If it wasn't the wind doing the damage, a heavy snow pushed against buildings with the same ferocity.

They found Callie's father in the barn, cutting a piece of wood with a handsaw. He looked up when he saw them approach. Callie held her breath.

"Daddy, this is Miles."

Miles approached her father and held out his hand. "Nice to meet you, sir."

Callie relaxed. Her daddy would appreciate Miles manners.

Her daddy pulled off his gloves and took Miles' outstretched hand. "Hello, Miles. Good to meet you."

He quickly put his glove back on. The barn was colder than even outside. "Don't you and your folks live over on Durand Road?"

Miles nodded. "Yes, sir. Been there my whole life."

"What school did you attend?"

"Graduated from Owosso, sir."

Callie's daddy folded his arms. "Good grades?"

Callie cringed. Perhaps she should get Miles out of the barn and soon. Callie's friends often had to endure her father's prying questions, but with a boy how far would he go?

"Yes, sir. I'm not perfect, but I try hard."

Daddy smiled. "Glad to hear." He picked up his saw. "Well, you two have fun. I think the other girls are out on the pond now. They rushed through their chores like squirrels getting ready for winter on the last day before snowfall. I think they'd like to meet you, too, Miles."

Miles grinned. "Nice to meet you, sir."

Her daddy smiled, too. Callie adored her father, but she also knew not to cross him either. Then it happened. Her father and all his glory. "Not too much kissing out there, okay, Miles?"

Callie wanted to run. She wanted to go over and slap her father on the shoulder. But she also knew that probably wasn't a good idea.

Miles stumbled over a reply, but instead backed away, put his hat back on, and turned to head for the door. With his back turned to her father, Callie's daddy looked up and winked at her.

She was mortified.

* * *

Blaine couldn't help herself. As Callie told the story of their meeting with her daddy, Callie blushed telling about the kissing statement. Blaine laughed as she watched her. "What did you do?"

"For the first time in my life I actually gave my daddy the look Momma often gave him."

"What did he do?"

He just grinned, picked up his saw, and kept working. "What did your father do when he met your boyfriend?"

Blaine grasped for a reply. Something needed to come quickly. "We can't seem to manage to find the time to go and see him. Kyle always has an excuse. Always." Her vivid imagination always came in handy.

"Back in my day, Blaine. It was the first and most imperative thing to do. Meet the folks. My Daddy insisted upon it."

Blaine added more, "My father never asks about Kyle. Or my love life."

"Why not?"

This woman asked too many questions. "Just 'cause he doesn't. He's too busy." Blaine shifted the conversation. "So how did the date go, Callie?"

Callie smiled. "He held my hand for the first time."

Their conversation mystified and surprised Blaine. Why would parents really care who their child dated? Was that normal? Blaine's girlfriends would always comment about having the boyfriend 'meet the parents.' It was a woman's choice regarding who and when she dated. The whole story now seemed archaic. Strange.

"Callie, why was it important for your parents to like Miles? It should be a woman's choice to be able to date whomever she likes. Why should they care?"

Callie looked over at her as if her question was as strange as Blaine perceived it. Her forehead wrinkled, "Don't you care what your parents think of your boyfriend?"

Blaine shrugged. "I don't know. I guess I never thought about it before."

Callie shook her head. "You kids these days." The woman then retracted. "I'm sorry, Blaine. I don't like it when I sound like an old woman."

Blaine agreed, but looked away so Callie wouldn't know any better.

"I know that making choices these days are your right. What you think is best. Women these days handle their own lives. But back in my day, doing anything without a parent's approval was not wise. Parents live through so many things. They've gone through making life-changing choices. They have experience. They've seen what happens to young girls who often don't think decisions through as well as they should."

Blaine didn't like how this conversation was heading. She liked being independent. A free thinker.

"Consider this." Callie turned in her seat to Blaine. "If you want advice from someone, good advice, who do you go to?"

Blaine knew she was probably headed right into a trap, but she knew Callie wouldn't let her off the hook without answering. "I don't know." Blaine then thought hard for a good answer. "Probably someone knowledgeable about a topic. An expert on something."

"That's right." Callie nodded and patted her hand. "You ask someone who knows about the issue. If you have an accounting question, you ask an accountant. A legal issue, you ask a lawyer. Right?"

Blaine knew the path. Her grandmother had taken her down it many times.

"My parents had been happily married for over twenty years. They didn't do everything right, but they worked hard at not only being good parents, and, hard workers, but good role models for what a good marriage should be." Callie smiled. "So why wouldn't I ask them their advice about a boyfriend?"

There it was. Blaine shifted in her seat, and crossed her legs. If only Blaine had that prerogative.

Thankfully, Callie didn't ask anything more. Why did older people find things like this so explainable, and why did adults her age only want to seek out their own solution?

"God tells us, wise people ask."

Blaine shrunk in her seat. She was sitting next to a religious person. The trip suddenly went south.

Chapter 7

Blaine sighed. Now what could she do? She couldn't move to a new seat now. How rude would that be? Did she care? Religious people gave Blaine anxiety. She'd heard about them from her friends. She watched their behavior on the news every single night. They believed that women didn't have rights. That guns should be legal and safe for everyone to own. She shook her head. And above all, they believed God was the answer to everything.

The only way around this was to keep Callie on her story. Keep her talking about Miles. That would steer her away from telling her about her sins, about Jesus, about...

"So, what happened next?" Blaine smiled, intentionally.

Callie followed the hook like a line of women at a Coach store sale.

When Callie came into work the next Monday after Miles visited her house, Clarence was all smiles. She'd left home that morning, thankful to be away from her prying sisters and their endless prattle about Miles, but it wasn't any different here at the store.

"How was your weekend?" Clarence winked at her.

"Fine."

"Did you do anything special?"

"Not really." Why was this man fishing? "Has that shipment of shoe laces come in yet?"

"No. I expect it today or tomorrow."

Callie took off her coat and hung it on the hook behind her desk. Turning to her desk, she noticed a card propped up against her record-keeping books. Her name was scrawled on it. She went to reach for it, but realized that Clarence was eyeing her from across the room. She sat down, took the card and, slipped it into her purse, stashing her purse in the large drawer of her desk. As she did, Clarence went back to work.

She grabbed a pencil and began making notations in her notebook on the weekend sales. Looks like it had been slow, but January always had fewer sales than other months. February would be the same. She wasn't sure how Clarence could keep the store going and pay her at the same time. The war wasn't helping.

Many Americans were fearful of an attack on the mainland. Callie and her family had talked about it. They'd even planned what they would do if it did happen. If they were apart, they all agreed to get back to their farm as soon as they could. Nothing like this had ever happened in the United States. The fears from Pearl Harbor still were fresh, and worries mounted over the news coming in from all over the world.

Callie had learned of more of her high school friends enlisting and now heading off for boot camp. Clarence struggled to order tires for the store. He'd told Callie that this was just the beginning. He suspected gas would be next. Callie wondered if she would be able to keep her job if the bus stopped traveling out to the gravel road by her home.

* * *

"I can't imagine a country in war like that." Blaine looked over at Callie. "Things like tires and gas were actually rationed?"

Callie nodded. "Normal life changed. Many were worried, and the talk in the store was who was going, who had been lost and, sadly, who might be next. Clarence had two brothers fighting; this would be the third of his five brothers to go off to fight."

"How scary, especially for the parents of those already fighting." Blaine added, "Wondering if they'd ever see them again."

Callie looked out the window. "Miles' mother was a Godly woman. She loved the Lord. I often thought if anyone could handle three of her six boys fighting it would be Gertie, Miles' mother.

"For many of us, the Depression years were still alive and real. Yes, families were getting back into life. Jobs were available now, but suddenly, after so many years, now there weren't enough men left to do them. Farming was prevalent and needed, but so were manufacturing jobs. The car industry in the area was sprawling and getting bigger every year, but now many possible workers were going off to fight for their country."

"Callie, what did Miles' note say?"

Callie smiled, "I loved that note to death. I kept it for years. Miles had written only one sentence in it. 'You're my sunshine on a winter day.'

* * *

Miles began dropping by the house every Friday night. Callie had saved up enough the year before to buy a used player piano for her family for Christmas. Every so often Callie could afford to purchase a new, fun roll for it of the latest tune. On many a Friday evening, all her sisters' friends and Miles would stop by to play music together. They loved playing, dancing, and singing to the new tunes. Songs like "Pistol Packin' Momma" by Bing Crosby and the Andrews Sisters, and "You'll Never Know," by Vera Lang were just some of their favorites.

One particular evening, the fun had gone on for hours and the house grew quiet as one by one had to leave for home, leaving Callie and Miles alone in the piano room. Miles was a master at playing the piano. He could play almost any tune that was played for him. After everyone would go home and Callie's sisters would head up to bed, Miles would sing to her. She loved it.

On one particular night she just sat on the bench beside him, listening to him play for her. Callie smiled as he began to sing to her as he played. "You are my sunshine, my only sunshine. You make me happy, when skies are gray. You'll never know, dear, how much..." Miles stopped singing to pick up Callie's hand, "I love you." He looked into Callie's eyes, and then sang, "Please don't take my sunshine away."

Callie stopped breathing. She'd never had a man, besides her father, tell her he loved her. Miles raised her chin and kissed her. The softness of his lips, the moment she'd often dreamed about as she grew into a woman, the sensation she felt deep within her heart, made her close her eyes and then he repeated it. "I love you, Callie."

***

"I remember thinking, at that very moment," Callie exhaled, "life couldn't be any better than that second." She looked over at Blaine with tears in her eyes. "I will never forget that moment and what it felt like."

Blaine blinked. She knew that moment, although she never felt it like that with Kyle, but she did remember a first kiss with someone else. It was sentimental and almost stupid to think about, but she imagined most girls remembering their first kisses. Always. No matter who the guy was.

Callie looked over at her. "Do you remember that moment?"

Blaine smiled. "Doesn't everyone?"

Tears filled Callie's eyes. "I'm so glad I got to have it with Miles." Callie wiped her eyes with a tissue and then giggled. "Everything was perfect, until my sister walked through the door." Callie laughed some more. "I truly believe my father put her up to it."

"What did she do?"

"Later that night my sister sat on the staircase while Miles and I sat on the couch in the front room. We were just talking. She was supposed to be in bed, which made me even more sure my father had put her up to it.

"She'd have never gotten away with staying up so late. She was an entrepreneur even way back then. She told Miles if he would give her a quarter, she'd go upstairs to bed." Callie smiled, "Relentless should have been her name, not Mary."

Blaine giggled, "What did Miles do?"

"From that night forward," Callie laughed, "Miles never lacked quarters for my sister Mary." Nodding, she added, "She grew quite rich that winter."

Callie grew quiet again and looked out the window. "Then, unfortunately, came spring."

Chapter 8

"Oh Blaine, I'm sorry. Here I've just been blathering on and on about Miles." Callie leaned forward in her seat. "I haven't even considered you don't want to hear all of this."

Blaine was growing annoyed a bit, but tried to be polite. "Who doesn't want to hear a love story, Callie? But sometimes..."

Callie shifted to look Blaine in the eye. "But what?"

Blaine pulled at the collar of her shirt, "I don't mean to be disrespectful," she leaned back and shook her head, "but men like that don't exist anymore."

Callie grimaced. "Do you really believe that?"

Blaine wiped her nose with her sleeve. "And I'm sure Miles was great, but..."

"I'm sorry."

"No need to apologize. That's just my perception. I hate it, but it is what it is." Blaine had had enough of life's misfortunes to know.

Callie turned back to her and smiled. "I'm sorry the men in your life have been poor examples."

Blaine picked up her purse and rummaged through it for her phone. She wasn't sure if she should continue talking. She'd only known Callie for what, like an hour? Why did she all of a sudden feel the need to dump on her? But it happened without much effort.

Her voice went up an octave in pitch. "I don't know a single person who is happily married and living..." Blaine made quotes in the air with her fingers, "happily ever after. My friend's husband never goes to work.

He expects her to kill herself by working a thankless forty-hour-plus job and also take care of their three children." Blaine's voice grew exasperated. "All," she waved her hand in a circular motion above her head, "at the same time. Every time I see her, I wonder if it will be the last time I see her. She's exhausted. The kids run over her like she's nobody. Then, there's my grandma. Her husband left her when she was pregnant with my mom. She raised all her kids alone. And that's not even including my own father," Blaine raised her voice, "who, by the way, I have never seen!"

Callie touched her arm. "Sweetheart, I'm sorry. What about um...the boy who dropped you off at the station?"

"Kyle?" Blaine shook her head. "What about him?"

"Does he love you? Do you love him?"

Tears sprung immediately to Blaine's eyes. "Sounds like you've lived a pretty pristine life so far. I don't think you understand real life. Real life isn't like this. Women like me can only attract men like my boyfriend. We cater to them. We do everything in our power to keep them. 'Cause maybe that's all we can attract.

"Real life shows up. They expect so much out of you, pretty soon, you don't even know who you are anymore. Worse than that, you strive to continue to be the person they want you to be, and even then they'll find some hooker and use them to meet their needs." Blaine looked at her for a reaction. "I'm sorry, but that's real life."

Suddenly, for Callie, the reason for her trip began to make a little more sense. It wasn't about Mason at all. Even though those were her plans, God placed her here, right now, for perhaps this.

Blaine wiped her eyes again with the back of her hand. "I'm sorry, but I truly believe that men only exist for one reason and it isn't to make all our dreams come true."

Callie wondered if she should say something. Anything. But she had to know. "So, you aren't in love with…?"

"Kyle?" Blaine smirked. "In love? What's that? I'm just trying to find my way. Kyle just happened to be on the road to getting there."

"Is he in love with you?"

Blaine shook her head. "Who really knows?"

Callie looked sincere. "Do you want him to love you?"

More tears came then. "I once thought I did, but now I can't figure out a way to get him out of my life. He's controlling. Manipulative. He only thinks about himself. Always."

"I'm sorry, I should have been more sensitive. It's just that..." Callie wrung her hands in her lap.

Blaine wiped the tissue over her cheeks. "What, Callie?"

Callie looked over at her and smiled. "Every time I get on this train to head home, I think of Miles. Actually," Callie shook her head and wiped a tear off her cheek, "it isn't often I don't think of him, but this train brings out my story. I relive the moments. The good parts."

"The good parts? From what I hear so far, it was far from bad."

Callie smiled. "If you'd let me continue with my story, you'll see that it didn't stay that way."

Blaine asked, "You mean, it doesn't end happily ever after?"

Callie looked over at her. "It depends on what kind of happily ever after you mean." She tried to appear cheerful, even though her heart ached for this young woman. If somehow Callie could help this young woman believe that true love did exist, not just Miles' and her story, it might make this entire trip even more worthwhile.

Something prompted Callie to add, "I won't bore you any further if you don't want to hear anymore. I can keep it all to myself." She smiled. "You won't hurt my feelings if you don't want to listen. I'm sure, to a young woman like you, it may sound like a story, too good to be true."

Blaine seemed to lighten up a bit. "I'm sure it's a wonderful story."

Callie knew she was just trying to be polite. "What if I told you it wasn't as wonderful as it started out to be?"

Blaine shook her head. "Excuse me, Callie, but I need to use the restroom."

* * *

Blaine closed the door to the small restroom and sat on the edge of the closed toilet. Men were scum. All men. None cared about women like the movies made them out to do. This old woman who shared her seat on the train was delusional. There was only one thing that men wanted. She'd dish it out. Just like all the other women. Once they had that and could play around for a few months, then the real man would always come out. Just like Kyle had. They all pretend in the beginning to be something they really aren't.

What if Callie's story turned out to be no different? Would Blaine even want to hear it? Deep in her efforts to run from Chicago? Leave Kyle for good? Unfortunately, in Blaine's world, she wasn't sure she had any choice.

* * *

Callie wondered if Blaine would return to her seat. She looked down to see her things still sitting on the floor.

Yes, her love story resembled that Disney-like perception, but it was far from that. Many marriages start out with moments such as the ones she had shared with Miles. But, as with most relationships, time keeps moving and even the greatest of love stories are tried by meeting a monthly mortgage, paying electric bills, weight gains with pregnancies, and flat tires.

Blaine did return to her seat. She was quiet for a few minutes. She pulled a mirror from her purse and reapplied her mascara.

Callie sighed.

Blaine looked over at her. "Something wrong?"

Callie shook her head. "No, I was just thinking about flat tires.

"Flat tires?" Blaine grimaced as she dropped her mascara tube back into her purse.

"Flat tires during the war were not just flat tires. A real concern grew when someone got a flat tire," Callie pushed on. Perhaps if she kept the story moving, Blaine would soften more. "The war made tires scarce."

* * *

"I'm not sure what we're gonna do, Callie," Clarence answered after hearing about the store not being able to order tractor tires. "It's not gonna stop there. This is just tires, but what about other things like car replacement parts?" He looked up from his inventory list. "Even nylons."

Callie blushed. The problem was just getting larger. Today it was tractor tires, tomorrow it would be more things. What would happen with her father's car repair business if he couldn't buy replacement parts? How would people get to work? If their jobs weren't within walking distance, they wouldn't be able to report to work. Callie would lose her job if the bus stopped traveling to Flint every day. Then how could she help her parents at home? She sighed.

"So, how's Miles?" Clarence stood by her desk. Tucking the clipboard under one arm, a grin replaced his frown.

Callie looked down at her figures. "Miles is fine." She couldn't refrain from grinning, and with her luck, probably blushing. Miles had the same effect on her, every time she looked into his soft, kind, green eyes.

Callie looked up at Clarence. She'd avoided eye contact for fear he'd be bold and ask her how she felt about Miles. He went back to looking over his list. "He's going off to war soon."

Callie picked up a pencil to sharpen. She scooted her chair back and went back to the pencil sharpener in the back of the store. Clarence followed her.

"Callie, how will you do with that?"

Callie inserted the pencil into the sharpener and began turning the crank. She hated to think about Miles leaving, but as with all women across the United States, she wasn't alone. Fear nearly strangled her heart every time she thought about it. Sadness would fill her soul in the middle of the night for no apparent reason, and it would keep her awake for hours if she allowed it. She stopped sharpening her pencil, but didn't turn to face Clarence. "I'll hate it."

Clarence grabbed her shoulders. "We'll all hate it." Clarence turned on a heel and went back to the front of the store. "Hard enough with the other brothers there, but Miles," Clarence sighed. "He's the baby."

* * *

"Blaine, can I tell you something?"

Blaine sighed, looked down at her hands, but nodded. She didn't look up.

"I know the world has changed since 1942." Callie shook her head. "So much. I don't know how men are these days. I haven't dated since then." She laughed. "Never had the desire, nor do I now."

Blaine shook her head. "So? What does that have to do with me?"

"I tell young women like you my story only to give you hope. Inspire you. Challenge you to," Callie breathed a quick prayer, "not give up on anyone. Life is hard. Marriage is harder. Things don't always turn out as they first seem."

That comment caused Blaine to look up. "So, your life with Miles didn't stay as perfect as it started?"

Callie smiled and grabbed the young woman's hand. "Hardly."

Chapter 9

Callie put her hand over her chest. The pain came and went. Sometimes it would travel down her right arm. It was probably something she'd had for breakfast, aggravating her acid reflux issue. In the hurry of the morning, she'd forgotten to take her tablet. Her ear ached, too. Perhaps the walk to the train had aggravated more than she thought.

"Did he go off to war?" Blaine leaned her head back on her seat. The train whistle echoed through their car. It distracted them.

"I love that sound."

"The whistle?"

Blaine nodded. "It's almost a comforting sound. You don't often hear them in the heart of Chicago. More like horn's blaring from irritated cab drivers and roars from trucks needing mufflers."

"I think of the importance of being on this train and having others have to stop at the tracks to allow us to pass." Callie smiled. "Makes me feel important."

Blaine smiled. "I can see how you'd think that."

Both women looked out the train window as they crossed in front of a line of headlights.

"The next two months flew by. Then Miles got the letter."

"The letter?"

"Of where to report and when. We'd been having such a wonderful time. The winter had flown by as we'd spend each Friday night at my house listening to music. Sometimes Miles would save enough money to take me to a movie. We'd try to go to a happy one and not view the war movies, but on this one particular night, we got in the wrong movie theater. Before we knew it we were mesmerized watching the fighting and battle going on right in front of us. For some reason, we stayed and watched."

"You didn't watch the news?"

Callie laughed. "We only had radios, dear. No televisions."

Blaine laughed now. "Of course."

"They would film the war from Japan, the South Pacific, and then everyone would race to the movie theatres to watch our boys in action. Some people could sit and watch our boys fighting for our country, even dying for it. But with Miles planning to go off in a few months, it wasn't something I had the stomach to watch."

***

That night the movie theater was cold. Callie kept adjusting her sweater closer around her neck. The sounds of war seemed to drown out her thoughts. She couldn't move. Miles seemed to be reacting the same way. Callie wanted to ask him if they could leave, but she couldn't get her eyes off the big screen.

Glancing around, everyone stared at the screen as though they were viewing a glimpse of what was happening to their boyfriends, brothers, sons, grandsons...as if watching would keep everyone on the screen well. Safe. Yet, deep down, everyone knew that this wasn't a theatrical production. It was real. Men were actually being killed.

Callie looked over at Miles to see a bead of sweat make its way down the side of his face. He scowled. A cannon-like blast erupted from a tank, approaching what seemed to be a small village. Children ran from the streets, doing their best to reach their parents' outstretched hands for safety. Callie didn't know how much longer she could sit still and watch. The horror ripped her heart apart and she realized she was fighting to breathe. A bomb went off close to a tank, and she flinched. She nudged Miles. "I'm leaving."

He continued to stare at the screen. "Miles." She rarely raised her voice in a theater, but for this she didn't care who was disturbed by her urging. Miles continued to ignore her. "Miles, I'm leaving." For some reason he'd heard that, and soon was following her out of the noises of war filling the room. Another explosion made her jump.

Once outside, Callie kept walking. She pulled her sweater closer and started buttoning the front. It was spring, yet the temperatures had yet to warm the nights.

"Callie?" Miles called her from behind. "Callie, hold on."

Callie couldn't stop. She wanted to be as far away from the sounds of war as she could get. She knew that what went in would cement itself in her heart, keeping her even more awake at night. Miles finally reached her and pulled her arm back. "Callie, can you stop a second?"

Callie could feel the tears streaming down her face. She didn't want Miles to see them so she stared at the sidewalk as Miles fought to get her attention.

"Callie, look at me." She shook her head.

"Which movie have you liked better? South Pacific or Yankee Doodle Dandy?" Miles picked up her hand, squeezed it tight, and smiled at her.

She pulled her hand away and kept walking. "No fair."

"Answer the question."

Callie grew frustrated. "Miles, I don't think this is the time..."

"If we don't change the subject, we'll both start crying."

"I'm not crying."

"Okay, well, then don't let me start. I'm a horrible crier. My face gets screwed up into a horrible contorted mess, and once I start..."

Callie wiped the back of her hand over her cheek.

Miles called from behind her. "It's just embarrassing."

Callie stopped.

Miles walked around, and stood in front of her, "What Callie?"

"I can't do this."

"I know." Miles pointed back to the theater. "I should have gotten up sooner. Left first."

"No, Miles." Callie looked up at him. "Us. I can't do us anymore."

Miles' facial muscles relaxed and then he began to scowl. "What? Do what anymore?"

"This!" Callie walked around Miles and continued down the sidewalk.

"Callie, stop."

Callie shook her head. She could hear Miles run up to her from behind. He turned her around. "Callie, what are you saying?"

Callie looked up into the face of the man she'd fallen in love with over the past few months. She loved his face. His smile. His kindness. His returned love. And that single dimple at the edge of his mouth. It took all her courage to say, "I've changed my mind. Take me home."

Miles shook his head, but seemed to realize how serious she was and that she meant what she was saying. He stuffed his hands into his pockets and said, "Okay. Let's go." He turned and left her on the sidewalk and walked back to his car. She followed. What had made her say that? What had she just done?

* * *

Miles came into the store a few days later. His face was solemn, his smile gone. Clarence had been behind the counter and came out to meet him. They whispered something. Clarence looked down, grabbed his hand with both of his own, and shook it. All Callie could do was stare. Miles looked over at her and flashed her a grin and a dimple, but then as fast as it came, it disappeared, and his eyes grew moist.

Callie didn't know what to do. She knew what news he'd gotten. He'd been called up. Boot camp. She hadn't talked to him since he dropped her off in her driveway that past weekend. She looked down at her tally sheet and pretended to keep working. She heard Miles steps growing closer. Soon Miles' shadow was over her desk; her figures on the sheet went dim. Despite his presence, Callie couldn't look up.

"Good morning, Callie."

Callie nodded without looking up.

"Can we go outside and talk?"

Callie shook her head. "I have work to do."

Clarence called from the other side of the room. "Go ahead Callie. I'll hold up the fort for awhile."

Callie sighed and whispered, "It won't work."

"I just need to talk to you," Miles implored.

"I've made up my mind."

She looked up to see Miles crossing his arms. "So what do you mean? Is this it? Has nothing happened over the last few months? It means nothing?"

"It's no use, Miles. I'll pray for you and your safety, but I can't sit here and..." Callie gulped.

"Okay." Miles backed away from her desk. Callie looked back down at her bookkeeping sheet, although tears blurred her eyes too much for her to see it. She wiped them away quickly with the back of her hand so they wouldn't end up smearing her tallies.

"I'm sorry, Miles." She looked up. "May God protect you and keep you safe."

He lowered his arms and turned. "I love you Callie. I always will."

As he left her, Callie felt her whole world crumble to pieces. Like a solid piece of earth hit by a strong wall of water, pieces of her started dissolving into an ocean. Layer by layer. Her pencil dropped, she gasped for air. Something was pulling her to stand up. A force she never knew possible. As the front door of the store slammed and the bell tinkled to announce a new customer, Callie stood up so fast it knocked her chair backward with a slam to the floor. Clarence looked back at her, startled. All she could do was holler his name. His amazing, beautiful name. "Miles!" She was heading out through that same door. Right behind him.

"I hate this!" The scream startled Miles as he was getting into his car in the parking lot.

He heard her and got back out the car. He didn't move. He just stood just inside his car door. If she were to officially break it off with him, he didn't know if he wanted to hear it. He'd rather not hear her say it. That way, he could pretend that it didn't really happen. But she said something else as she stood just outside the door of the store. Her hands were clenched by her side. He battled the eagerness to jump into the car to make the horror of it all go away, but just then he saw her shoulders start to shake as she raised a hand over her mouth.

He'd be the man. The one to swallow his pride and listen to what she had to say. If she wanted to end it, he'd take it like a man. Just like the upcoming boot camp. If he could fight in a war, he could start with a battle with Callie. He left the car door open and approached her. She was now visibly sobbing on the porch of his brother's store.

As he approached her, he wasn't quite sure what he was going to do. Should he just stand there and take the verdict or hug her and leave? He hated seeing her cry. He felt a single tear trickle down his cheek. In that split-second he knew what he wanted to do. What he needed to do.

He wrapped his arm around her tiny waist, drew her close to him and kissed her solid and hard on the mouth. The taste of the kiss was salty from their tears, but the bond solidified more as she wrapped her arms around his neck and pulled him closer. She returned the kiss almost as exuberantly as he delivered it. When it finally ended they stood in the embrace and he drew her even closer. Their foreheads touched and Callie whispered, "I just don't know what I'm going to do without you."

* * *

"I knew at that very moment, with that one single, solitary kiss that I would never let him go. No matter what was to happen. I would love him forever." Callie wiped a tear now lingering on her cheek. She may be on a train headed back to her home in Michigan, but at that moment, reliving that kiss made Callie feel young again. She was back in Flint and in love. She closed her eyes remembering it. From the smells of his jacket, to the coolness of the spring morning outside.

"Did he leave?" Blaine grabbed Callie's hand.

"The next day. On a train." Callie looked out the window of the train now barreling down the tracks at top speed. "For Florida."

"What happened that night?"

"It wasn't a very happy night. I had to go back into work and finish my job for the day."

"His brother couldn't give you the afternoon off?"

"I was working. I needed the job and, despite my boss being my boyfriend's brother, he still expected a day's work for a day's wages. That's how it was in 1942."

"I'd have quit," Blaine announced. "There's always other jobs."

"Not many. It was a job I needed to keep. It paid well and the hours were perfect for a single woman. But, we did get together again that night and said our goodbyes. It was horrible, but I also knew he'd return."

"How did you know that?"

"Cause Miles had never lied to me before." Callie leaned her head on the back of the train seat. "At that moment in our relationship, he had never broken a promise."

Chapter 10

Curious to hear the rest of Callie's story, Blaine could see she appeared agitated. Perhaps she felt she'd revealed too much personal information, yet Blaine knew she hadn't pushed Callie to talk about her past. Glancing over at the elderly woman, she clutched her shirt in a fist at her chest.

"Are you okay, Callie?"

Callie looked at her with a perplexed look, but then relaxed, smiling. "I feel badly that I haven't been able to let Mason know that I made it onto the train."

"Why don't you call him?"

"How?"

Blaine was unsure of why the woman couldn't call. "Don't you have a cell phone?"

Callie shook her head. "No. What would an old woman like me do with a cell phone?"

Blaine wanted to say, 'call your grandson,' but then she added, "You could borrow my phone. Who's his provider?"

Callie gave her a quizzical look. "God."

Blaine laughed right out loud. "What?"

"God is our provider," Callie claimed decisively and without hesitation.

Blaine shook her head. "Well, maybe, but what about his cell phone provider?"

Callie laughed. "Oh, I don't know. I thought you meant who takes care of him."

Blaine knew she wouldn't get anywhere with her questions. She picked up her purse and pulled out her phone. "Do you know his phone number?"

Callie picked up her purse. "Yes, he gave me the number before I left this morning. He just got a new one." She began digging in her purse. "Somewhere."

Callie then proceeded to take out several slips of paper, two sales receipts, a twenty five cent coupon, and a fast food Monopoly playing piece. "Oh dear, I wonder if I need that one on my board..."

Blaine giggled. "Callie, what if you never find..."

"Ah, here it is." Callie smiled at Blaine. "Can you dial your phone, dear? I have no idea how to work those new-fangled things."

"Yes, I can do that."

Callie smoothed out the wrinkled piece of paper that had her grandson's number on it. She smiled and handed it to Blaine. "I appreciate this. Oh."

Blaine asked, "What, Callie?"

"Does that thing do the word thingy?"

"What?" Blaine squinted. "What word thingy?"

"Oh dear." Callie squinted. "I can't remember what to call it. Word, no. It's like you type into the phone."

"Text?"

"I think that's it. Mason has a hard time answering a phone call at work, so if you could do that thingy?"

"Text?"

"Yes. Then he doesn't have to stop working."

"Got it. Hold on." Blaine entered Mason's phone number into her phone. "So, what do you want to tell him, or do you want to do it?"

Callie shook her head. “No, honey. I wouldn’t know the first thing about how to even attempt to do it.”

Blaine nodded as she spelled out Mason in her contacts. “Go ahead when you’re ready.”

“Just tell him I made the train and all is well.”

Blaine smiled, yet jealously filled her heart. How special it would be to have someone care whether you got to your destination. Blaine thumbed the send message button on her phone. “There.”

“All done?” Callie laughed. “You’re quick.”

“I told him who I was and then said you were well and on the train.”

“Do you think he’ll do that?” Callie pointed to Blaine’s phone. “Text. That’s it, right?”

Blaine nodded. “If he texts back, I’ll let you know.”

Callie nodded, patted her hand, and said, “Thank you.”

Blaine looked up. “Sure, my pleasure.”

***

"What was it like for him?"

Callie shifted in her seat toward Blaine. "Who, honey?”

"Miles? Boot camp?"

"Oh, Miles."

"Remember, Callie? You sent him off. To boot camp?" Blaine seemed to think repeating herself wasn't getting through to the older woman. Maybe she should just mind her own business.

"Boot camp." Callie glanced back out the window and seemed to stop interacting for a few moments. Then she turned back to Blaine. "It was the longest three months of my life."

"Three months sounds like a long time."

Callie nodded. "When a relationship is just starting out, it seems like forever."

"Three months? Boot camp doesn't last that long, does it?"

"I don't know what it is now, but just after Pearl Harbor boot camp usually lasted around six weeks. But for Miles, he left early and got home late. He left me in the spring and I didn't see him again until the middle of the summer." Callie looked out the window again. "He wrote every day and I to him, but it couldn't replace seeing his face, smelling his aftershave, or even feeling his kisses." Callie turned again. "Nothing prepares a sweetheart for war. You don't know how long he'll be gone. What life will be like without him. And worse," Callie turned back again to face Blaine, "if you'll even see him again."

Callie continued. "I thought of Miles every night. Every single night. During the day, while I was working, I didn't hurt or miss him as much. I was busy and didn't have time. But as my sisters had boys coming to the house in the evenings, I would often watch with envy as they sat close and talked. Their boyfriends were too young to go off to war.

"War makes a girl feel so alone. On those evenings, my mother often called me into the kitchen to help her with something. I was too young and naive to know what she was trying to do, but her conversations would redirect my thoughts."

* * *

"I think we're going to have a bumper crop of tomatoes this year." Callie's mother was busy snipping the fresh beans out of the garden. She sat in a chair by the kitchen table with a bowl in her lap and another one close by on the table. Callie's mother snipped beans, like most women knitted or even played the piano. She snipped with a swift motion of snipping and cracking the beans as she tossed each into the bowl on the table. Soon it created a rhythm all its own.

Callie pulled out another chair from the table and grabbed a handful of the beans from her mother's bowl and followed with a motion all her own. "So many beans, too."

Callie's mother nodded. "Yes. These are just the first row. I haven't even picked the next two yet."

The only noise was the snip sound, the snaps of cracking beans, and then the clink the finished beans made in the metal bowl.

Callie could feel her mother's eyes on her. Looking up, she caught a glimpse of her staring at her, but quickly diverted her eyes when Callie saw her. "I think Esther is liking that boy."

Callie nodded. Her youngest sister just had a new boy stopping by. His hair was dark, his eyes a deep blue. He was a handsome boy. She hoped the handsome part wasn't overpowering her sister's wisdom in choosing wisely, "He seems nice."

"He has a lot of older brothers. Two sisters, too. Do you know them?"

Callie shook her head. "No."

"Me neither. Been trying to ask a few neighbors."

"Nothing?"

Her mother shook her head. "No one has heard of them. Too close to the creek. Don't much hear about them this far west."

"Mary seems to like Bert quite a bit, too."

"You girls have grown up too fast for me. Too many changes. Too many boys. Too fast."

Callie laughed. "But Mother, we're at that age."

Her mother looked up and smiled. "But not all at once."

Again, the snapping bean sounds filled the room.

"Have you heard from Miles?"

Callie nodded. She missed him more than she even thought possible. "It seems he's just disappeared. I didn't know how much I liked him until..." why was she confiding so much to her mother? This felt odd.

Her mother snipped two beans at once. "Until he was gone."

Callie swallowed hard to prevent herself from crying.

"I don't quite understand that feeling of lonesomeness. Once your father and I were dating, we didn't quite ever have a time without each other. Although to think about it, I don't think I would have enjoyed it much either."

"But Mother, this is different. So different. What if he's gone for a long time? What if he forgets about me while he's gone? What if...?" Callie couldn't speak her next thoughts. She looked up at mother who now looked at her with love.

"It's a scary time. For all of us. Who knows how long this war will last? A future is not promised to anyone, but especially for those going off to war." Callie's mother sighed.

Callie could barely see the beans now as tears slipped down her cheeks. Her mother handed her a handkerchief from inside her apron pocket, but then continued snipping beans.

"Callie, you need to make up your mind." She stopped her motion for a moment and tapped Callie's hand. "He needs you fully or not at all."

"Make up my mind?" Callie wiped her eyes and looked at her mother.

"Miles doesn't need a reason or a distraction from what he is about to do. You need to make up your mind whether you love him or not. Will you wait for him or look around for another while he's gone?"

Callie shook her head. "It's too soon."

"It's war, Callie." She stopped snipping and looked up at Callie. "He needs to know what he'll have when he returns. If you like him or even love him, tell him now. But if you're having second thoughts about him or really don't think you want to spend the rest of your life with him, he needs to know that, too. And then..."

Callie looked at her mother as her eyes went back to snipping the beans.

She looked up again. "He needs to know what will await him when he returns. If you love him, you have to be faithful. If you're unsure about any of it, you need to let him know." Again, she returned to her snipping. "If you do love him, you need to give him one thing before he leaves."

Callie asked, "What?"

"Your faithfulness. Your unswerving, unchanging faithfulness."

Callie wiped her eyes again and began snipping beans.

"He deserves that. Do you understand?" Her mother looked up at her again.

"I think so."

"No matter what happens."

* * *

Callie looked over at Blaine. "My mother rarely gave me worthless advice. When she spoke, it was important to listen."

Chapter 11

Blaine wasn't sure how all of this had happened. She had been looking forward to plugging in her headphones and blocking out the world on the way home. Home? Was she now trying to even fool herself? What if Callie knew she wasn't heading home, but just running away from Kyle?

Blaine looked around her. No one knew her secret. She'd tried to leave before, but had never been this successful. She'd make it as far as Michigan City before totally freaking out. What if she ran away and then couldn't fend for herself? Kyle made great money. She'd left him without a plan. But this time, she was determined. She wasn't going back. If she did, she would never contact him again.

She had a friend who might take her in once she arrived in Lapeer, but other than that she really didn't know what she was going to do. Spending Christmas alone sounded horribly sad. Her friend thought her visit was to see her new baby. If she could hold out through Christmas, and maybe even the New Year, she'd come up with an idea of where to head. Where to go. A new place and a new beginning.

"Blaine?"

Blaine looked up. Callie stood over her and a sudden lurch of the train caused her to stumble after her trip to the restroom. She nearly fell into Blaine's lap. Blaine held Callie's arm, to steady her. "Careful." She stood up and allowed Callie to maneuver back into her seat, then sat down. "Sorry, Callie."

"Where were you? You seemed miles away."

Blaine shook her head. "Just thinking of the coming New Year."

"Hard to believe it will be a new year." Callie smiled. "I never thought I'd live to see any year past the year 2000."

Blaine wanted to change the subject. Get Callie back to her story. "So, what was it like to have him gone?"

"Miles?"

Blaine nodded. "Miles." She smiled.

* * *

The letters came every other day. Callie never knew Miles liked to write so much, but she was so thankful he did. Boot camp was quite the grueling experience for him. He described in detail the weather, his new friends, even being beat up by the drill sergeant. His letters made her feel like she was right there with him.

Yet those three months felt like three years. Each day she felt anxious anticipation while returning home from work. Would a letter be propped up on the counter by the back door? Worse yet, would she have to place it aside so she could help her mother put dinner on the table, often having to sit through dinner before having the chance to open it? Callie felt rude opening it at the table and not reading it for everyone to hear.

If she didn't know any better, she thought perhaps her father wanted to watch her squirm and eat like a hungry young calf so she could help clean up and rush upstairs to read it. "Another letter today, Callie?"

Callie put a mouthful of tuna noodle casserole in her mouth and nodded. "Yes, Daddy."

"Sure get lots of them."

Callie nodded as she chewed.

Mary looked up and winked. "What are they about?"

Callie added, "None of your business."

Callie's mother patted Mary's hand. "Eat your food."

As soon as the dishes were piled on the counter for her sisters to wash, Callie would escape to her room, shut the door, and rip open the letter. She loved the salutation the most. '*My dear Callie,*' or only one word which always made her blush '*Beautiful.*' Callie knew she wasn't beautiful at all. She had plain brown hair which she could barely keep in curls, especially during a humid Michigan summer. As she left work, even hairpins couldn't keep her looking half way decent. Her dresses were beginning to show wear, and her shoes had scuff marks, and a heel on her left shoe kept falling off. Yet reading his words, made her feel like a princess.

Then he'd add. '*Oh dearest, I miss you so. I think of you each moment of the day. The drill sergeants are brutal. We go from sun up to sun down, but I take at least fifteen minutes each night to slip under my bed covers with a flashlight and write as much as I can before they come in for inspection. Oh, how I miss you. Hope work is going all right. Clarence isn't working you to death, is he? Guess what? They've made me the drill caller as we train. As the men march, I call out little ditties to keep them marching and to keep up morale. I love to march. I'd so much rather do that than run. I've made up several wonderful ways to keep everyone's spirits up. They like me to call. I add a bit of rhythmic music as we go.*

Looks like I'll be graduating soon. They're cutting boot camp short so we can be shipped off sooner. We need to pray hard, Callie. We need to do our best to keep up our spirits. God will care for me. He will be there to care for you. I'm sure of it. Please keep praying for me, Callie. All my love, Miles.

Callie would often cry as she read the letters. She missed that man. Her heart would ache reading about his sore muscles and tiredness. He probably shouldn't be writing so late into the night. Why didn't he rest? Yet, she was so thankful for his letters. It kept her alive. Functioning.

She placed the letter on the stack in her bureau drawer, smoothing them down with her hand. There were so many now. She would never throw one away. On the weekends, she often pulled out a few of them to read over again. How long would it be before she could see him again? Only God and the United States government knew.

A car pulled into the driveway. Callie didn't look down from her second floor bedroom window, certain it was one of her sisters' boyfriends. She wasn't in the mood to see the girls flirt and cuddle with their boys. She felt a tinge of guilt, yet still praying they never had to kiss them goodbye like she had had to do with Miles.

Callie lay down on her bed and began to cry. She'd thought long and hard about what her mother had said. Callie knew she had to make up her mind about Miles. It wasn't a question whether she loved him. She did, or she wouldn't be telling him so in all her letters. Telling the truth was important to Callie.

Could she stand by him, despite what their future might hold? That's what kept her from agreeing to love him through the whole war. But then she began to predict the worst that could happen. If he lost a leg, she could still love him. Perhaps he would come home in a critical medical situation. All these thoughts haunted Callie. The only thing Callie was reluctant to agree to was having to stand at a grave. That scared her the most. What if he wanted to marry her before he left for war? Could she be a war widow?

Her mother called from the base of the stairway. "Callie, can you come down? Miles' mother is here to see you."

Callie jumped up off her bed and glanced down at their driveway. Miles' car was parked in the driveway. She went to the mirror and wiped her eyes. She hoped no one noticed she'd been crying. Red blotches always appeared on her face when she did. Callie picked up her compact and powdered again.

As she came down the stairs Miles' mother was at the foot, looking up at her with a smile. "Hello, Callie." Callie had only been to Miles' house a few times since he'd left for boot camp. She held out her hand. "Hello."

Mrs. Bennett held out her own hand and clasped Callie's in her own. "How are you?"

Callie could feel her own mother's gaze on her. She knew if she were to look her way, she'd probably resume crying again. Being truthful sometimes hurt. "Lonely," she told Mrs. Bennett.

She smiled. "Me, too, sounds silly to admit when I have so many others at home." Tears filled her eyes as well. "But none of them are my Miles. My baby."

Callie's mother broke the discomfort. "Let's go into the living room." She led the woman to one of their most comfortable chairs. "Well, what brings you to visit, Mrs. Bennett?"

"I just got a letter from Miles."

Callie gasped. "Everything's okay, right?" She inched to the edge of her seat.

"Oh, Callie, yes. Everything is fine." She waved off Callie. "Dear, he's fine."

Callie eased a bit, but couldn't officially relax with Miles' mother in the room.

"Well, he's asked me to come see him."

"He has?" Callie felt a tinge of sadness fill her heart, but then she felt guilt. "I mean, how wonderful." Why wouldn't Miles want his mother to come visit? She looked down at her hands, twisting her apron around her hand.

"And he wants me to bring you."

Callie looked up. "What?"

"Would you like to go?"

"To see Miles?" Callie edged closer to the end of her seat. "Um, well, it all depends."

"On what, Callie?" Miles' mother grinned.

"Well, I'll have to take off work and I'm not sure Clarence will let me go for..."

"Probably two weeks."

"Two weeks?"

"Honey, we're going to California. Not sure two weeks will even be enough. Don't worry about Clarence. I'll take care of that. Would you go with me?"

"California?"

"I just got word. Boot camp is over and they're transporting them to the West Coast. As soon as he arrives he just has a few days and then they're shipping him overseas." This time the tears came without hesitation. Callie looked over at her mother, who just smiled at her. "Okay. Yes. Of course, I'll come."

Mrs. Bennett stood. "Then, it's all settled."

Chapter 12

The next few weeks were a whirlwind, as Callie tried hard to finish up monthly bookkeeping for Clarence before her trip to California.

"Can you be sure you have all the bills paid for September before you leave, Callie?"

Callie nodded. Paying all the bills for a six-week period was going to keep Callie busy, but having a few weeks off to go see Miles made it all worth the work.

"Are you excited to see Miles?"

Callie continued sorting through the bills.

"I can't believe Mother is going." Clarence poured more ice into a barrel by the front door. He always had cold pop bottles on hand for their afternoon customers.

Callie looked up. "Why do you say that?"

"It's just odd, that's all. She hates traveling. Leaving my father. None of it makes much sense," Clarence carried bottles of soda from a back room storage area to the front of the store and placed them in the cooling barrel.

Looking back to her recording sheet, Callie added, "Why is it so odd that a mother wants to go see her son before..."

She probably shouldn't have said anything, yet Callie was unsure where Clarence was going with this whole conversation. He walked back to her desk and folded his arms. "She's not a traveler. Never has been."

Callie couldn't take it any longer. Clarence had been defensive since she told him they were both going out to meet Miles on the West Coast. "Miles is her son."

"I'm her son." Clarence shook his head. "So are my four other brothers."

Looking up again, Callie said, "I don't believe she thinks any less of any of the rest of you." Callie grew annoyed. "Or your brothers."

Clarence walked away, muttering as he went.

She was good at her job. She worked hard. Going back to record a few more bills on the accounts payable ledger, Callie convinced herself Clarence was angry with her for leaving because he needed her. She needed this job, but she desired to see Miles more. If she came back and someone else had taken her place, so be it. She'd do the best she could to finish well before she left.

The day drew on and Callie ate her lunch at her desk. It would save her the half hour she normally went out to get the latest newspaper for her father to read. It helped her take a break from sitting at her desk. Today, she wanted to finish tallying up the accounts payable ledger so tomorrow she could start writing out the checks to pay the bills.

She'd worked for a six straight hours and was just about ready to get up for a break, when Clarence came to her desk and set something down on it. "Could you find room in your suitcase for this?"

Callie looked at what Clarence had set down on her desk. "He does love these chocolates."

Callie glanced up at Clarence. "I'm sorry. I know this trip is important to you. Go love on my brother for me. Tell him to stay safe. There are no atheists in foxholes. May God be with him." Miles' brother smiled and pushed his hands into his pockets, whistling as he went to the front of the store.

Callie sighed and pulled the box of chocolates closer to her purse. That would remind her to not forget them. She smiled, knowing Miles would love them. It was Clarence's way of showing his affection for his brother, and a peace offering to Callie that he was giving his approval of her trip.

* * *

The days lingered on like it was the week before a holiday. Callie thought she'd never get through the week. She and Gertie would leave on the train early Saturday morning out of Durand. The depot in Durand was one of the biggest in the state. Callie had taken the train a few years ago to visit her mother's sister on the west side of Michigan. It had just taken two hours, but going across the whole country would take much longer. She loved traveling, but she'd never done it alone. Thankfully, she didn't have to do it alone because of Gertie's invitation. It would give them a chance to become better acquainted.

Miles' mother was sweet. She always had a good time while visiting her, which had included a few after-church lunches during the summer.

The only consolation of such a long trip was what would be at the end. Miles' last few letters had been about his preparation to leave Florida and head to California. Gertie and Callie would follow behind, making the trip through the northern states of the country. She hadn't gotten a letter in awhile, so she hoped his trip was going well. He'd promised to write as soon as he arrived in California, but Callie probably wouldn't receive them until her arrival home in a few weeks.

Callie hadn't gone that long without hearing from Miles throughout their entire dating relationship. She thought about all of this as the bus from town meandered down the country roads to her home. As the bus came to a screeching halt, Callie stood up from her bus seat. Glancing out a bus window, it seemed so dark. Long summer nights were giving way to shorter fall ones. She'd finished all her assigned work but had to stay an extra couple of hours to do it. She continued to worry that her job might be given to someone else before she could return. Surely Clarence wouldn't do that to her.

As she stepped down the steps of the bus, she looked up to see her father's pickup idling at the end of the road. She smiled and approached the truck. Her father rolled down his window. "Want a ride, sweetie?"

"What are you doing here?" Her father had never come to pick her up at the end of the road without a good reason.

"You have some long days ahead. I thought a ride tonight might be nice."

Callie went to the passenger side of the truck as her father leaned over the seat and opened the door for her. She slid in, "Thank you."

He smiled, grinded the rusty truck into gear, and headed down the road. "You all packed?"

"Almost." Callie placed her purse on her lap, as the bumps in their dirt road jolted the truck like a roller coaster ride.

"I hope you have good weather. Fall has been holding off." Her father shifted again into a faster gear.

"Wonder what California weather is like in September."

Her father laughed. "I wouldn't know. I've just heard what others say."

The truck roared into another gear. The ride from the end of the road was only about three-quarters of a mile to their farmhouse on the north side of the road. Dust began seeping into the car as Callie's father rolled up his window.

"Callie?"

"Yes, Daddy?"

Her father held out his hand in a fist. Callie opened her hand under his and a roll of money fell into her open palm.

"What's this?"

"Take it. It's from your mother and me."

"Oh, Daddy, this isn't necessary."

He put up his hand in protest. "Keep it. We did well this summer with hay, and your mother sold some of that bumper tomato crop of hers. It isn't much, but maybe you can take that handsome boyfriend of yours out to dinner one night."

Callie held the money out to him. "You need to keep this. You'll need it for spring crops."

Her father shook his head. "Who taught you to sass your daddy?"

Callie knew her father was teasing, but giving her any money wasn't easy.

"Just take it. Your mother wanted you to have a little extra."

Callie looked at the money in her hand. "Thank you."

"You work hard. It's the least we can do for how much you've helped us out this past year."

This would be the longest Callie had ever been away from home, her parents..., even her sisters. She felt a tinge of hesitancy grow in her heart, but then she thought of Miles. For the first time, she realized, this was part of being faithful to him. A new sense of excitement filled her heart. She couldn't wait to see him.

Chapter 13

The next morning, she met Miles' mother at the train station. Her father had driven her in his truck. He pulled up to the curb to drop off her luggage at the sidewalk, then turned to kiss her forehead. She tried hard not to burst into tears as she watched him stride around the back of his truck to head back home. After he slid into the driver's seat, he pulled out a handkerchief, wiping his eyes and nose.

Sitting on a bench inside the depot, Callie found Mrs. Bennett. She stood, smiling as Callie approached her.

"Ready for a train ride?"

Callie took a deep breath and walked toward her. "I think so."

Miles' mother looked concerned. "Are you okay, dear?"

Callie nodded. "I've never really been away from home before. I'm a little nervous."

"Are you changing your mind about going?"

Callie shook her head. "No."

The older woman grabbed her hand.

Callie hated admitting this trip was her first big trip away from home. Of course, she was old enough to travel, but inside she felt much too young to be traveling so far away.

"Well, let's start the trip well. You don't have to call me Mrs. Bennett the whole trip. How about Gertie?"

"If you'd like."

Gertie grabbed Callie's shoulder, squeezed her tight, and led her to a counter across the busy depot. "I would like. Now, let's get your ticket."

* * *

"How much did your ticket cost?" Blaine interrupted Callie's story.

"Um, not half as much as this one going home from Chicago." She turned to Blaine. "But, to be perfectly honest, I don't even remember."

"Let's Google it."

"Let's what?" Callie giggled.

"Or better yet, let's ask Siri."

"Who?"

Blaine picked up her phone. "Siri, how much would a train ticket have cost in...what year did you go to see Miles, Callie?"

Callie tried hard to remember. "The summer of, let's see, '42."

"Well, that didn't work. Maybe we need to be a little more specific." Blaine pushed her phone again. "Train ticket prices in 1942." She fiddled with her phone for a moment and then smiled. "Twenty dollars? Does that sound about right?"

Callie grinned. "I have no idea."

"How long did it take you?"

"To purchase the ticket?"

"No, Callie. The train ride."

"Two days. A very long two days."

Callie glanced over at Blaine. Since Chicago, she'd been inquisitive and curious about Callie's story. Why was she so enamored?

"We slept, ate, and chatted on the train for two days. By the time we arrived in California, we knew each other much better, that's for sure."

Blaine smiled.

"Dear, are you getting tired of my story yet?"

Blaine shook her head.

Callie loved sharing her story with Blaine, but added, "It's okay if you don't want to hear anymore."

"If I wasn't listening to you, I'd be wasting time on my phone. And I think," Blaine held up her phone, "I'd rather hear your story than talk to a boyfriend I'm not even sure I want to say is my boyfriend anymore."

"Well, then, do you want me to tell you about that trip?"

Blaine smiled. "Please."

* * *

Callie didn't really mind the train ride all that much. Seeing the terrain, watching pastures full of cows, fields as far as you could see, all of it reminded her of home. All she could think of was how much her father would enjoy seeing the large farms through Illnois and Iowa.

"I'm so excited to see mountains, Callie," Gertie said as they whisked past the fields of corn ripe and heavy on the stalks. "I've never seen mountains before, have you, Callie?"

Callie shook her head. "No, I haven't either." She liked thinking of Miles traveling through this exact place just days before. Callie viewed every click of the tracks as just a little closer to the one she loved.

It was nice to get to know Miles' mother better. They didn't have much in common, but the boisterous, talkative woman was full of fun. She loved talking to the other passengers and plying them with questions. Soon, many asked her for directions and followed her many trips to the dining car to get ideas on what to purchase to eat. Oh, how Gertie loved to eat.

"I love this roll," she'd announce to everyone around her. "Did you get one of these? They're delicious with this ham." Her announcements brought smiles to the other passengers and many would head to the dining car for their own share of the train's offerings.

Callie's belly fluttered and the constant train swaying only aggravated her nervous stomach. Her thoughts were as unpredictable as the train's next jerk. What if Miles would have preferred she not come for a visit? Perhaps he only wanted to see his mother. Worse yet, what if he'd found a California girl who made her look like a country bumpkin? There were too many miles on this trip to not have inconceivable visions permeate her soul.

She'd gone to numerous lengths to prepare herself for the trip. Her mother had trimmed her hair, and she'd even rummaged through her mother's old buttons to find some which matched her worn, outdated sweater. She'd borrowed one of her sisters' cute new spring hats. What if that California girl now on his arm wore the newest, latest fall fashions? Callie couldn't compete.

She smoothed down her skirt, which would never make the trip without wrinkles inevitably growing deeper as she sat. Perhaps she should have not taken so much time removing them the night before leaving home. She planned not to change out of her outfit until after arriving in California. She wondered if Miles would even notice, but what if he did?

She'd brought a book her mother had on a shelf at home. It appeared interesting but she could only read two or three paragraphs, as interruptions from Gertie were constant. When Gertie rose to use the restroom, the sudden silence made Callie realize how much Gertie's chatter had been a constant since Michigan. She smiled to herself as she thought of Miles and his quietness. Perhaps there was a reason for it.

The scenery grew even more spectacular as the train began to shift downhill into what appeared to be more hills and valleys. Later that afternoon, off in the distance, Callie could just make out a mountain range. Callie had never seen such beauty. She wished she could be sharing it with her family. Her mother would love seeing it. The green mountains emerging ever closer began to show the first signs of red-dipped autumn trees. How would she ever explain this beauty to anyone? The contrast from mid-Michigan was astonishing. Seeing a mountain for the first time filled her heart with gratitude. What a world God had created for their enjoyment. Seeing a mountain for the first time took her breath away.

As the afternoon sun began to disappear behind them, the spectacular view kept all the passengers transfixed. At one point, Callie had even gotten a glimpse of a moose standing proud in one of the mountain streams. She pointed it out quickly to Gertie, who just didn't turn her head fast enough to see the majestic animal, but several other passengers remarked about it.

Callie couldn't nap. When Gertie took a long nap that afternoon, it allowed Callie the opportunity to relax. She took in every turn, looking forward to the tracks revealing something new and different. The United States was beautiful. She could now see the majestic mountains and the miles of prairie mentioned only in school books.

Soon the night made it impossible to see outside. Callie grew tired from her early morning trip to the depot, but the train seat made it almost impossible to get comfortable. Above all, Gertie snored. The noise reminded Callie of her father's afternoon naps during haying season. He'd often try to sneak in a nap just after his lunch, when the sun was the highest and hottest. His snoring just made Callie and her mother laugh as they canned tomatoes or made applesauce from the apples now burdening the orchard trees.

Her mother once whispered, "You should try sleeping with that every night." They'd laugh as another roar would erupt from her father's rocking chair.

During the early morning hours of their third day, Callie grew weary. It was just an hour or so before they'd be at their destination. And even though the scenery continued to be far more beautiful than she'd ever imagined it to be, Callie could barely keep her eyes open. She longed for a real bed and a good night's sleep. The only thing keeping her awake was the ache and excitement in her heart to see Miles. To finally have him squeeze her tight and whisper loving things in her ear. She longed to hear his voice. Feel his lips on hers.

Callie had heard horror stories from girls back home who had boyfriends away at boot camp. Some had even promised to marry or wait for them to return home, only to find them seeking other women's attention while away. She hoped Miles would stay faithful to her. She thought she knew him well enough. But what if she didn't? What if, when she arrived, she could sense that things weren't the same?

Why did she have to worry? She'd inherited the dread and fear from her mother who often worried about all their chickens dying in the night or whether Callie would make it home during a winter snowstorm. The relief she saw on her face upon arriving home from work made her believe that her mother had been fretting away the day as she ironed her father's shirts, or made pies for dinner. The fold of skin in her mother's forehead always gave it away. It would pinch together and her mother would often mumble to herself.

Worry was a bad disease. It robbed a person of not only their security, but their hopes. Rarely did any of the worries come true. Yet her mother's logic was, "If I don't worry, something worse will happen. I'll be prepared either way." Callie just wished she could break her own habit of doing it.

Before she could think much more of anything, the train made its first stop after crossing the California state line. Callie watched as passengers gathered their belongings to leave the train. She loved watching people. She'd imagine why they were traveling and what they'd do once they left the train. She'd see couples hand in hand and imagine them being on their honeymoon. Perhaps the older man leaving the train with just one suitcase was a salesman, and he had great riches stored in his luggage to share with his wife on a trip back home. The thoughts of what might or could be were endless and so tantalizing to imagine.

Gertie nudged Callie from her dreams. "We're almost to our stop, I believe. Our ticket says this is the last stop before Fort Ord. It's the place Miles told us to get off the train."

Callie took out her compact and opened it. She dabbed her nose with her powder puff and used the mirror to apply some lipstick. Her mouth grew dry and she felt as though her heart would actually beat out of her chest. She longed to see Miles again, but at the same time she felt as though she could crawl under a seat and never come out until she reached home again. What was causing her to be so nervous?

"I can't wait to see Miles." Gertie patted her hand as Callie placed the compact into her purse. "But I'm probably not as anxious as you are."

Callie smiled and looked down at her lap. If only she could iron her skirt before seeing him.

As soon as the train stopped Gertie stood up, gathering her purse and belongings. "Come on, Callie, let's go see our boy!"

Callie blushed. Our boy? It sounded as though they were going to see a tiny child who'd been abandoned on the side of the tracks somewhere. But as she rose from her seat, she glanced out the train's window closest to her, hoping to see Miles standing on the side of the platform, yet it was overflowing with GIs.

As she descended the stairs behind Mile's mother, she glanced from one soldier to the next. Girls were being kissed, hugs lavished on everyone. Where could Miles be? Once on the depot platform, she huddled directly behind Gertie in the throngs of people. It had been easier to look over the crowd from the steps of the train; now all she could see were shoulders of those crowded around her. The smell of sweat and perfume lingered in the air.

Timidly, she grabbed Gertie's hand as they made their way through the crowd. No one stopped her. No one hugged her. Her worst nightmare was coming true; Miles was nowhere to be found.

Chapter 14

"Where could he be?" Miles' mother looked lost to Callie. "Do you see him, Callie?"

Callie shook her head. Gertie led the way through the throngs of brown uniforms, bumping into those around them as they made their way to the nearby depot. She realized Gertie couldn't see her shake her head and answered, "No, I don't." Her heart sank. They were counting on Miles being there. What were they going to do now?

Gertie turned to her and tried to talk, but the excitement of others meeting loved ones drowned out what she was trying to tell Callie. Callie shook her head. Miles' mother pulled her through the crowd toward a depot door. Once inside, they brushed off their outfits and were able to talk without shouting. "I don't understand it. Where's Miles? He had to have seen us get off the train."

Callie could only shake her head. Then it struck her. What if? Her hopes sank. Her eyes grew misty.

Gertie must have noticed the fear in her eyes. "Callie, what's wrong?"

"What if..." Callie couldn't get the words out. They couldn't have come this far only to find Miles didn't even want them there. Could she get stuck at the depot with a woman who now would no longer become her mother-in-law? How uncomfortable would that be?

"What if what, sweetie?" Gertie didn't understand Callie's reaction. "Callie, talk to me."

"What if?" Callie choked back tears. "What if he's gone?"

"Gone where?" Then Miles' mother understood. She put her hand over her mouth. "Oh, Callie, no."

Callie now felt the tears sliding down her cheeks. "We've missed him." That fear hadn't even crossed Callie's mind. What if he'd been shipped out before they were even able to arrive in California. The thought made her weak in the knees.

* * *

"Missed him?" Blaine shook her head. "Like he was there and you couldn't find him?"

Callie looked over at her new friend. "I'd never really given it a thought until that moment, even though it was war. Things like that happened. Miles might have been shipped off before we even arrived. All we could think of was that he was gone. For good. And we'd come all the way across the country to mourn his going, instead of reuniting just one more time before he was sent overseas."

"No way! Tell me that didn't happen!" Blaine seemed almost as agitated as Callie had felt that day so long ago.

Callie looked over at the young girl. "We were alone. Two women from across the country. Tired, sore from the trip, and only desiring one thing: To see Miles, and he was nowhere to be found."

Chapter 15

"You missed him? Seriously?" Blaine didn't want to believe the story. "You traveled all the way across the country and you missed him?"

Callie laughed. "Life is like that sometimes. Often, our biggest nightmares seep in before we have to time to react or prepare ourselves."

Blaine leaned forward. "I can't imagine going all that way to find him gone. Shipped out. How could the Army do that to you?"

"The Army never asked the girlfriends about shipping troops off to fight." Callie smiled again. "If they did, there wouldn't have been anyone available to fight."

* * *

Miles' mother and Callie sought a place to sit down and think. Everyone around them laughing, kissing each other, and hugging. Callie now led the way and she knew she needed to keep moving through the crowd. She turned to see Gertie's face which was ashen, the color drained, and tears ready to spill onto her cheeks. Callie nudged Gertie in front of her and through the crowd in search of a place where they could sit and talk about what to do next. She continued to scan the crowd, hoping beyond hope that he'd show up. Around the next corner, past the crowd in front of them, but he never did.

Callie knew that if he were there, he'd have found them by now. She spied an empty bench just inside the depot and maneuvered Gertie through the door. The crowd thinned a bit when they entered the lobby. Callie stepped past Gertie and took her hand. "Here," she said, and pointed to the empty bench on the south wall of the lobby. "Let's sit down a minute."

"Callie?" Gertie glanced at Callie as she sat down beside her. "What will we do? I'd assumed Miles would be here. Waiting for us."

"Well." Callie tried putting on her adult face, even though her stomach quivered like this was the first day of school. "I wanted him to meet us as much as you did, but it appears that he isn't here." Callie scanned the crowd again.

"So," Gertie removed a handkerchief from her purse, wiping her eyes, "let's look at the address Miles sent us. Perhaps we could ask someone. Speak to another soldier." Gertie's eyes darted back and forth as she also was scanning the room, but no one paid attention to the two ladies seated on the bench in a depot.

Gertie took out a small piece of paper and began to unfold it as if it were their last hope of survival. Callie looked at the address on the paper, in Miles' handwriting. "May I have it for a second?"

Gertie said, "Of course. What will you do?"

Callie stood up and found the nearest available attendant. She politely asked, "Sir, could you help me?"

The man stopped from checking off a list on a clipboard. "Yes, what can I do for you?"

"We were supposed to meet my boyfriend here, and he doesn't appear to have shown up. We have this address..."

Before Callie could finish the man pointed to a counter across the room. "You may call a cab from that desk over there. Excuse me, please." He checked off another item on his list and turned his back on Callie.

She'd never encountered someone so rude. It broke her heart to think that someone couldn't stop for a few seconds to help her. Lead her to the counter. Ask the man across the counter what their next step could be. She breathed in and, instead of losing her temper, strutted up to the counter. A man seated behind the counter kept working, but said, "Give me a second." Callie set the small piece of paper on the counter and waited.

The man was counting something on his sheet. His lips moved as his pencil went down another list, one point at a time. He suddenly stopped and wrote down a number on another sheet. "I'm sorry," he said as he looked up from his list, over his pointed nose and spectacles. "How may I help you?"

"We were expecting someone to meet us here, but for some reason," Callie fought back the tears that were ready to emerge, "he isn't here."

"That happens all the time, sorry to say."

"Could you give me directions as to how to get to this particular address?"

The man disregarded Miles' piece of paper, but added, "We have two ways of transportation from the depot to your destination. You may either call a cab or take a street car from here to get closer to Fort Ord."

Callie nodded.

"I'm assuming you're going to meet your man, at Fort Ord?"

"Why, yes, how did you know?"

The man laughed. "Everyone these days is coming to meet their honeys before they ship them overseas."

Callie wanted to cry. She wanted to sit down and sob. What if they were too late? What if they had come all the way across the country and President Roosevelt had given the go-ahead for troops to be gone early? Just as she was about to burst into tears, she felt a touch on her arm. She thought it was probably Gertie, so she didn't instantly turn. The grip tightened and soon she felt a tug pull her around. As it did, she smelled a familiar smell. One that sent her back to her hometown. A familiar Friday-night smell.

There he stood. In his Army uniform. Her Miles. Smiling. "Hello, Beautiful!" Behind him stood his mother, also grinning while dabbing at her eyes with her handkerchief.

Suddenly, everyone in the room went dim as Callie fell relieved into his arms. Even Miles seemed a bit caught off guard as he nearly fell backwards in surprise. "Callie, Callie," he whispered as he planted a big wet kiss on her lips. It felt like heaven until she remembered Gertie standing behind them. She hadn't stopped dabbing her eyes and was still smiling. Callie felt her face grow warm, but she looked into Mile's eyes. She loved how they twinkled in excitement.

She then did her best to gain her composure. She took her arms from around Miles' neck and ran them down his uniform jacket. He was so handsome in it. His hair slicked back just right, flashing that smile. She'd memorized the crooked bent of it and the dimples at each corner of his mouth. Stepping back from him, she smoothed the front of her skirt nervously. He noticed her discomfort and said, "No need for that, dear, you look so beautiful." Callie felt the warmth in her face, yet smiled.

"Well, girls," Miles turned to his mother, "where to?" As he pushed the two women through the crowded depot, he began to recite all the places he could take them that week. After a recitation of the list of what sounded like incredible places to visit, he added, "I'm so glad you're here." The three got into a cab at the curb and headed for the only place they wanted to go that late in the day. The whole incident had made them all hungry.

Callie had been so thankful for Gertie's chaperone on the trip out, but she couldn't deny that in the next hours, days, and for the rest of that week, she hated sharing Miles. She understood Miles need to give his mother attention, too but, shamefully, she was embarrassed at how much she wished it was just her and Miles enjoying their time together in California.

The trio went to see the Pacific Ocean and Fisherman's Wharf. Callie loved to sit on the beach and watch the abundance of marine life on shore. Pelicans, sea lions, and otters, and occasionally, if they were watching closely, they saw a dolphin jump out of the water and into the air. Callie could have sat for hours to watch their silver backs bounce out of the water and slip back under the deep, blue waves of the ocean. She'd never seen anything like it.

Callie saw many things she'd never seen, and probably would never see again. Despite all of them, she knew the only thing drawing her attention was her sweetheart. Her man. She tried to enjoy every single moment of their visit. Miles would often steal a few minutes to themselves by grabbing her hand and leading her down to the beach. He'd duck her behind a mound of sand and steal a kiss. Every time he did it, he'd flash his sweet smile. She couldn't resist him or his advances, nor did she want to.

At one point of the trip, Miles pulled out a blue plastic box which snapped open as he presented it to her. Inside, on silky fabric, was a beautiful crystal necklace, complete with earrings to match. It took Callie's breath away. She'd never gotten a gift of jewelry from a man.

Miles pulled the necklace from its box and motioned for Callie to turn around. He clipped the back clasp, and as she turned back he held out each earring for her to put on her ears.

Once it was on, Callie turned for Miles to see. He winked "Perfect."

Callie kissed his cheek. "Thank you. They're beautiful."

"I got them at a tiny gift shop down by the shore." Miles grinned. "I couldn't resist getting them for you."

"I love them." Callie felt the beads between her fingers. She couldn't wait to show her sisters.

Miles handed her the box and then looped her arm around his elbow. “To tell you the truth, I wanted to buy you an engagement ring instead.”

Callie patted his arm. “What?”

“I couldn’t find one I liked well enough. But I will. I’ll find one and it’ll be perfect.” Miles grinned and pulled her closer. “Will you say yes?”

Callie shook her head slowly, then looked up into his eyes, and nodded. “I would be honored.”

Miles strode on down the beach with Callie on his arm. “I knew it. I knew you’d say yes.”

Callie murmured, “I love you, Miles.”

He pulled her closer to him and kissed her temple. “I love you, too.”

* * *

"I think that week was one of the best weeks of my life." Callie looked over at Blaine. "I remember every day, every kiss, every moment together, but underneath all the amazing moments of that week was an underlying fear. Like a foreboding cloud." Callie shook her head. "I wondered if that would be the last time we'd be together. It seemed there was an impending storm just hanging low and ready to dump on Monterey Bay."

* * *

At the California depot, dread filled Callie’s heart about what would soon happen. She hated to think about it the whole week, trying her best to relish each moment, but the fear in her heart wouldn’t go away.

Gertie seemed anxious to return home. Callie just wanted to cling to Miles forever. She couldn't even imagine her worst fear. What if this was it? What if she never saw him alive again? She just couldn't fully comprehend how she would get through this goodbye. Tears kept wanting to surface, but she'd wipe them away as quick as they came. She couldn't allow Miles to see her anxiety. Her despair. Yet being brave at this moment took more courage than she could ever imagine.

He continued to smile until they pulled into the depot parking lot. Then a slow realization of what was happening seemed to overshadow his spirit.

He paid the cab fare and helped the driver open the trunk and remove their bags. Callie wished her suitcase was big enough to slip Miles in it and take him home. There were plenty of soldiers left at the Fort. They didn't need Miles. Her Miles. She reached for his hand and slipped hers into it. He squeezed it tight, looked back at her, and smiled. Again, she wished that Miles and she were the only two people heading for the train. She squeezed Miles' hand tighter. If she held onto it, it helped to endure this moment. He seemed to sense the panic through her hand because he looked back with tears in his eyes.

* * *

"I never really knew how he felt that day." Callie wiped at a tear slipping down her cheek. "I can only imagine the agony in his heart. His mother and I were going home. Headed back to the safety of the Midwest, but he would soon be traveling across an ocean to a war. But there was one thing we knew: if something were to happen, we'd see each other again." Callie looked over at Blaine.

"You would?" Blaine shook her head, confused.

"Of course. We both loved Jesus, even way back then. We somehow knew that, if this was the end, it would not be the forever end. God was the keeper of our souls."

"How is anyone ever sure about things like that?" Blaine seemed to want to argue.

"Have you ever heard the phrase 'a peace that passes all understanding'?"

Blaine shook her head.

"It's an amazing feeling, that kind of peace. It's hard to even explain. But somehow, deep within, you know everything will be okay. God plants it in your heart when you're unsure of life. Unsure of things ever being normal again. And it gives you confidence, no matter the outcome."

"Well, of course," Blaine snickered again. "You did end up marrying the fellow. You can say that now."

"Now I could, but then, that peace was with me for the next two years. Two years of wondering if he would come home, if we'd get a telegram telling us bad news, if he'd return home a whole person, or even worse."

"Whole?"

"Many didn't. Some came home without a leg. A few without fingers. Back then, we hadn't a clue how our men would return. I'm so thankful they now know how to help soldiers coming home, so much better than after that war." Callie sighed.

"How horrifying." Blaine's face contorted with the ideas.

Callie looked over at Blaine. "That afternoon in California was the last moment I saw the Miles I fell in love with. The dimples would soon show something other than a sweet smile. When the war finally came to an end, my Miles was replaced by a man scarred from fighting. A life changed forever. I'm so thankful God allowed me to not know that as I kissed him goodbye in California."

Chapter 16

The discomfort in Callie's chest grew stronger as she shared her story of leaving Miles in California. She'd eaten too many sweets since leaving Chicago. Sugar always provided enough heartburn to keep Callie's esophagus raging for hours. She began to rub her chest to see if that would ease the pain a bit.

What Callie wouldn't give to go back to the days when she could eat whatever she wanted. She looked over at Blaine, who now had been fumbling with her phone. It appeared she was debating on whether to text or call someone.

Callie decided to just ask. "Are you going to call your boyfriend yet?"

Looking over at Blaine, Callie noted again what a beautiful girl she was. She imagined her to be around Mason's age, perhaps still in college. Her skin was firm, with just a slight bit of peach above each cheekbone, her soft blonde hair tied up at the back of her head in a ponytail. Yet Callie couldn't get over the dark circles around her eyes. The tiredness made Callie believe that she'd been through a rough few years.

"I'm not sure if he's even worth talking to anymore." She set her cell phone in her lap, even flipping it down so all you could see was the flowery cover. "Dealing with him just gives me grief."

"Life goes so quickly, Blaine. One moment you look at yourself in the mirror and you're young. It seems the next day, an old woman is looking back at you."

Blaine looked away and sighed. "I guess I just don't know what I want."

Callie knew it was time to push. "Tell me a little bit about...what's his name?"

Blaine looked back at her. "Kyle. His name is Kyle."

"Do you love him?"

"He's all I have."

"That's not what I asked."

Blaine looked down at her lap and flipped her cell phone over, then back over again. She hesitated, but then looked up. "I don't think so."

"Then why are you still with him?"

Without much hesitation, Blaine answered, "I have no clue."

Blaine looked at Callie as a tear slipped down her cheek. "I'm never perfect enough for him. He says I need to work harder. Lose more weight. Run more. Buy more expensive makeup. You name it. Every day he tells me to change. Something. You just get tired of hearing it after a while."

"Do you want to change?"

"I only change for him." Blaine looked over at her. "I know in my head that I need to leave him. Run away but, somehow, he has this pull on me. His venom draws me closer. I know that doesn't make any sense. It's just the way it is. And then now..."

Everything Callie wanted to say or thought she needed to say wouldn't come out. She waited a moment. She actually managed to keep her mouth shut, which was no easy task.

"Did Miles ever make you feel worthless? Unloved? Yet have this draw on your heart like you couldn't imagine being with anyone else? Almost like..."

Callie so wanted to set this young woman straight. Tell her what real love was all about. Explain to her the importance of a man loving you sacrificially. But the only way she knew how to do that was continue with her story. Would it work? Would it help? "What question did Kyle want you to answer for him? You know, the one he kept repeating at the depot?"

Blaine shook her head. "It's crazy. Ludicrous. If I answer how he wants me to answer it, I know I'll regret it for the rest of my life." Tears edged her eyes. "But if I answer it the way I want to answer it," Blaine pointed to her chest, "our relationship will be over."

Callie sensed the need to be silent. She closed her eyes and pretended to rest.

***

Callie's story was a beautiful one. Blaine knew it was silly to be so engrossed, but what else did she really have to do? The train was barreling down the tracks to her new life, but what would it even be? Was she really going to have the courage to leave Kyle for good? She doubted she had enough guts to do it.

Life would never be a fairytale for her, like it seemed to be for Callie. At only 22 years of age she'd been alone for so long, she felt so much older.

Even when her grandmother was sick, she cared for her the best she knew how. Mainly because she'd have been alone quicker if she hadn't.

She didn't really deserve happiness anyway. Yet, despite knowing it in her head, her heart felt different. What she wouldn't give for a story like Callie's. Yet, she was pretty sure it would never happen for her.

Chapter 17

"What was it like to have Miles off to war? To not even to have him in the States anymore?"

Callie had a hard time explaining her life while Miles was away. She'd shut so much of the fear, doubt, and waiting out of her mind for so many years, it was hard to remember what had happened while he was away. She closed her eyes, as if wishing it to come back just so she could explain her fears from those years to Blaine.

All she could remember fully were Miles' letters. They were still stored in her attic. She'd never been able to bring herself to throw them away.

* * *

Letters came about every other day for the first few months. It was so hard to stay at work, knowing that a letter might have arrived that day. Many days Callie's anxious motivation to arrive home became stifled once walking back through the farmhouse's kitchen door at the end of a long day at work.

Her mother knew what she wanted to hear, and a shake of her head would greet her before her voice. She'd have to wait another twenty-four hours for a nod, smile, and her hand outstretched to her with an envelope in it. It became a ritual, an unspoken way to ease Callie's loneliness.

The radio broadcasts each night caught everyone's full attention. Callie's father never missed a night of sitting close to listen of the overseas news. They'd follow the broadcasts as much as they could, knowing morning would come all too soon. Farm chores, cooking and cleaning, and Callie's job forced them to retire before anyone really wanted to.

The next day, the ritual would begin all over again. The walk to the bus, the endless bookkeeping chores, a short lunch, another afternoon of pencil scratches, and then the long walk home after being dropped off by the bus. Letters came almost every other day, but when a long streak came without them the radio brought no comfort. Callie would awaken in the middle of the night with thoughts of Miles. Was he safe? Why hadn't he written? What if the next day brought nothing again?

On letter days Callie couldn't reach her bedroom fast enough, carrying the precious envelope in my hand, to peel it open and read how Miles was surviving across the world from her. It was hard to believe that the envelope, carrying the sweet thoughts of Miles' love, had traveled across the ocean to bring her such joy and relief.

Each word brought visions of Miles washing his face using his helmet as a sink, cleaning his rifle, thinking of him enduring the endless hot sun. The words brought nothing but more imaginations of what he was enduring serving his country. Callie knew he wasn't telling her all the events of his day. Many times, some of the words or complete sentences were blackened out.

She knew his letters were censored by the military. Callie would often hold the letters up to her bedroom light, trying to decipher through the blackened ink, but to no avail. The blackened words left her with more questions. Was he hungry? Often, she sensed he was tired beyond making sense. He would ramble on about something, only to conclude with sweet sentiments. She'd feel herself blush as he told her how much he missed her and what life would be like for them if they could marry soon.

Reading the letters over and over made them soft, but she couldn't help herself. She'd clutch them to her chest and often her tears would smear the ink. Some of them she'd put under her pillow, thinking the words would seep into her soul as she slept.

Letters were her link to Miles. Her only hope that he was safe. If they failed to arrive, Callie's suspicions would grow deep. Her mother knew her heart. When the letters would stop for three or even four days, tears would fill her eyes as she'd shake her head at the end of one of Callie's work days. Those days only made Callie long for the next day to start.

* * *

“You know what, Blaine?” Callie leaned her head back and closed her eyes for a moment. “I'm not feeling all that well.” The pain in her chest gnawed at her well-being. She hadn't felt exceptionally well after her walk to the train.

"Want me to get you something in the food car?"

Perhaps that's what she needed, something to eat. Callie opened her eyes and leaned forward to grab for her purse. She pulled out her wallet and handed Blaine a twenty-dollar bill. "A sandwich and an iced tea would be nice," Callie added, "thank you for asking. Get yourself something, too. My treat."

Blaine held out the twenty. "That's not necessary, Callie. You've pretty much fed me this whole trip already."

Callie grabbed Blaine's hand and folded it up with the money in it. "I don't mind. Really. Get us something sweet, too."

Blaine smiled and stood up. "I'll be right back."

* * *

Callie missed her conversations with Miles. His letters being a link while he was gone to war, but now she had only her memories. What she wouldn't do for just one more chat. Face to face. One where you could see the expression on his face, and hear the lilt of his voice.

As she drifted off to sleep, she thought of one of their walks they used to have after they were first married. As if it were planned, Callie soon found herself in the midst of one of those walks in her dreams. Miles felt for the fingers of her hand and slipped his into hers. He bent closer to her and kissed her ear as they walked almost synchronized down the dirt road by her house. It was so good to have him here with her. "You know which letters I loved from you the most?" Miles squeezed her hand. She looked up into his face, now narrow from weight-loss and stress. She shook her head."The ones which seemed dipped in your perfume." Miles grinned. "When I opened them up at the barracks, every single man commented about the aroma."

Callie giggled. "I didn't dip them in perfume. I just sprayed them a little."

"Well, whatever you did," he picked up her hand as they continued to walk, and kissed the back of it, "it made me very happy."

Callie could feel herself blush.

"You're turning red." Miles laughed now, too.

"Stop." Callie looked away. She hated how she would blush so easily.

"I'm so glad I suggested for you to do that. Whenever I'd read your letters I could see your face in my imagination, but that was all. But when you began to spray them with your scent, that's when I couldn't help but feel you in my whole being. Maybe because I could now smell you." Miles walked with her in sequence, almost step for step.

"I knew someday I'd have that beautiful smell as my wife." Miles roared in laughter and pulled her hand closer to his chest. "And then, I'd be able to do more than just smell you."

Callie hit him. "Stop. That's enough. If you don't stop talking so romantic, we may have to walk faster to get home sooner."

"We could do that." Excitement etched his voice.

"We will. But let's walk a little longer." She was so happy she didn't have him only in letters now.

"Callie, I need to tell you something." Miles stopped in the road and looked into her eyes. He put his finger under her chin and kissed her full on the lips. Sparks of joy penetrated her heart.

"What?" She pulled away.

"I wish I could have bought you a car before I left for home. Or allowed you to use mine. I just wasn't thinking, but when I was overseas, I kicked myself for not thinking of it sooner.

"Every time I got a letter from you and it was doused in the wisteria perfume, it was all I could think of. What if other men could smell you on that stupid bus and tried to steal you away from me?"

"That was never a possibility, Miles. You know that." Callie gazed into his eyes. "Right?"

He nodded. "I was just so mad that I didn't think of it sooner."

"I did fine. See, I'm here." She picked up his hand and brought it to her cheek. "I didn't choose anyone else."

"There were moments..." Miles stopped talking. He dropped her hands, began to stroll away from her, forcing his hands into his pockets.

Callie went after him. "What? What moments?" She reached him and turned him back to face her again.

"I couldn't get past the fact that I hadn't thought of it before I left. I fought demons in my heart that you'd choose another. I couldn't bear to think of it." He looked at Callie with tears in his eyes. "Usually out on patrol. In the dark. The worst thoughts filled my mind. I'd try to chase them away with prayers but nothing ever worked, except..."

Callie cocked her head, "What?"

"The smell of your letters. I would pull them out of my coat pocket. They'd grow damp in the night air or grow rumpled in the rain, but I couldn't help it. But I didn't care; the smell of them made me remember your love. Your promise to wait for me."

Just then a small truck roared past the two of them standing at the side of the road. Dust flew everywhere.

He grabbed her hand and began leading her back to the farm. "It's funny that just a single smell can solidify your heart so much."

* * *

Callie awoke from her faraway dream with a stabbing pain in her chest. The pain made her sit up straight, just as Blaine returned to her seat. She held out a sandwich. "Does this look good?"

All she could think of at that moment was what her mother had told her to do. Mean what you say. Don't promise him anything that you can't follow through and do. He deserves that. And now she knew why.

Chapter 18

"Callie, are you okay?" Blaine placed a bag in her chair and handed Callie a drink. "Take a sip, maybe that will help."

Blaine picked up the bag from her seat and sat down. She'd bought whatever she wanted. The tofu, fish, and vegetables-only diet Kyle always made her follow was over. Why had she allowed someone like him to have so much control over her life that she could never eat what she wanted?

Callie seemed to be moving in slow motion.

"Here, Callie. Put your food on this." Blaine took her drink out of her hand and put it and the straw on Callie's tray.

"Oh my!" Callie exclaimed. "How convenient." The old woman sighed.

"I thought you've been on a train before, Callie? Didn't you know they had trays for your food?" Blaine was puzzled by her slow movements.

"Of course." Callie seemed to be coming to reality again, "Not sure why I had forgotten." Callie stared at her food as if she wanted to proceed but couldn't move well.

Blaine picked up her own straw and removed the paper protecting it. "Let's eat; I'm starved." She unwrapped her sandwich.

Callie picked up her straw and unwrapped it as if with great determination.

Something seemed wrong with the older woman. Blaine couldn't figure out what, but the smell now emanating from her sandwich took over and she took a large bite. It was quite good, despite being just train food.

Callie managed to get the straw into the hole on the plastic lid of her cup. She picked up the cup now and was taking a drink.

Through bites of meat and bun, Blaine murmured, "You okay?"

Callie nodded and began to unwrap her sandwich. "I'm sorry, yes."

Still having a mouthful, Blaine mumbled, "Are you sure? You seemed miles away."

Callie unwrapped her own sandwich and seemed to sharpen. "Oh wait." She stopped before biting. "May we pray first?"

Blaine's sandwich was halfway eaten. She placed the half uneaten portion back on her tray and said, "I guess."

Callie bowed her head and murmured a short, but necessary prayer, it seemed. "Dear God, we thank You for this bountiful feast of which we are about to partake. Amen."

Blaine mumbled an accompanying, "Amen," looking around to see if any other passengers had noticed. No one was paying any attention. She picked up her sandwich for another big bite.

Callie began to eat as well.

Blaine took another large bite of her meal, but realized how fast she was eating. She set the sandwich down and picked up her drink, realizing at that moment she wouldn't have to ask for Kyle's permission to have one again soon. It was delicious and she needed to stop eating so fast so she could really enjoy it.

Callie began again, "One day the letters just stopped coming. All of us grew worried, for we knew that if or when the letters stopped, there had to be a reason." Callie sipped a bit of her drink.

Blaine wanted to ask a simple question. The usual response to what the possibility of lack of letters could mean, but before she could, Callie answered it for her.

"You knew that if the letters stopped coming, perhaps he was in an intense battle and couldn't write. Oddly, that was what you hoped for. Maybe he didn't have paper, a pen, or even a pencil to write. But you just couldn't imagine what the alternative would be. You couldn't go there." Callie stopped eating for a bit and leaned back in her seat. "But the thought, or the fearful idea that something could seriously be wrong, not only kept you awake at night struck such fear in you that life at home came to a standstill."

* * *

Every day felt like years in Callie's life as she awaited one letter. Any news. It had been almost a year since she'd told Miles goodbye at the train station in California. How would she find out the news that perhaps something was wrong? It wouldn't be officers at her front door, nor would she be the recipient of a Western Union telegram. Miles' family would hear the news long before she did.

One morning as she arrived at the store, Clarence was much quieter than usual. She sensed the silence as news. She wanted to ask. She wanted to beg him to tell her what was wrong, but then again, she didn't. He wouldn't keep information about Miles from her? Would he? Her thoughts battled each other, keeping her in turmoil for over an hour after arriving at work.

The figures on the page blurred. She couldn't concentrate. She was paralyzed by her own fear. Did she want to know or not? Callie watched Clarence stack cans of coffee by the door.

She wasn't doing any work, which made her feel guilty. Upset by getting paid to work and not putting figures down on a page, would eventually force her to ask.

The morning had started off as a humid, sticky August day. The heat was unbearable in the stuffy office. Reaching up she switched on a fan, sending her bookkeeping papers fluttering in all directions. Many settling around her desk and on the floor.

She stood up, grabbing for items to stabilize the others now threatening to sail to the floor. It'd take her another few minutes to put them back in order again. She looked up to see Clarence making his way to her. She'd been nervous all morning, now revealed in her shaky hands. He was about to say something. She knew it would be the news she'd been dreading to hear for a week. Instead of wanting to stand and listen, she crouched to the floor and began picking up the sheets.

As she tried to pry a sheet of paper off the floor, she felt Clarence bend down and help her with others by the desk. She looked up into his face as he said, "Are you okay today, Callie?"

She tried hard to keep her composure, but those words just made her melt inside. A tear escaped and slid down her cheek. "Um, yes." She wiped it away quickly.

Clarence stood up with her and handed her the sheets of bookkeeping files.

She blurted out, "What do you know? Have they come to tell you anything yet?"

Clarence seemed concerned, and answered, "What? Who?"

"The military. Is he hurt? Or is he..." Before she could finish her sentence, Clarence grabbed her hand.

"Callie. What are you talking about? We haven't heard anything about Miles. Is that what you mean?" He shook his head and then seemed to understand. "No letters. You haven't received any either?"

Callie released everything now and she began to sob. "None. For a week."

Clarence took the bookkeeping sheets out of her hands and placed them carefully on her desk and then did something he'd never done before. He pulled her into his arms and hugged her. "Mother hasn't received any either. I didn't think. I didn't put the two together. No, Callie. The government hasn't paid us a visit nor has a telegram arrived. I'm sure Miles is fine."

Callie gulped. "But you were so quiet this morning. I thought perhaps you've heard something and you couldn't tell me." Embarrassed, Callie just couldn't stop her tears.

Clarence took her by the shoulders and pulled her away from him, looking directly into her face. "If I had heard something, I wouldn't come to work and ignore you. I would have stopped you at the door and told you." He pulled her into another embrace. "I wouldn't have kept something like that away from you. Ever!" Drawing her tighter, he said, "Callie, I'm sure he's fine."

Then he added, "But your desk will be much more of a mess, if you don't turn off that fan."

Just then, Callie noticed her papers were still fluttering to the floor. She stopped hugging Clarence and turned to switch off the fan. Papers were strewn all around them. A grin gradually appeared on Clarence's face. Callie looked up at him and realized how silly her reaction had been to his quietness of the morning, and began to laugh herself. It would probably take her all the rest of the morning to pick up and sort through the mess now scattered around them on the floor.

"Not sure what you should be more upset about. All these papers in a mess, or your boyfriend's brother hugging you." Clarence laughed and headed back up to the front of the store. "Miles would be furious."

Callie felt her face grow warm from not just the heated day, but his comment. She sighed and bent over to pick up more of the papers off the floor.

* * *

As she made her way home from work that night, Callie suddenly realized how exhausted she was and how thankful for Friday. She hadn't slept well all week and it was finally matching her mood. No wonder she couldn't keep her composure. As she got off the bus, she saw one of her sisters running toward her. She waved something in the air.

She knew what it was before she could even see the printing on the envelope. A letter had finally arrived and her mother knew how worried she'd been. She picked up her pace to meet her sister as she heard her cry out, "Callie, it's from Miles! You got a letter today!"

* * *

Blaine looked over at the woman, who now seemed to relive that moment in her stupor.

"I would have been an absolute mess." Blaine glanced down at her cell phone in her lap. Sixty years later, technology now arrived within minutes. Women awaiting news from the war now would know within minutes or hours that someone had been injured or killed overseas.

"Miles' mother got a letter the same day. We were so relieved. He'd been fighting, as I first thought, and didn't have time to write. It's a moment I will never forget, even some seventy years later. From that point on, I tried hard not to panic when letters failed to arrive. Soon I realized there were other things much worse." Callie leaned her head back and gazed out the window as snow began to fall. Large flakes floated to the ground, swirling away from the train like mini tornadoes as the train sped down the tracks toward home.

Chapter 19

Callie felt herself roused by a jolt. As another jerk passed through her body, she became alert to where she was and what she was doing. She must have fallen asleep. Her eyes popped open and as she looked up. Blaine was smiling at her.

"Feel better?"

That was an odd thing for the young girl next to her to say, but Callie managed to answer, "Yes, why?"

"You seemed upset by the last thing you told me and went to sleep," Blaine told her.

"I wasn't upset. I've told that story so many times, but every time I do it takes me back to that week all over again." Callie took a handkerchief from her purse and wiped off her face and mouth. Despite cold temperatures, she felt sweaty. She couldn't possibly be having a hot flash at her age.

Callie rarely shared Miles' and her story with anyone. She wasn't quite sure why she felt compelled to tell Blaine. The young woman seemed intrigued. Their trip wouldn't last much longer, and somehow it brought her joy to relive her love story. It could often mask the pain of losing him.

Callie continued: "One day, the phone rang at the farm. I'd been kneading bread dough with my mother and was covered from head to toe in flour." Callie smiled. "But Mother was covered worse. She was such a good cook, but a messy one."

* * *

Callie ran to the phone to pick it up but as she did, she realized the voice on the other end was broken, someone trying to speak sounded very upset. "Hello? Who is this?" Callie brushed off her hands on her apron hanging at her waist.

She then realized who was on the phone. Her heart sank. Surely Miles' mother wouldn't tell her bad news over the phone. The woman spoke through tears, "Can I come over?"

Callie felt her knees grow weak. "Gertie, what's wrong?"

"I just received a telegram."

Callie wasn't sure how the words came out, but she had to know. She had to ask, "Is he alive?"

"Yes, Callie. He's alive, but has been wounded in action."

Callie somehow managed to thank the woman, but couldn't say anything more. She heard Gertie hang up the phone at her end. Callie sank to her knees. Her mother was beside her and took the receiver from her and placed it back on the wall mount. She took Callie's hands, helped her stand and hugged her tight, slowly murmuring in her ear, "It's okay. It will be okay. Don't cry, sweetie."

Callie did cry. She cried as she tried to fix her hair and change her clothes for Gertie's arrival. Her sisters stood in the doorway of her room with sympathy on their faces, yet silent.

Callie heard a car door slam shut in the driveway. Wiping her face with the back of her hand, she managed a smile for her sisters as she made her way past them and down the stairs to greet Gertie.

Callie opened the door as the autumn wind blew a cool breeze into the kitchen. Gertie and Callie hugged. Gertie's face was puffy and red.

Tears flowed. She pulled a handkerchief from her coat pocket and blew her nose.

Callie's mother escorted Gertie further into the kitchen and they sat down at the kitchen table. Gertie held out an envelope. "You read it and see what you think."

Callie slid open the top of the envelope as the letter slipped out easily. Her hands shook as she read each word slowly. She read the first few words, but knew her mother would want to also know what it said, so she began again, out loud.

"*To the parents of Miles Bennett: We regret to inform you that your son, Miles Bennett, has been wounded in action as of September 6, 1944. We have shipped him to the States, as of yesterday, and he should arrive at the Army hospital at Fort Ord within the week. He will be transported to Indiana within a few weeks. Please be advised to travel to the Veterans' Hospital in Indiana at your earliest convenience. The Army would like to extend to you our deepest sympathies and hope for a speedy recovery.*"

"What do you think, Callie?" Miles' mother looked at her with hope and sadness in her eyes at the same time.

"I don't know." The letter gave no comment as to the extent of his injuries or what had happened.

"It's concise and to the point. I hate that they don't tell you anything more specific."

Callie nodded in agreement. "Are you going to see him?"

Gertie nodded. "Of course. I need to prepare a bit. The garden has produced so well this year. I'd planned on spending the next few weeks canning. I hate for all of it to go to waste. I was hoping one my daughters-in-law could help."

Callie's mother had picked up the letter herself and turned it over. "If he was wounded on September sixth, I wonder when they sent this." She pulled her glasses from her apron pocket and examined it again. "This was postmarked for September tenth, but it's the fifteenth now. Surely, he's back in the States."

Silence flooded the room. It was so unusual for Gertie to be so quiet.

Callie wanted to go. She was just about ready to ask if she could, when Gertie inquired, "Will you go with me, Callie?"

Callie sighed in relief and nodded. "Of course." Tears began sliding down her cheeks. "When do we leave?"

* * *

The next few days were a whirlwind of getting her clothes prepared to leave. Her mother helped her press them and place them in a suitcase. She even baked batches of cookies to take with them, on the premise that Miles always loved her baked goods. Callie hoped that it wasn't just Gertie and herself who would be eating them. She didn't want to think that Miles wouldn't be able to enjoy them.

Thoughts of dread, fear, and mystery went through her mind as she ironed clothes. Was he hurt badly? Did he have all his limbs? Or even worse, would he recognize her? The one that haunted her the most and kept her awake at night, was if they were too late and the trip home was too much of a strain on his injured body.

The night before the trip, Daddy had to listen to the radio. He wanted news. He thought if he could figure out where the fighting was, perhaps he could figure out in which battle Miles may have been wounded.

Callie couldn't listen. She escaped the family time and had gone upstairs to her bedroom. Her clothes were packed. All she could do was sit and wait for morning to arrive. They'd leave on the train the next day.

How would she ever sleep? She glanced out the window and noticed some of the trees were beginning to show signs of the upcoming fall weather. Here and there a few yellow leaves began showing through the dusty green ones. She wondered how long she'd be in Indiana with Miles. Would they be all turned or, even worse, all on the ground before she could return home?

Her sister soon joined her on her bed. Callie stroked her hair just to find a small piece of straw. Her sisters had been busy in the fields haying with their father. Callie was proud of how hard they worked.

"Are you sore?" Haying season never failed to cause her sisters pain.

Mary nodded. "And tired."

"I bet."

This kind of conversation usually caused a slew of accusations about how Callie never went out to help in the field. Yet, tonight her sister didn't tease. "Are you scared?"

Callie was afraid of what she'd find in Indiana. For all she knew, he might be fighting for his life right now. "I'll be fine," she assured.

"I would be so upset if anything happened to Bert like that." Mary had been dating Bert for over a year now. Their relationship had grown. Callie could see Mary liked him. "He told me last week that he's enlisting right after school is out." Callie's sister began to cry. "I'm not sure I can be as strong as you."

Callie let her sister lay her head down on her lap. "I'm not all that strong, but I do know that God cares for Miles very much. I've been praying for so many months that He would protect him. He can't let us down now. If I think otherwise, I just go crazy."

"You've been so strong. I'll have to follow your lead," her sister added.

Callie kissed the top of her sister's head. She'd tried hard to keep her life as private as she could without realizing how much her sisters were watching her. They were both about to be consumed with their own fears for their boyfriends. Esther's boyfriend had a feeling he'd be called up before even finishing his senior year of high school. Every man was needed. The war was failing to end.

"How long will you be gone?"

Callie had no idea. She wanted to tell her that it wouldn't be long and soon she'd bring Miles home with her and everything would be fine again, but she just didn't know. She shook her head. "I don't know."

Over the next few hours, Callie and her sister chatted about many things. Callie opened up about her relationship with Miles, and Mary did the same. Thankfully, the conversation took Callie's mind off Miles for a while. It was two in the morning before they stopped talking and tried to sleep.

Her sisters were growing up. They were no longer high school girls just excited to have the interest of a boy. They could now relate to Callie's fears. Soon they'd be awaiting word from overseas.

As she heard Mary's breathing ease into sleep, she prayed for her sisters and their boyfriends. She hoped her example made them strong when it was their time. After her prayers she tried hard to sleep, but all she could think about was the next day. As eager as she wanted to be to see Miles, a shadow of what might be clouded her dreams.

Chapter 20

A rocking train with its jerks kept Callie awake most of the trip to Indiana, despite running on little sleep the night before. The train's movements hadn't prevented Gertie from sleep. She'd dozed off just after leaving the train station.

The silence left Callie again contemplating the fear in her heart. Callie considered every possibility. Yes, he was injured, but how badly? Was he now missing a limb? What if he lost his hearing? She'd heard so many stories of those returning from fighting, she couldn't shut out the comparisons. Howard, from the other side of town, had lost his sight. What if Miles wasn't able to see her? Her head throbbed with all the what if's.

Callie shifted in her seat, sighing. Why couldn't she turn off the fear? Why did she have to consider each possible outcome of what she'd find at the other end of the journey? Her mother called it their worry syndrome. If you considered every possible avenue for your suspicions, from an assortment of different angles, then what would really happen or whatever the outcome wouldn't be half as horrible as what a person could imagine.

Trust was impossible at this point. It was one thing to trust God for a warm home, plenty of food to eat after a busy day on the farm, whether a picnic would be rained out or turn into a spectacular Michigan day, or one of her family members would recover from severe flu. But this? This event had never happened to Callie. In her twenty-three years of life, the worst thing she'd ever suffered was the death of her grandparents and a move from her childhood home in the city to their new farm in the rural part of mid-Michigan.

After nearly two years of having Miles overseas, even the missing mail days seemed to dim. What if he never returned home? She would love him in whatever way she found him in Indiana. They could deal with a loss of a limb. She'd help him. God forbid if it had taken his vision, she'd now be his eyes. Picking up her purse, she took Miles' small photo out of her wallet. He was so handsome; what if his injury made him look different? Then she looked at that smile. The one with the dimples.

It was a silly request, almost absurd to ask for, but at that moment her silent prayer was that God wouldn't erase that grin, or his dimples. But if He did take away even that, she'd remember every moment that it could have been worse. He might not be here at all. Anything else seemed trivial to losing him and having to go visit a grave at the local cemetery.

Whatever they were to face, they'd do together. Miles wouldn't be alone. She was there to help him. God always promises strength in the worst situations. A single tear slipped down her cheek. Callie wiped it away just as Gertie began to stir in her seat. She'd do her best to help him.

"Callie, sweetheart." Gertie sat up straight in her seat and wiped her face. "How long have I been sleeping?"

Callie smiled and patted Gertie's hand. "Two hours."

"Two hours?" Gertie sat forward, pulling on the hem of her skirt. "My, oh my; I'm so sorry. I just didn't sleep very well last night."

Callie didn't want to tell Gertie she hadn't slept the night before either. Part of it was Mary's fault, but Callie didn't care. She smiled, thinking of Mary's joy. She knew how it felt to be perfectly, happily, in love. The thought of Mary and Esther feeling the same made her smile.

"What time is it?"

Callie looked down at her wristwatch. "Eleven-fifteen."

"We should be there in less than two hours."

"Yes, I believe so."

"Are you excited to see Miles again?"

Callie looked over at the woman still appearing groggy from her nap. "I miss him so much. It will be good to see him." There was no reason to share her fears with Gertie. Even she didn't need to hear her uncertainties out loud.

"I miss him, too, but I miss all of them. Hard to have three of my boys overseas."

Callie knew all this, but hearing Miles' mother say it gave her great empathy. She'd been selfish to think only of herself.

"I've been a mother for over thirty years now, and even having one gone makes me lonesome. I miss hearing their feet hit the floor and their rumble down the steps to be the first one to the outhouse. We have leftover food now at dinner, because I just can't cook for just three. And there's something to be said when you lay your head on your pillow at night and realize they're all gone and the house is empty. But with Miles..." She stopped for a moment. Her eyes filled with tears. "He's my baby. My youngest. Since the war began, I had great fear that even one would have to enlist. It was hard enough to have the older ones marry and move away."

Miles was the youngest of seven children. Callie understood, and nodded.

"You think the day will never come. I can remember when they were all small. I was so busy. Every single night I would crawl into bed and dream of at least three or four hours of uninterrupted sleep. I wasn't even sure it was possible." Gertie laughed. "If nature didn't call, I could probably get a whole eight or nine hours straight now." Gertie giggled some more.

Callie laughed; her mother rarely shared how she was feeling or what she was going through with anything. It was nice to have an older woman's perspective on life.

"Listen to me prattle on. I'm sorry."

Callie shook her head. "I'm happy you're finally awake." For once, the older woman's stories, were a welcome distraction.

Gertie turned to look out the window and Callie suddenly realized that her worries about Miles alone had been selfish. At least he was home. It gave her courage to face the unknown.

***

As the train pulled into the station, Gertie again took over and headed off the train before Callie could even pick up her bags to follow. Two people wedged between them. Gertie called back to her. "I'll wait for you when I get off."

As both women descended the steps of the train, a hot, humid day met them as they approached the depot in the small Indiana town. September often resembled May when cool days were followed by lingering summer days.

"Heat!" Gertie shook her head. "Not sure why I didn't think that south of Michigan would be warmer. I can't imagine living in a southern state." Gertie didn't stop. "Can you imagine living in a place like Florida, or worse, Alabama, in the middle of the summer? I can't imagine. I just can't imagine."

Gertie continued talking, but Callie couldn't concentrate on the weather or southern parts of the country. Determined, she needed to compose herself. Reacting badly would only hurt Miles' feelings. Right? She needed to be encouraging, but not overbearing. Hopeful, but not let the fear in her heart show on her face. She'd never been good at hiding her fear or her emotions. She should have been preparing herself before now. Perhaps even now it was too late.

"Callie," she heard her name, but was distracted by her thoughts. "Callie, dear." Gertie touched her arm.

She came to. "Yes."

"Should we call a cab?"

Callie nodded.

"Okay. I think we have to go over here."

Thankfully, Gertie seemed to be thinking clearly. She forced herself to smile. It didn't come easily, but she concentrated on good thoughts. Soon she'd be with Miles. She hadn't seen him since leaving him in California. It seemed like such a long time.

Gertie took her hand and led her out the side door of the small depot and out onto the nearby street. "This will cost us a fortune, but I don't know any other way to get to the hospital."

Callie managed a nod.

She breathed the Indiana air. It was hard to find any fresh air to take in, but she did her best. With the deep breath, she tried to stifle the turmoil in her soul. Prepared herself for what could be ahead. Miles.

Chapter 21

"What do you want to do in life, Blaine?"

"Excuse me?" Blaine wanted to hear what had happened to Miles. She wanted to hurry up and get to the hospital and see what condition Callie found him. She only wanted this old woman to stop asking questions and finish her story.

Callie turned in her seat to face her. She even pointed a finger in the air as if she were scolding her. "If money or time were no longer an issue, what would you do with your life?"

Blaine looked as another Michigan town sped by the window. She'd never actually been asked that question, but she thought carefully for a moment. "You mean that I didn't have to have a job?"

Callie nodded. "Sure."

"Well," she thought for a moment, "I'm too young to do what I really want to do."

"Pretend age doesn't matter either," Callie added.

Blaine picked up her water bottle for a drink. She needed a few minutes to decide. Why did Callie want to know this? And right at this moment? Why had she turned her attention toward her life?

"Blaine, what would it be?"

Blaine shrugged her shoulders. "I don't know."

"As you young ones always say," Callie shook her head, "Seriously?"

Blaine began to giggle a bit and then felt disturbed. It was a simple question. Why was she having such a hard time answering Callie? She thought for a moment and just couldn't think of anything, so she said something off the top of her head to get this woman who now seemed intent on her answer, off her back. "Travel." she nodded. "Yes, I'd travel."

"To where?"

Callie seemed so determined for Blaine to answer. It began to feel intrusive. Nosey.

"I don't know. Maybe France."

"Why France?"

Again, more questions. "I don't know, Callie. It sounds like a pretty place to go."

That answer did it. Callie turned in her seat and muttered something to herself as she looked out the window.

"What did you say?"

Callie turned back to her. "Life is wasted on the young."

Blaine now felt scolded. Mocked. "What does what I have to do in life have anything to do with what happened to Miles?"

"A simple question. It should have a simple answer. What do you want to do in life?"

"Did you know?" Blaine had always been great at shifting the attention off herself. She'd been interrogated by Kyle enough to know. "When you left the train depot that day, did you know what you wanted to do in life?"

Callie nodded. "Absolutely."

Silence hit the pair. Blaine looked at the woman waiting for a response, and none came. "Well?"

"From the moment I was a little girl, I only really wanted one thing in my life." The old woman reached for her purse and pulled out a tissue, dabbing at the inner corners of her eyes. This interrogation was making the woman cry. She sniffled a bit and dabbed some more.

"What was it?" Blaine now felt bad. She hadn't meant to make Callie cry.

"I wanted to be a wife. I wanted someone like Miles in my life for always. I wanted to be a mother and raise as many children as God would allow us to have."

"That's a nice thought."

"I wanted to buy a little home, right down the road from my parents, and teach my daughters to bake pies. I wanted to be a wife and a mother. That was all."

Blaine thought that was a splendid goal in life. "Nice."

"No." Callie began to get agitated. The tears were still coming, but she did her best to dab at them before they streaked down her face.

Blaine grew more uncomfortable. She had done her best to answer her question. Or had she? What did she want to do?

"That's all I wanted, at that moment in my life. I wasn't an amazing, attractive woman. I had dreamed of the day when a man like Miles would walk into it. As I left the train station that day, I decided it didn't matter."

"What? What didn't matter?" Blaine now saw a bit of the connection.

"The rest of life. It didn't matter if I found a man with one leg or no legs. It wouldn't have upset me at all if I had found him blind or even deaf. I had imagined the worst. Challenged myself by asking 'what if'. But as we left that station in a cab and headed to my beloved Miles, nothing else mattered. Not one thing."

Blaine thought she now saw why Callie had asked her the question.

"Nothing else mattered but Miles. I wanted to spend the rest of my life seeking to make up for the months we'd been apart. I wanted to get him well quickly so we could head home and be married as soon as possible. It didn't matter what kind of injuries he'd sustained. I wanted to be his wife. The mother of his children. Whatever his injuries. It really didn't even matter what was wrong with him. I just wanted him."

Blaine smiled, and nodded.

"But I never expected or even surmised what I would really find behind the front doors of that veterans' hospital. But I'm so thankful." Tears flowed without hesitation. Callie's wadded-up tissue was no match for the excess tears now flowing down her cheeks. "I'm so thankful God put that in my heart at that exact time. Because, Blaine, if He hadn't done that, I might have walked away that day. I might have decided then and there that I needed to find a new man. A whole man. Instead, God gave me the desire to do anything but leave the man now lying in a room in that hospital in Indiana."

Callie turned away from Blaine, as if to say she didn't want to finish her story. As bad as Blaine wanted to hear it, she also understood that she might not.

Callie appeared to want to be left alone for a while. She had cried awfully hard that last few minutes. Whatever state this woman had found her soon-to-be fiancé couldn't be anything so horrible that she couldn't marry him. Could it?

Blaine had imagined herself marrying Kyle at one time. In the beginning. They seemed a solid pair. A good match. She loved his eyes. He looked so adorable after a night's sleep. He'd push his hand through his long black hair, and even with it standing on end he was still very handsome. She loved how he ate a bowl of cereal every morning in his boxer shorts. He'd been attentive to her during their first few months.

But then, real life changed their relationship. He'd often tell her in the morning, "Go brush your teeth." It seemed logical for him to tell her that. But then he'd just be annoying about it. That's about the time the compliments, the way he looked at her, changed. As if he was trying to mold Blaine into something he wanted her to be, not into someone he just wanted to be with.

The weight issue began to rear its ugly head. Often on their movie-binge nights when popcorn just wouldn't do it for her and she'd run to the phone and order a pizza. He once laughed at her doing it, but then he'd just shake his head, flip off the television, and head to bed. She'd often be the only one up to eat the pizza once it arrived.

She was in a relationship that was one-sided. It wasn't something that brought her joy. In fact, it brought her more heartache and fear than anything else.

What had once felt safe and secure now seemed to threaten her future with sadness and frustration. Why was she putting herself through it? But, more importantly, as Callie had asked, what did she want from her life? She hadn't even really thought about her dreams for a long time. She was too busy fulfilling Kyle's dream of what he wanted her to be.

What did she want out of life? What did she want to do? She looked over at the woman who now seemed to be worlds away and not sitting next to her on a train. Callie seemed to know. Callie knew what she wanted to do. Did she?

Just as she began to think of something, find an idea, force herself to decide what she really wanted to do in life, Callie startled her and began her story once again.

"Gertie and I left the station that day, and I was determined to do whatever it would take to find Miles and fulfill my dream. I hoped it was still what he wanted in life, too.

"Gertie seemed more hesitant to see Miles now. She walked behind me. Again, I knew God had instilled in me hope and determination. I plodded on and walked into the hospital as confident as I could."

Blaine then realized that a trip into Michigan had turned into something much larger. She was hearing the life story of this stranger and, somehow, it was helping her to envision her own life. In a new way.

Callie now smiled at Blaine. "It's funny how, when something tragic happens, all we can think about is getting life back on track. Everything gets into perspective. You realize what you really want, and you will do anything to get it."

* * *

Approaching a nurses' station, just inside the door of the hospital, Callie asked for Miles. "We're here to see Miles Bennett. We haven't been told much and were wondering..." The nurse held up a hand as a phone rang nearby.

"Just a moment." The nurse picked up the ringing phone. Said a few words. Callie didn't seem to comprehend what she was saying. Her words were blurred out by Callie's thoughts.

She hung up the phone and then returned to speaking to Callie. "What's the last name again?"

Callie repeated her question. "Bennett, first name Miles. "Could you tell us..." the phone rang again.

"I'm so sorry. It's been a crazy day today." She picked it up and answered it again.

Now holding up a finger, she grabbed a clipboard and handed it to Callie. She cupped the phone receiver for a moment and whispered to Callie, "Find his name."

Callie looked down at a list of names. There were columns and numbers listed beside the names. She slowly went down the list, looking for Miles' room number. Once finding it, she pointed it out to the nurse still on the phone. The nurse nodded and continued to answer the question of the caller, "Yes, that's fine. We'll look forward to hearing from you soon. Thank you for calling."

Callie waited a moment while the woman wrote something down. "Take this paper down the hallway and then to the left. Tell the nurse at the desk that you'd like to talk to a doctor." The nurse looked again at the clipboard she'd handed Callie. "Uh, Dr. Thomas."

She handed Callie the piece of paper. "Can we see him?"

"Yes, the doctor will see you right now. I'm pretty sure he's out of surgery."

"No, I mean Miles."

The nurse grimaced. "I'm sorry, not before you talk to Dr. Thomas."

Callie's heart sank. Why wouldn't they allow them to see Miles first? That would be best, right? The anticipation of finally seeing him was delayed again by a doctor's visit. For what?

Callie turned and picked up her suitcase, making her way down the hallway of the hospital, with Gertie close at her heels. Gertie was uncharacteristically silent.

Once at the next nurse station, Callie and Gertie were ushered into an office. They were told to sit in the chairs opposite a desk and the doctor would be in to see them shortly. Callie placed her suitcase beside her on the floor. Gertie did the same. Glancing around the room, Callie saw college diplomas and certificates in frames placed in various places on the walls. The desk was stacked with papers and clutter. The curtains were drawn shut, closing out the sunshine of the hot, unusually humid September day. It seemed to make the room unbearably warm.

Callie wished she could stand up and take off her coat, but the space was small. It seemed like hours instead of minutes before the doctor opened a door at the side of the room and walked in. Callie thought she should probably stand as if he were a judge entering a chamber, but then he motioned for both travelers to stay seated. He stretched out his hand and introduced himself. "I'm Dr. Thomas."

Sitting across from them, he placed a few more papers he'd carried in onto the stack of papers on his desk. Callie wasn't sure they'd stay in place as the pile shifted to one side. "I'm so sorry my office is such a mess today. We've had so many casualties come through in the last week or so. I haven't been able to process my notes as quickly as I normally would."

Callie nodded. "It's fine. We understand. I'm Miles' girlfriend and this is his mother. Can you tell us how he is? We haven't heard a word since the telegram arrived a few days ago."

"We need to find a better way of sending out those telegrams. I'm sorry for the delay in getting his health details to you. Some men we can process quickly and get the information out sooner. But in cases like Miles', we need to run more tests to determine just what we're looking at."

Callie was confused. "I'm sorry, is he okay?"

"He will be, but unfortunately in cases such as this it takes time to evaluate the damage. Decide the plan moving forward."

It was now or never Callie held her breath, "Doctor, what are his injuries?"

"I'm happy to say he doesn't really have any injuries. No outside wounds, that is."

Callie sighed in relief, but all kinds of questions began pouring into her thoughts.

Before she could wade through all of them and ask the question, Gertie finally spoke up. "So, why is he here, if he doesn't have any injuries?"

"I'm sorry to say," the doctor picked up a piece of paper and read it off to them, "Miles is shell-shocked."

He muttered, "This is a common occurrence among the troops coming home these days. We're still investigating what happens to a person when this occurs. Many seem to arrive here dazed and confused and we start certain procedures..." Callie couldn't seem to get past the diagnosis to listen as intently as she should to the additional things the doctor was saying. She'd never imagined this in her thoughts on the train coming into town.

As much as she wanted to be prepared, this wasn't something she'd even considered.

Chapter 22

"What did that mean, Callie? Shell-shocked?"

Callie seemed so far away at that moment. Blaine wasn't sure she was going to come back to reality to answer her.

Blaine asked, "Is that like PTSD now?" Blaine had heard the term many times during invasions of Iraq and Afghanistan. Surely, it probably was the same thing.

"I'm not sure." Callie seemed to rally her thoughts. She continued, "So many things happen to man, or now even a woman, during war. Trauma is suffered from images they see or the fear of what will happen if shooting begins. Can you imagine the waiting and watching for an enemy to shoot at you?" Callie sighed. "Can you imagine how traumatic that would be? I never will know the things Miles saw right before he had what the doctor then described as a 'nervous breakdown.' He didn't remember anything. In fact, he was in total disbelief when he woke up to find himself in a hospital. The nurses and doctors kept trying to explain what happened to him. All Miles could remember was walking through a deep jungle with his gun up and ready to shoot. He remembered nothing after that."

"So, what did you find when you finally got to go see him?"

"Not what I expected." Callie grimaced. "He looked perfectly well. No bandages or casts. No head wound or even a scrape. He looked tired and worn out, but nothing else."

"Did he know you?"

Callie nodded. "At first, yes, but as we sat with him for a few days, we then started to see the damage. There were moments he didn't quite remember my name. He seemed always to know his mother, but not me."

A tear slid down Callie's cheek. "The Miles I had sent off to war had come home and, at times, didn't even know who I was. He would smile and hold my hand, but there was a faraway look in his eye. He would look at me, puzzled, and Gertie would remind him who I was." Another tear slid down Callie's cheek. "Of all the ways I thought or imagined I'd find him, this wasn't one of them." She wiped her cheek with her hand. "Never would I have imagined Miles sick like this."

"So, what did you do?"

"I sat beside him and would often hum one of our favorite songs. For some reason, the music soothed him. He would either hum along or smile back at me and say, 'Honey, you are so tone-deaf.' Normally his comments about my singing made me mad, but once he would start to hum along or sing, too, it brought me great joy. At least he was remembering something. Often, he'd fall asleep humming and holding my hand. For a few short moments, I would see my Miles, but at other times..." Callie'e eyes grew misty. "He just didn't know who I was."

The train stopped at another depot by the side of the tracks. Blaine glanced out a window. She'd been so engrossed in the story, she'd forgotten to even listen to the conductor announce the next train stop. For a second, she wondered where they were. Perhaps Battle Creek? Or had they arrived in Lansing yet?

She placed her hand on top of Callie's and massaged it. As much as she wanted to hear the rest of the story, she knew it was taking a toll on Callie. She wanted to stop her, but she also wanted to hear more.

Perhaps Blaine needed to change the subject. It was almost too sad to listen anymore.

"I'm sorry. I don't mean to blubber so."

Blaine shook her head. "No need to apologize. That must have been a very hard time in your life."

"I guess the part I hate about it the most is how decent, honorable, brave men left home and often would return so unlike their former selves. Sitting at home and listening to the radio broadcasts gave us no clear picture of what could be happening to our boys. They'd try to tell us through the letters, but I always knew when Miles wasn't telling me everything.

"Many went only on adrenaline due to lack of sleep. Others saw atrocities that we could only imagine in our most hysterical nightmares. What would it feel like to stand before another man with his gun raised to shoot you and yours raised to shoot him? Was there ever a split second that a man with a gun would think to himself, why am I doing this? Men, who just a few years before, only used a gun to hunt or for target practice out in the back forty.

"Yes, they were trained, but what has to change in a man's heart to shoot another man in cold blood? What makes a man take up a rifle and know that, without a doubt, he'll shoot the enemy? So many thoughts have to enter your mind. What will those around him think if he doesn't shoot? Will he be classified as a hero or yellow? They'd probably court-martial someone who ran away instead of doing something they'd always known to be a sin. Killing someone.

"I had no clue what had gone through Miles' heart overseas. I knew the man lying in the bed was my boyfriend. The person I wanted to marry. But who was he really? Had he come back to me as Miles, or just a likeness of the man I'd given my heart to?"

Callie's tears had stopped now. She looked over at Blaine. "As the months continued I soon learned who had come home from war, but at that moment, despite the fact that he was sitting or lying right beside me at any given moment, my Miles had gone off to war and would probably never fully return."

***

The train's whistle blew. As Callie looked out the window, she watched cars stop to allow the train to go through a city. She remembered seeing that on her way home from seeing Miles in Indiana. The train ride, back to Michigan, had seemed so much longer than it had been traveling to Indiana.

She looked over at Blaine, who smiled back at her. "Please don't feel you need to go on, Callie. I understand."

"If I don't go on, you won't know the whole story of Miles and me." She smiled back. "I can't stop now."

***

Callie thought about her future with Miles to take her mind off the Miles she left back at the hospital. Soon she realized, she was fooling herself. They'd have a different relationship from this point forward.

When he asked for her hand in marriage, she'd be marrying a stranger. As she sat at his bedside, there were moments he would come back to her and smile up at her with that same adorable dimple, yet there were also moments he seemed frantic, distant, and far away. Often, she felt he'd look right through her.

Watching him right after a shock treatment was the worst part of their visits. He'd come back with this far-off look in his eyes. Disoriented. Sometimes you wondered if someone had taken away his soul. How could these treatments be good for him? What did shocking a man's system have to do with bringing him back to life?

The doctor assured them it was the best treatment for men like Miles. His body had gone through something so traumatic that the only way to bring back the real man was to shock his system back to life. After treatments, Miles wouldn't sleep. He would toss and turn, and often-times found it hard to even go to sleep. He'd stare off at a wall for hours, only responding to drinking some water; if a doctor or nurse entered the room, he'd stare at them as if they were a threat.

Soon his exhaustion would take hold and sleep would follow. Usually Callie could stay with him after a morning treatment, but when he'd finally drift off to sleep before bed, Gertie and she would leave him to sleep. Whenever he would wake up after a treatment, he would tell his mother that it was as if he didn't know where he was. That was usually when he wouldn't know Callie. Miles sometimes would awaken to thinking he was on patrol, or he'd lift his hands as if he had a gun in them. It would take some convincing of a nurse or even his mother that he wasn't overseas, but home safe. He'd reach for something. Try to sit up quickly. Every single time he'd ask for the time or if it was his shift to stand guard.

Once he realized he was in a hospital, he'd ask why or ask for some of his buddies. He'd search the room for any sign of them and often ask, "Where am I?" His mother seemed to be the only calming person in his life. She'd sit down by his bed, hold his hand, and once she realized music would calm him she'd begin to sing. Callie realized now where Miles got his musical talent. She knew every single church hymn. Some Callie had never even heard before, but as Miles' mother would sing she soon learned them herself.

Miles' seemed particularly receptive to "How Great Thou Art." He'd stop sweating, stop twitching, and listen intently. As if hearing it for the first time.

Both Callie and Gertie would leave the hospital exhausted. They'd have done their best to calm Miles. Watching him suffer more was beyond them both. Seeing the fear in his eyes, was like watching a child wake from a nightmare.

Only music would calm him. Only music brought him relief. So, soon, Callie found herself humming while she sat by his bed. She couldn't carry a tune like Gertie, but she could hum. After about a week she realized not only did it calm Miles, but it also brought her great strength to sing his favorite hymns.

* * *

Gertie suggested they go home after two weeks. "I hate to leave him," she'd told Callie, "But I have others at home who need care. And the animals." It would be hard for her husband, Floyd, to take care of the animals by himself. "And my garden. We'll need the produce through the winter. I need to get canning. The tomatoes must be bulging with ripeness now."

Callie would nod. As much as she didn't want to leave Miles again, she knew that his care was beyond her expertise. She wasn't sure how long she could endure his response to treatments and, above all, she had to think.

And that's what she did after being with him for fourteen days. The two women headed home with a promise to return when they could. They doctor told them to give him a good six months' worth of treatment. Callie knew she needed to get back to her job. They needed the money now more than ever. Who knew how long it would take for Miles to return to work?

Yet, as the train left the station in Indiana that day after an incredible hard goodbye to Miles who was again suffering from another treatment, she thought of herself. Maybe she should get away to think. Her desire to take Miles home and help him recover had been replaced by insecurities she needed to understand.

What if she didn't want to marry him after all? Even when the thought came to mind, Callie tried hard to push it away as never an option. But on that long trip home from Indiana, it did push in with such force that it took her breath away, only to be replaced with fear. Would she give up on their relationship now? After all they'd been through?

Chapter 23

Callie didn't mean to ignore Miles' mother on the trip home. She tried hard to interact and listen to her for a short time, but kept getting distracted. She was thankful when Gertie finally fell asleep.

Callie knew fear wasn't of God. Her family survived the Great Depression. She'd been a tiny little girl when her mother had her little sisters. The pregnancies were hard on her mother, and Callie often would be found washing dishes on a stool her father had propped up for her, while her mother was nursing a baby or just too tired to do dishes.

After her sisters grew and became strong enough to help, they'd also be propped up by the washtub to scrub clothes or sent out to draw water from the pump behind the house. They were little, and yet they managed to help their sickly mother as their father went off to find work. Some days he'd come home with a little money he'd earned from fixing someone's car or from helping a neighbor chop wood. But the money he earned was little and often only bought them enough food for a day.

As the next day crept into another, the girls would mend their dresses before a tear would give way to a large rip, just one more time. Hoping it would at least keep them covered for another few months. New clothes were never thought about, holes were cut into shoes so their growing feet would have room to breathe.

Food was another need. A few potatoes were a luxury. A vegetable from the garden produce, a great blessing. A cup of milk from a neighbor's cow would be divided three ways. Sometimes Daddy wouldn't get any at all. He'd give his quarter cup up for them and say, "My girls have growing bones. Mine are all grown."

Even amid the hardships of growing up in the 1930s, nothing prepared Callie for this decision. For this was her choice. No one else had to decide if the man she'd sent away who was now lying in a hospital would still be the man she'd marry.

Yet she knew, deep in her heart, that the love she had for Miles just wouldn't disappear or be forgotten. Perhaps he'd somehow, some way, return. What if he came back again as the Miles she'd grown to love? Could she accept him back with open arms? Would she?

The vicious, fearful thoughts wouldn't leave her as the train back into Michigan chugged on down the tracks. At each turn or bend in the road, she'd have another fear seep in. Could she calm him as Gertie had been able to? The doctor assured her she could. It was only Miles responding to his mother. He'd known her much longer than Callie.

All of it made sense. All of it seemed reasonable, but her positive thoughts would quickly fade when she saw the fear in Miles' eyes after each treatment. She could only imagine what was happening in those treatment rooms to make him so afraid. His fear brought her fear.

One thing she did know for sure, she loved Miles more than anything in the world. She loved him with her whole heart. Was her love enough to keep them together? At one time she'd never imagined a life without Miles, and now she wondered if it would even be possible. What if he never responded to her or couldn't love her back? Could she live with that for the rest of her life?

What would her mother say if Callie even thought about changing her mind?

At the thought of her mother, Callie recalled the memory of her mother's admonishment, the moment before Miles went off to war. 'You're promising him, Callie, that you will support him and love him even if he doesn't come back as he was before he went off to war. Don't give him false hope."

A promise was a promise. No, she hadn't taken her vows yet that said, 'until death do us part,' yet her mother had been right. If she accepted his hand in marriage, it was much the same thing. What if he had been in the States the whole time and an accident had taken a limb, or a tractor accident had caused him a head injury? Would she still marry him?

Gertie began to stir from her nap. As much as Callie wished she could disappear and go find a seat by herself to continue to think, she knew his mother was mourning as well. Startled awake by a loud clack and jerk of the train, Gertie sat up straighter in her seat. "Oh my, I've done it again, Callie. I'm sorry."

Callie smiled. "It's okay. I know you're tired. So am I." Callie's face could never keep secrets. From anyone. Her mother, father, or her sisters. She must have looked even more tired, as Gertie glanced over and patted her hands folded in her lap. "Are you okay? Why don't you go to sleep for a little bit? I'll watch for our stop now."

Callie couldn't sleep now. She wasn't sure she'd even be able to once they got home. Someone walked by with what smelled like coffee, and she even thought about going for a cup herself.

"What are you thinking about?"

Answering her would be horrible. Callie tried hard to think of something to say that didn't sound like the doubts flooding her thoughts. "Just Miles."

"Hard to see him like that." Gertie sighed. "So hard."

"Do you think the treatments are working?"

Gertie shrugged. "I'm not a doctor I don't know why they think shocking his system will somehow get him out of the stupor he seems to be in." Shaking her head, she continued, "I want to think of his illness through a mother's eyes." She smiled. "If I could just take him home.

Nurse him, in his own room. Tuck him into bed at night. Feed him. He's so skinny." She looked over at Callie. "Just love him as a mother, he'll come around better that way than how they're dealing with it. I know nothing about this kind of illness, disease, whatever it is." She gulped back tears. "I wish I knew how to take care of my boy."

Callie nodded. "Maybe we need to just bring him home." The idea froze in Callie's thoughts. Really? Did she want him home to care for? She nodded again. "Yes. It seems logical."

"But we didn't go to medical school. I've helped many a woman deliver their babies. I have cures for chicken pox itch, applying salve to a burn, and even taking care of bleeding udders on a cow, but this, this problem isn't anything I've had to ever deal with."

Gertie grabbed her hand and held tight. "But, Callie, I do need to know. I need you to be as truthful as you possibly can."

Callie reluctantly nodded. "I'll try."

"When and if he asks you, will you still marry my boy?"

Callie put her head down. This was it. Should she be truthful or lie? Lying wasn't something she ever wanted to do. Especially to a woman depending on her. She remembered her mother's words and slowly she looked up into the woman's eyes. The mother of her beloved Miles. As the word 'beloved' siphoned through her thoughts she also thought of Jesus. Odd that it would come into her mind at that moment, but it did. 'And God so loved the world that He gave His only beloved son, that whosoever believeth in Him, would have eternal life.' Beloved.

God loved His son. He was beloved to God. Despite what was happening to Miles at that very moment, he was still 'beloved' to Callie. She knew she couldn't out-love God, but she could have beloved thoughts of someone else. She looked into the eyes of her boyfriend's mother and nodded, "If he asks. Yes. I will still be his wife."

* * *

"That moment sealed my fate." Callie looked deep into the eyes of Blaine. Blaine blinked back tears. "He was my beloved and I did love him. Despite his illness and injury. He was mine and I'd promised him. I'd promised to wait for him. Come what may."

Blaine looked into the sorrowful eyes of her new friend on the train, and knew without even asking, she never changed her mind from that point forward.

Chapter 24

"The next few months," Callie went on, looking at Blaine with a mixture of melancholy in her voice, "I did many things." Callie looked down at her hands. "I struggled between wanting to be with Miles through his treatments and recovery, and needing to work."

"On my second trip to Indiana, Miles seemed greatly improved. He asked me to marry him. He promised me he'd get me an engagement ring as soon as he could return home. They wouldn't let him out of the hospital to go shopping," Callie looked down at her finger on her left hand. It still held the diamond Miles had purchased for her just before the wedding. The ring had been fixed nearly three times over the years, but the diamond remained. She would never remove it.

"Our engagement wasn't anything spectacular and he didn't get down on one knee or place a gorgeous engagement ring on my finger. He asked. I accepted. But it was enough." Callie winked at Blaine. "It was February when he asked me, so soon I was planning a wedding."

"What month did you plan on getting married? Could you even be sure he'd be well enough to get out of the hospital?"

"June. We planned for June. That was the doctor's best determination of when Miles could be released." Callie sighed. "We had no clue whether it would be for good or not, but we decided it didn't matter. If he could get out for a few days, we'd be okay with that, too. Then he could return for more treatments if needed."

* * *

"This lace will be the death of my poor fingers." Callie's mother sucked on one of her fingers. "I'm afraid I'm going to stain this satin with blood and never get it out."

Callie went to her mother and picked up the skirt of her dress to look at the handiwork. People from all over came to her mother when they needed a formal dress. "Mother, this is beautiful."

"Do you like it, Callie?"

Callie fingered the dainty lace as tears formed in her eyes. "I absolutely love it."

Callie's mother put down the dress and blew on the end of the finger she'd been sucking on. "Are you okay, sweetheart?"

Callie knelt beside her mother's rocking chair. "Of course." Then she looked up. "I think."

"Wedding jitters?" Her mother smiled and picked up another edge of lace and began stitching it again.

"I guess." Callie sighed.

"I had the jitters when I married your dad, but in a different way."

Callie looked up. "A different way? Aren't all wedding jitters the same?"

Her mother smiled and shook her head. "No." She picked up the last stitch and examined it closely. "No, they aren't." She dug into another seam with her needle. "For some young ladies it's the thought of spending that first night together. For some it's the thought of leaving their parents and going across the country to live with this man they love, but they don't really know all that much. For others, it's the fear of marriage." Her mother giggled. "Will he soon figure out she really can't cook?"

Laughing, Callie felt assured. "I can cook."

Her mother looked up for a moment. "But can you do it with a baby on your hip crying with a fever, and a toddler throwing up on your shoe at the same time?"

Callie shook her head. "Who can?"

"But for me, my fear seemed greater. Bigger at the time."

Callie shifted to another knee. "Why?"

"Callie, I don't know if I should tell you this, but you're old enough to understand. Your father and I had to get married fairly quickly."

"Well, I knew that, but..."

"You see, I wasn't sure, but I suspected that we might be having you a little sooner than nine months after the wedding."

Callie looked up from her dress to her mother's face. "What?"

"I'm not proud of the fact. I wasn't sure, because I'd never been pregnant before, but with my queasy stomach in the mornings and my appetite growing more ferocious each day, I was fairly certain something was happening. Your father laughed it off as if he didn't care, but I knew he was almost as scared as I was. We pushed our wedding date up much sooner and forged ahead."

"Did Grandma know?"

Her mother nodded. "I couldn't keep it from her. She was mortified, of course." Callie's mother wiped her eye with the back of her sleeve. "I had failed as a daughter, but she always told me that failing only meant I needed to get busy and make it right. The best you knew how."

"What did Grandpa do?"

"He didn't know. I don't think. I told Mother not to share it with him. I had already disappointed her; I didn't want to fail him, too."

"Do you think he knew?"

"Maybe. I was never sure if Mother told him or not. But back then, you don't discuss those issues with anyone. It's embarrassing, and soiling the family name was outrageous. Thankfully, my mother loved me and knew that mistakes happen. She set me on a course to fix the damage and quickly. She concentrated on helping me find an appropriate dress to go to the courthouse with."

"You went to the courthouse?"

Her mother nodded. "The local judge came to town each Friday, and we were just days away from him visiting. We worked hard and fast on a Sunday dress I had barely worn. Mother had a pretty hat that matched perfectly. I was married just six weeks later."

"But, wait," Callie counted on her fingers. "I was born in August, and you were married in September. That doesn't add up. I should have been born in June."

"After we got married, we assumed I was already pregnant and didn't try to prevent anything else from happening sooner. Within about two months, I realized I really was pregnant and the other time was just a false alarm."

"We kept it from everyone. The false alarm. I was thankful my behavior hadn't caused the family name to be tarnished. My mother knew I had intercourse before marriage, and for me, and that was shameful enough."

"What did you worry about?"

Callie's mother set down her needle. "I worried about whether I'd be a good mother. I was only eighteen years old. Almost a child myself. But now, as I look back, God prepared me for you even before I really had you growing underneath my heart." She stroked Callie's cheek with the back of her hand. "I wouldn't have traded you for a million beautiful weddings."

She picked up her needle and began sewing again. "That's why I want you to have the kind of wedding I only dreamed of having. You've been a good girl and have waited for your wedding day."

Callie sighed again. "I hope I'm making the right decision."

Her mother stopped sewing again. "We talked about this, young lady, remember?"

Callie nodded. "I will marry him."

"Yes, you will."

"But what if..."

"No what-if's," Callie's mother said sternly. "This man needs and deserves your allegiance. He's fought boldly for his country. You need to be loyal, too."

Callie nodded. Callie's were different than others, but what if Miles came home different? Worse yet, that he couldn't remember her at all, as he did before he went off to war.

Soon, letters from the hospital arrived, taking up where they'd appeared to leave off before he'd been treated. They were full of hope and sincere wishes for their future. He talked about having children. Raising them in a home of their own. He talked about going on their honeymoon and how he was saving his money to go on a special trip north. They could visit relatives, he said.

Callie picked out perfect wedding-day shoes at work. Clarence had just gotten in a beautiful selection of white ones made of a satiny material. They would be beautiful beneath her dress. Clarence laughed as she tried on two pairs one afternoon, trying to decide which pair would look best.

"Those look nice on you," Clarence admired from across the store.

Callie felt herself blush, but she only had five minutes left of her lunch hour to decide which pair to purchase.

Clarence came from across the store. "Miles is one lucky man."

Callie hated hearing her soon-to-be brother-in-law talk like this to her. She needed to change the subject as she sat down, began unbuckling the pretty shoe, and then taking it off her right foot. "Have you heard from Miles?"

Clarence came over to her and folded his arms. "No. Just what Mother tells us."

"How are your other brothers?" Miles' other brothers were still overseas, each stationed at opposite ends of the earth. One in Japan and the other in Germany. "Betty and Irene tell us they're well. Mother hears from them, but not as often as the girls." Both of Miles' brothers were married. One brother was due to arrive home shortly before the wedding.

Clarence left her to put the shoes, back on the shelf. She carefully folded the paper over them, so they wouldn't appear to a customer that anyone had tried them on. She then placed the boxes back on the shelves.

"No one in our family thought Miles would be the one to suffer in this way. He's the baby of the family. We worried about him the most. Hard to believe he's the one suffering in a hospital."

Callie nodded.

"What do you think from his letters? Does he sound okay?"

Callie smiled. "He sounds just like the Miles we always knew." It was true, but she often wondered what troubles hid beneath the words.

"Then," Clarence said as he smiled and went back to work, "everything will be fine."

Callie went back to her desk. Without saying anything she prayed. *"Oh, God, please help him to be right."*

* * *

The wedding day drew near. The worries in Callie's heart gave way to excitement and the anticipation of having Miles home from that point forward. He'd been in the hospital for so many months; Callie had only been able to go visit him twice. Both times she saw a bit of a difference in his moods, but blamed it on treatments he'd received the day before her visits.

It was just a day before he was to return home from the hospital for good when Callie received a phone call from doctor Thomas. He introduced himself to Callie again and told her that Miles' mother had told him to call her.

"Is everything all right?" Callie breathed into the phone. "Miss, I need to have a bit of a consultation with you before Miles returns home. I hear you're about to get married."

Callie said, "Yes, at the end of the week."

"Well, congratulations. I wish you both the best."

Was he calling to congratulate her?

"May I call you Callie?"

Again, Callie nodded, even though he couldn't see her. "Yes, please."

"I don't mean to scare you with my phone call. But it's customary for us to release our men into good hands. Sounds like I'm doing that, but I have a few things to tell you. Things you need to watch for, as far as Miles care is concerned."

Callie gasped. This was it. This was what she was suspecting all along. They hadn't been telling her everything.

"Miles' body has been through many treatments in the last few months. We're still trying to determine if it's the best course of action, but we're never truly sure that it has been enough."

"Enough treatments?"

"Correct. It's always different for each patient. Some are completely fine when we send them home, but some..."

This was it. Callie's hands began to shake. She began to sweat, though the day was a bit chilly, even for May.

"Some men react differently. There are a few things I need you to watch for. Unfortunately, not just in the near future, but as he grows older. Major, significant life changes could cause him to go into shock again. If he does have a problem, I need you to notify another doctor. Tell him of his treatments here. Tell him about the nervous breakdown in New Guinea."

"What kind of major life changes? Like a job change?"

"No, probably not something like that. It would have to be more significant."

Callie wasn't sure what that could be. "I'm sorry, can you give me an example?"

"Perhaps a sudden death in the family. Losing a child. An automobile accident, anything traumatic."

"What do you look for?"

"A sudden change in his demeanor. If he starts getting unusually quiet or disruptive. He could change again or worsen. It's not uncommon for a patient like Miles to often revert back to the state he came home in. He could have another breakdown."

Callie sank into a nearby chair.

"It's highly unlikely, but it could happen. Just keep a close eye on him and I'll be sending you release papers which will indicate some of the symptoms to watch for."

Callie was holding her breath, but let it out to reply, "Okay. Thank you."

"One more thing."

"Yes."

"You need to watch for suicidal attempts as well."

Suicide attempts? Callie's heart sank.

"Again, we hope it's just a precaution, but we need to be on alert for anything that could put him back into the state he came home from the war in."

She hung up the phone with shaking hands as tears sprung to her eyes. These weren't just precautions but perhaps a glimpse of their future. A glimpse she didn't want to see. Just a few minutes ago, she was going to soon be Miles' wife. And now, after the phone conversation, she was now going to be a caretaker. From this day forward.

The only words she could hear as she wept after hanging up the phone were her mother's words. "Make it for life, Callie. Don't promise it without making it for life."

At that moment, Callie knew her life would never be as carefree as before. She now had to become serious and grow up. Miles needed her and, as she had promised, she'd be there for him. No matter what lay ahead. She'd promised.

Chapter 25

The next day, Miles walked through the door. He came into the room, and before Callie realized it she was up in the air and he was twirling her around the room. "We're getting married. We're getting married." In front of Callie's mother, he planted a solid, hard kiss on her lips before she could do anything. She relaxed in his arms, which made her feel secure and safe despite the phone call from about a month before.

Her worries about their future. The doctor's phone call. Her fearful thoughts seemed to float away with each kiss and sweet whisper in her ear. Her Miles was back. He needed some good cooking and even a haircut, but he had returned just as he was the day she'd sent him off to war.

They sat outside the first night on the porch, chatting about their honeymoon plans. If his car would make it on the trip or whether he should find a way to get some new tires for it before they left. They'd planned a trip to the northern part of Michigan, on a lake they both enjoyed visiting during the summer.

"I have something for you." Miles got to his feet and began digging in his pocket. He pulled something out and sat down. He picked up Callie's left hand and slipped a beautiful engagement ring onto her finger. It glistened as it reflected off the evening sun now setting in the west.

Callie gasped. "Oh, Miles, it's beautiful."

"Do you like it?" Miles added to her excitement with a broad smile, showing his dimples.

She leaned toward him and, as she did, he turned his face for a sweet, long kiss. She wrapped her hands around his neck and pulled him closer. Their kiss took her away from the afternoon worries of the upcoming wedding, and she imagined doing this for perhaps the next seventy years.

As she sat back to admire her ring, Miles kept nibbling on her right ear. She was happy that, soon, they'd be alone and that kind of affection from him could be behind closed doors. Then she wouldn't have to blush as she did now on the front porch swing.

"Two days," Miles whispered in her ear.

"Are you sure you want to marry me?"

Miles sat back and glanced at her. "I think I should be asking you that question."

Callie pushed a strand of hair behind her ear. "Are you sure this is what you want now? You've been through so much." Callie couldn't look at him.

Miles took her chin in his hand and kissed her softly. "I've missed you so much. I can't imagine living my life without you. Ever."

Callie kissed him back. "I do love you, Miles."

He kissed her, too. "I love you, Callie, and I can't wait to make you my wife."

The next few days were full of activities. Flower gathering. Church decorating. Preparing food for the reception. Her sisters were all giggles and nervousness. Despite the flurry of activity, Callie realized she'd soon be leaving home for good. They'd never be a family again with just three girls and parents. In two weeks she'd return to her work schedule, but then arrive home at a place Miles had found for them to live, closer to her job. She'd never have to walk the dirt road again at night or early in the morning.

Two days before the wedding, the thought struck her when she was upstairs trying out some different hair styles for the wedding on Saturday.

It was just before dinner. Soon the girls would be coming in, hot and sweaty from getting the yard ready for the reception. Her mother was baking one more cake to frost the next day. She decided to head downstairs to help prepare their dinner.

Coming into the kitchen, she found her mother sweating as she took the last of the cake out of the oven. "That's the last one. I'll start decorating them tomorrow."

Callie then offered to bake some chicken for dinner. Her mother sank into a chair and picked up the night's newspaper and began to fan herself from the ninety-degree temperatures of the unusually warm June day. "July must be coming. It's so hot today."

"I hope it will be warm on Saturday."

"Me, too, Callie girl. Me, too." She stopped fanning for a moment and glanced at Callie. "Your hair is nice. Is that how you're planning to wear it?"

Callie nodded and put her hand below her hairline and fluffed up the bottom curls. "What do you think?"

Her mother nodded. "Very flattering. Will you help me do mine on Saturday?"

"Of course."

"There's a fresh chicken on the counter. He needs to be plucked just a little more. Get some scalding water going."

Callie did as her mother asked. "Potatoes?"

Her mother nodded. "There's a bit of asparagus left in the cooler. Let's cook that up before it goes bad."

Callie got out a sharp knife, grabbing a few potatoes from the bin to peel. She sat down beside her mother.

"Are things better now?"

Callie looked up. "Better?"

"Miles. Do you feel better having him home now?"

Callie smiled. "Yes, I do."

"Good." Her mother set down the makeshift fan and began helping to cut up the potatoes after Callie peeled and washed them. The cold water felt good on her warm hands.

"Mother?"

"Hmm?"

"Do you see a change in him?"

Callie's mother cut up a potato and glanced up at Callie. "No, not really. He seems the same to me."

"Are you just saying that?"

"No. I truly believe he's fine."

Callie nodded. "So do I." She hadn't told a single soul about the doctor's phone call. She couldn't. That would be a secret she would hide forever.

"I wish he didn't have to go through those horrible treatments. He's so skinny."

"I'll fatten him up. With all the garden produce coming on fast and furious, it won't take long with some of my, yours, and Gertie's home cooking."

Callie's mother fanned the cooling cake on the kitchen counter. "We'll start it with this wedding cake."

Chapter 26

Callie woke early the morning of her wedding. She heard raindrops striking her west bedroom window. She sat up in bed, pulled off the covers, and hurried to a window. This was not what she wanted to hear on the day of her wedding. Their outdoor reception would be that afternoon. She didn't want to have to move the whole thing to the church basement in town.

The invitations had been mailed to one hundred guests. They wouldn't all fit into the cramped quarters of the church basement. She wanted to be outside. They'd worked so hard to prepare the yard to be just perfect for her day. She got up, pulled her bathrobe around her shoulders, and ventured downstairs where her mother was frying bacon for their breakfast.

"Good morning, Mother."

Her mother turned to her, and in a sing-song voice said, "Here comes the bride."

Her father turned from washing his hands and grinned. "Big, fat, and wide."

Callie gave him a scolding glance. "Daddy, don't say that."

His laughter filled the kitchen. "Ready for your big day?"

Callie looked out the kitchen door window. "As ready as I'll ever be. But, Daddy, it's raining."

"Oh, baby, it won't last all day. The clouds are too thin. No worries. By this afternoon, you'll never know it even rained this morning. We live in Michigan, you know."

That was the problem; they did live in Michigan. Where the morning could start out with crystal-clear, blue skies and end up having a hurricane-like deluge by lunch time. They'd have days in March that would start with a blizzard and end with a tornado watch. Summer was no different.

Her mother approached her from the back as she gazed out the kitchen window. "I hope the flowers stay nice. Those peonies on the side of the house were at peak form yesterday."

She turned Callie around and hugged her. "One thing is for sure, Callie girl, you'll be married by the end of the day, despite the weather."

Callie hugged her back. "This will be my last breakfast at home."

"That's why I made you these." Her mother bent down and pulled open the oven door. The scent of cinnamon and yeast filled the room.

"Cinnamon rolls? How in the world did you have time to make me those?"

Callie's mother laughed. "Sleep can wait until tonight. Today, my little girl is getting married." She reached for a pot holder on the counter and pulled out the pan of rolls. She had a bowl on the counter filled with white glaze. Picking up a large spoon, she began to drizzle the white glaze over the hot rolls.

Soon the sound of her younger sisters bounding down the stairs filled the warm kitchen with excited chatter.

"What are you going to do with your hair, Callie?" Her sister, Mary, remarked as she pulled a strip of roll from her plate and put it in her mouth. "Pulling it back?"

"Mary, don't talk with your mouth full." Her mother pulled back strands of her own hair. "What will I do with mine?"

"Put it in a bun, Momma," said Esther.

"You think?"

Esther nodded, putting a roll dripping with glaze up to her mouth and taking a large bite.

Callie thought the whole scene reminded her of Christmas morning, but the humidity in the air made her wonder if the style she'd decided on for her own hair would hold up.

"Stop talking about hair and pass me another roll, Pearl." Callie's father grinned as he demanded food.

The whole scene made Callie want time to stop. Her family and a fresh, cooked meal. She'd miss these days. The teasing from a family who loved each other. The moments of cherished fun and laughter. As much as she didn't want it to end, she also didn't want time to stop. Today she'd be marrying the man of her dreams. The one who still made her heart ache to see him. The one who could make her happy for the rest of her life.

But it did end. Soon everyone was upstairs preparing for the big day; hair being combed and makeup applied. Callie soon stood in her bedroom, dressed and ready to be taken to the church. She looked at herself in the mirror and hoped Miles would like to see her as well. She felt beautiful.

Her mother had finished her dress just three days before. She'd not wanted to try it on again until this last possible moment, and it zipped with ease. She looked down at the lace that had put welts on her mother's fingers from the pinpricks of applying it to the dress.

A veil, almost as long as her room, cascaded down from a pearled crown on the top of her head. The lace on the edges of her gown caressed the floor. At that moment Esther came bounding into the room, ready to ask her something, but stopped in her tracks. Her hands flew to her face and she gasped, "Oh, Callie. You're just..."

Just then Mary came to tell her something as well, with almost the exact same reaction. "Oh, Callie."

Callie turned in slow motion for them, causing her veil to curl around her legs.

Both girls sat cross-legged on the floor and swooned. "You look so beautiful."

At that moment, her mother came into the door to tell her something as well. She was busy placing an earring on her ear, with the other one pinched in her mouth. She nearly dropped the earring from her mouth when she saw Callie. Tears began to fill her eyes. "Oh, Callie."

Callie laughed at their identical reactions. "I think you all like what you see."

All three women laughed. All three said "yes" at the same time with excited laughter. Giggles from her sisters made her smile.

Her sisters were wearing blush-pink gowns with gathered bodices in the front making them look more grown-up. They were excited to finally have a chance to be in a wedding.

"I can't wait to dance with Bill," Esther commented, and Callie could see the excitement in her eyes. Bill would soon be leaving for his military duty in a few weeks as well.

"I hope Bert likes me in this dress," announced Mary. She swirled in the room. "I'm so glad you picked out this color, Callie. It makes my black hair shine."

"I guess it's time to go get married," Callie announced as she picked up as much of her dress and veil as she could and headed down the stairs to the car. On the way out the door, Esther picked up the handmade bouquets on the dining room table, and Mary passed the keys to her mother. "Are you driving us, Mother?"

Her mother nodded. "Daddy's coming in his truck behind us. He had to finish up milking before heading to the church. Cows don't care whether today is a wedding day or not."

Callie smiled, looking around at the yard as they headed out to the car. The rain had stopped, but a few droplets fell from the trees in the driveway as they did their best to fit their dresses around them and into the car. "We look like we're going to a ball," Callie announced as she wrapped her long veil into her lap.

"This is going to be such a fun day," Esther announced from the backseat. "I can't wait for the wedding to start."

Callie agreed. It might be the best day of her life.

* * *

A scent of candle smoke and lilies met Callie at the door of the church. She could hear the guests murmuring as she came through the back door with her sisters. The mahogany arch was the entrance to her new life with Miles.

Her sisters giggled nervously, their bouquets dropping tiny specks of baby's breath around their feet. They felt their hair for any stray strands and turned to Callie and smiled. Her father stood beside her as her mother went to an usher and was escorted under the arch leading into the sanctuary.

Soon, she'd see Miles. She thought of their kiss goodnight from the night before. He'd lingered on her lips longer than usual. Both fought their passion, desiring to kiss harder and longer. He looked into her eyes and said, "I can't wait to marry you tomorrow." She'd felt herself blush, unable to speak.

Callie looked into his eyes. All she could see were the tender, green eyes of her fiancé. She smiled at him and kissed him one more time. "Until tomorrow, my love."

Miles stepped back. "And tomorrow, we'll never have to part again."

Callie's heart fluttered now at the thought. Oh, how she longed to finally have Miles to herself. The war had ended in Germany, yet fighting still lingered in Japan. It filled every American with hope that soon everyone would return home.

Callie could only envision herself with Miles by her side. She couldn't wait to set up a house with all the wedding gifts that had been arriving all week. Performing every day chores with him.

Her father had arrived just minutes before, in his best suit. It was unusual to see him all dressed up. He now touched her arm, pulling her hand over his arm, grasping her hand. "Ready to get married, buttercup?"

He hadn't called her that since she was a little girl. She grinned up at him.

"You can still back out. The doors right behind us."

Callie shook her head. "Not on your life."

"You'll still come home and make me apple pie from time to time, won't you, Callie?" Her father always raved over her pie, but only when Callie's mother was out of the room.

She nodded and smiled. "Of course."

Her sisters now stood at the arch entering the sanctuary of the church. She stood off to the side so no one could see her before the wedding march started. She watched each sister glance over her shoulder and smile at her before they started up the aisle. A niece of Miles' was also standing up with them at the altar. She wasn't sure who was more excited among the three young girls. Each one looked so pretty in her floor-length dress.

As soon as her sister Mary left the arch, her Daddy escorted her to the arch. She breathed in deep, now smelling her father's aftershave. He'd shaved today and looked rather handsome. She was pretty sure it had been years since his suit had been out of his closet. When she entered the sanctuary, everyone stood.

She glanced up from the back of the church to see the crowd now standing as the pianist played the bridal march. The organ's loud notes resonated through the large auditorium and out into the hall. Loved ones filled the pews of the church, but Callie didn't notice any of them.

She wanted to see Miles' reaction. A very tall man blocked her view of him, standing in the row in front of Miles' mother. She wasn't sure who he was, but she hoped he would move just in time to see Miles' face. As they moved under the arch, she caught a glimpse of her mother raising a handkerchief to her eyes. She then looked again. Miles stood tall in his Army uniform. He did the only thing that could make Callie's heart skip. He smiled. Every guest now gazing at Callie disappeared from her thoughts. All she could see was that handsome soldier, now home from the war, gazing at her with tears in his eyes.

Before Miles had left for the war, she'd rarely seen him cry. Now, tears were a part of his being. He seemed shy about them at first, and then just gave in and let them trickle down his face from time to time. And then, there were those dimples.

Callie smiled back at him and he grinned at her. They couldn't take their eyes off each other, until Callie realized she was almost right in front of him.

Today was their wedding day. Years of loneliness were gone. Letters had stopped. She could now look to the future with hope and happiness, instead of insecurity and fear.

****

Soon they were back at the farm, greeting the many guests who had stopped the war long enough to enjoy a special day with them. The day, predicted by her father, had happened. The sun was shining and humidity from a Michigan June day made the sweat run down the side of Miles' face.

As Callie looked around at the crowd, some families were missing fathers, a few brothers were not around, many of Miles' buddies from school were not there to attend, but the ones who had survived their duty and were home seemed just as happy as the newlyweds.

News reports were predicting the war's end in the Pacific. Camps were being liberated. Soldiers were returning home each day. Callie and her family hoped that the predictions were accurate.

Callie's mother had used some of her best recipes for the celebration. Callie's aunts had chipped in some dishes. A large cake sat on the table by the back door. A few bees wanted nothing more than to sample a bit of the white frosting and nibble at the crumbs lying on plates.

A warm breeze made Callie's long veil twist in the wind as guests huddled around the couple to give their wishes for a blessed future. Much of the time, Miles held her hand. Never wanting to let it go, even for her to hug some of the relatives who had traveled such a long way to join in the celebration.

* * *

"But I didn't mind." Callie glanced out the window of the train. "I loved holding his hand." She looked down at her own hand. "It was strong, secure, and I knew that whatever life would hold for us, we could get through it together."

Callie looked up at Blaine. "That was it." Callie sighed. "My wedding day. I do remember every single detail."

"How long?" Blaine asked.

"How long?"

"How long were you married?"

"Sixty-one years. We were together that long." Callie smiled at Blaine. "That day was magical. It was everything I had ever dreamed it to be. And we were together. Forever."

"I think every woman alive hopes their wedding day can be that magical. That special."

Callie nodded. "I think so, too."

The train suddenly jerked. The weather outside the train seemed to change since Chicago. The clear blue skies were now hidden by thick, billowy, black clouds. "I think it's gonna snow soon," Callie said as she looked out onto the dusty, partially-snow-covered fields of mid-Michigan.

The train jerked again and began to slow. Callie looked out again on the winter landscape as a few snowflakes struggled free from the dark clouds above. "But something did happen on the honeymoon that set into motion the problems I was to encounter much more in the future."

Another jerk of the train made both women grab the arms of their seats. "What in the world?" Callie looked up at Blaine. "And that's when the first one came. Well," Callie shook her head, "the first one that I knew about."

"The first what, Callie?"

"The first of many."

Chapter 27

"We were staying with a cousin." Callie picked up her purse and began digging for something.

"What do you need, Callie?" Blaine thought perhaps she'd have the item Callie was looking for.

"I'm just so thirsty."

"Do you want me to go to the refreshment stand and get you something?"

"I thought I had more water in my bottle." At that moment Callie pulled a water bottle from her bag. "I was pretty sure I'd put one in there before I left Mason's house this morning."

Callie took a long time to open the bottle cap and then even longer to take a few gulps of the water. The liquid dribbled down her chin and she wiped it away with her coat sleeve. "I don't ever remember being this thirsty."

"Callie?"

Taking another long gulp of the water, Callie nodded. "Uh huh?"

"What started?"

"With what, dear?"

"With Miles. On your honeymoon? You said something started. You were staying with your cousin."

Callie tightened the bottle cap back onto the water and placed it down back in her bag. "They began one morning just before sunrise."

Blaine wondered if they'd ever get to the end of her story before the train reached their destination.

"What?" Blaine grew impatient. Callie seemed to be stumbling over her words more. Struggling to remember where she left off.

"Oh, I'm sorry. Sometimes my thoughts come faster than my words."

Blaine felt like she was in the middle of a great book and just couldn't keep reading fast enough.

"It was nearly morning. The sun was just starting to peek its way into a new day. Miles and I were sound asleep, cuddled together in bed. All at once."

Blaine held her breath.

"Miles sat straight up in bed and screamed."

"Screamed?" Blaine felt her eyes widen.

"Literally. A blood-curdling scream."

Blaine nearly spilled the drink she was holding. "What did you do?"

"I nearly screamed myself." Callie nodded. "It was horrifying. The screams seemed to come from his gut. Deep from within. He would sit up in bed, eyes wide with horror on his face. The first time was just so scary. I sat up in bed with him and tried to get him to stop screaming. I knew Cousin Deloise would surely come into the bedroom or, worse yet, they'd all think we'd gone berserk or something."

"Then what happened?"

"It was always so hard to wake Miles when he would do it. He seemed oblivious to his own terror. I'd shake his arm. Grab his face. Anything to get his attention, but when I would look into his eyes it was as if he wasn't there."

"What would happen?"

"The screaming would continue for what seemed like minutes, but it had to be just seconds. His eyes frightened me. He would be looking way past me. Not at me. Like he," Callie caught her breath, "didn't see me at all."

Callie picked up a tissue from her lap and wiped her mouth, which contained a few droplets from the water bottle. "I was petrified. Eventually, after he stopped and I thought I had him calmed down, my cousin did come and knock on the door. She whispered something to me from the other side, like, 'are you okay in there?' I assured her we were, but Miles was still very agitated and upset. He would be shaking all over. Sweat pouring from absolutely every pore in his body. His breathing short. His eyes lost.

"Once I could calm him, it took me a long time to convince him he was safe. I would push him back into his pillow and hold him close. That was about the only thing that would bring him out of the trance-like state. I'd hold him tight and he would grip me like I was the only thing to prevent his fear."

"Would he talk?"

"No. That's what scared me the most. As soon as I could get him to stop screaming, I'd stroke his face. Talk to him until his breathing would return to normal, but he would never talk. Not a word.

"Quietly and almost in a shallow-like state, but then his breathing would grow steady."

"Do you think he was dreaming about the war?"

"Oh yes, my dear. It was definitely nightmares about his fighting. But the odd thing about the nightmares" Callie shook her head, "Miles would never remember having them. He'd awaken in the morning just as normal as can be."

"Was he even awake when he had them?"

"I don't think so." Callie added, "I would do my best to help him remember or ask him about them in the morning, but he just didn't remember having them."

"Maybe that was good."

"Yes. Perhaps. But have you ever been awoken by someone screaming?"

Blaine shook her head.

"It wasn't Miles who began to lose sleep."

* * *

The train stopped and four passengers stood from their seats, moving into the aisle to leave the train. Snow now covered the ground, leaving two or three inches.

"There were times, in the beginning, we'd dream of having children. We'd talk about how many we wanted. When they'd arrive. Back then, any kind of birth control was rare. It wasn't something we wanted to prevent. But soon, we realized something was wrong. At the time," Callie rubbed her head, "we assumed it was due to the treatments Miles had received after his injury."

"The treatments made him sterile?"

Callie shrugged. "We weren't sure. Everyone around us began having families. It was an after-war phenomenon. Everyone believed children could erase the terror and fear of the world war now past. Almost to replace those we lost.

"It was time to get back to real life again. What better way to do it than to replenish the earth?" Callie smiled. "One of the best parts of having the war over was to have things return to normal. We could go to the store and purchase almost anything we wanted. The shortage of tires ended. Everyone could purchase them easily. With the men back, women returned home as homemakers again."

"I couldn't just be a homemaker and a wife." Blaine shifted uncomfortably in her seat. She wasn't sure why she said it, but it was too late now to stop it.

"No, I'm sure you couldn't." Callie smiled back at her. "Women are different now. Much more independent. I guess," Callie sighed, "we'd had a time without our menfolk home and now that they were back we decided we wanted to go back home. Let them fend for us for a while."

"I don't need someone to take care of me."

Callie looked over at her. "Yes, you are. I think women go through stages of wanting back home and then again being in the workforce." Callie leaned toward her. "You know, it isn't half bad to have a man go out and work. You can stay home and do all kinds of things."

Blaine couldn't imagine staying home all day. "Like what?"

"Oh, we had fun. If one of us knew how to sew, we'd teach the others. Or crochet, whatever was fun. And we'd have afternoon socials. So many things to do."

Blaine had worked almost as soon as she graduated from high school. What would it be like to have a whole week to do what she pleased? She'd probably choose shopping. Kyle would never allow her to just sit home. What man would?

"Life must have just gone on like it had before," Blaine surmised.

"For the most part." Callie turned her head away from Blaine and looked out the window.

"For the most part?"

Callie didn't turn back. For just a few seconds she was quiet.

Blaine still wanted to hear about Miles. The story brought tragedy, joy, but also a sense of belonging she'd never had the opportunity to feel. She felt pretty sure she'd never have the chance to feel that way with Kyle. She also knew she probably didn't want to. She leaned her head against the back of her seat.

Would there ever be someone like Miles for her? Men her age didn't feel the same way as they did back in the '40s. Did they? Who would want a wife who just sat home? Was it possible to find someone like that now?

Men today wanted women with careers. Who brought home just as much, or even more than they, on a weekly basis. Pulling their share. And kids? Who did she know now who would want more than just two or three children? No one. Kids were a pain. They cost couples thousands. Soccer practices, dance recitals, clothing alone, cost way too much for a woman to stay home.

Above all, she'd never been good at crafty things. Especially sewing. Did anyone do that anymore?

No, life was definitely different back then. Today, men wanted women earning enough to pay for their shoe fetishes. It seemed only fair. Blaine was pretty sure that living on a single income wouldn't cut it in Chicago. Was there anywhere that could happen?

Men today wanted skinny, exercise-crazy women. The selfish men of her day wanted the benefits of a sexy wife, a double income, so they could pursue their dreams. Every weekend would be spent on the latest craze, from skiing in the mountains of Colorado to dining in the fine restaurants in Chicago. Which Blaine enjoyed as well.

Blaine tried to imagine life as a stay-at-home wife. She laughed at the thought of even being a mother. She thought of her high school friend. She'd often text Blaine, feeling tired all the time and worn out. That didn't sound appealing at all.

Perhaps that was the problem in her life. She didn't have a goal. Unlike Callie, who seemed to know from day one what she wanted to do in life. What did she want in life? She really only knew one thing: she probably wouldn't enjoy a life like Callie had. But, at the same time, what did she want to do? For the first time in a long time, she decided to give it some real thought. She'd gone too long living out Kyle's dreams, and not her own.

Chapter 28

Callie was silent, seeming to look out the window. Blaine started thinking more about what she wanted to do with her own life. She was pretty sure the woman who had taken over the trip with her life story was now asleep.

Blaine closed her eyes and began thinking about the question Kyle had brought up to her during the past week. It was a life-altering one. She wasn't sure why he'd brought it up. It wasn't like they were contemplating marriage yet. She was pretty sure he was even flirting with another girl in his office. He talked about her all the time.

His question had brought panic. Self-doubt whether she could go through with it, or if she even wanted to. But what bothered her the most was what had made him ask her to do such a thing, yet he'd insisted he needed her to make a decision. It was a choice, really. To either have him exclusively or to share him with another.

She'd decided just a few days ago that she needed to get away to make her decision. As Callie was telling her about her own life, Blaine was soon realizing something. She needed to end her relationship with Kyle.

More than anything, Blaine began to consider what she really did want. She missed her independence. She'd been so busy helping Kyle have the life he wanted, she never realized she'd been missing out on her own.

***

Callie began to stir and looked up, startled.

Blaine put a hand on her shoulder. "You okay?"

Callie grimaced.

The look scared Blaine. "Callie, what's wrong?"

Callie shook her head. "Nothing." She tried shifting her heavy body in her seat. "I'm fine."

The wrinkles in her face and the look on her face didn't match her response.

"Drink some more water."

Callie nodded, but couldn't seem to bend down for the bottle sitting in her bag at her feet. Blaine decided to get it for her. "Here, let me help."

Callie leaned back again in her seat, closed her eyes, and sighed heavily.

Blaine grabbed the bottle and unscrewed the top, handing it to Callie, who now blinked and sat up.

"Thank you."

"Are you in pain, Callie?"

Callie took a sip. "I'm fine."

"You look as though you're in pain."

"Do I?" Callie took another sip of the water. A little dribbled from the side of her mouth. "Give me a minute."

Callie closed her eyes again, but held the water bottle in her lap. The baby across the aisle began to cry. Blaine glanced over at the mother, who now fumbled preparing a bottle from a diaper bag on her lap while juggling the baby fussing over her shoulder.

"Callie, how did you do it?"

Color began coming back into Callie's face. "Do what, dear?"

"Did Miles help around the house?"

Callie laughed out loud. "Well, he mowed the lawn."

"That's something, right?"

"But there was laundry, cleaning, ironing, cooking, dishwashing, childcare. You get the idea." Callie shook her head.

"He wasn't much help?"

"He went to work." Callie leaned toward her, "he was a good provider."

Blaine nodded. "My mom stayed home with us until she got so sick she couldn't even take care of herself, let alone us."

Callie looked over at her, concerned. "What happened to your momma, Blaine?"

Blaine's eyes grew misty and she wiped her nose with her finger. "I'd love to say it was cancer."

"Why would you love to say that?" Callie got a scowl on her face.

"Because that would be easier to explain. Or a heart attack or stroke, but my mother was killed in an auto accident."

Callie looked over as if waiting for more.

"She left us one night. All alone. We were sleeping so we didn't know. When we woke up, my brother and I, well..." Blaine shrugged her shoulders. "We were alone."

"You didn't know where she was?"

Blaine shook her head. "Daddy had left us years before. Soon there was a knock at the door. We'd sometimes let Mom sleep in the morning. It was a Saturday. She always loved to sleep in." Blaine smiled. "My brother and I were sitting in front of the television, eating out of the cereal box 'cause we were too lazy to get bowls and milk. It was easier that way and we did it often. The knock continued as we looked at each other as if to figure out what we should do." Blaine shifted in her seat and looked front. "It wasn't unusual for us to be alone like that. Mom often went to the store or to her friend's house next door, and we really didn't think anything about it." Blaine looked uncomfortably at Callie. "I know it sounds odd, but we didn't even know she wasn't home."

Callie nodded, as if she understood. "But then the knock got louder and someone shouted through the door. We heard someone say, 'police'." Blaine rubbed her hands down her pants as if they were growing sweaty just from telling the story. "It was the police. When my older brother finally got up and opened the door, I stood behind him." Blaine laughed a little. "It must have been quite the sight for the cop. This little girl huddled behind her brother, cereal boxes in hand." Blaine held up her hand like she was holding a box.

"What did he do?"

"At first he seemed puzzled. He asked if anyone else was home. I got brave and told him, we were just watching cartoons." Blaine stopped for a moment and looked over at Callie. "I'm sorry. My family was dysfunctional, but it was our normal. My mom was a horrible housekeeper and the floor was covered in Fruit Loops and Cheerios." Blaine laughed uncomfortably. "And dirty socks, blankets piled all over the floor." She motioned as if she were describing the living room scene of a well-lived-in home.

"What did he say?"

"He asked again if anyone was home and I ran into my mom's bedroom. My mom wasn't home. When I came back, I started to tell the cop that my mom wasn't there, but before I could my brother elbowed me in the gut and told the officer that Mom was next door. We didn't know where she was but we didn't want her in trouble by leaving us home alone." Blaine nodded. "My brother was smart enough to know that she could get in trouble if the cop knew."

Blaine leaned her head back. "But then he sat us down on the couch and started asking us questions. We grew more and more afraid. I remember cuddling as close to my older brother as I could get. I was little, but old enough to know what was happening. He put his arm around me as he lied pretty much at every question the officer gave him. Finally, the cop asked my brother to stop lying, that everything was going to be okay."

"He knew he was lying."

"Well, yeah." Blaine chuckled. "He was a horrible liar." Blaine sighed. "We had no clue where she could be.

"Pretty soon we were escorted to a police car outside. We thought we were going to jail. I took the cereal box with me, just in case." Blaine blinked back tears and even wiped one that had escaped down her cheek. "I was so scared. I thought we were in trouble because my brother had been lying. More police showed up at the house as we sat in the car. In our pajamas.

"We must have been something for the cop to stumble upon. He'd come to the house to inform us about Mom and her accident, but found us home alone.

"Soon a woman came and opened the car door and told us to get out. She bent down to our level and I'll never forget the softness of her hair and the pretty smile she had. She told us we'd be fine soon. That she would take us to a safe place.

"But my brother freaked out. Once out of the car, he dropped his box of cereal and headed for a nearby patch of trees we had beside the house. He was so scared. I tried to follow him, but officers came and soon we both were screaming and crying." Blaine shook her head and now the tears streamed down her face. She couldn't fight them any longer. "It was the scariest day of my life.

"Callie, my mother killed herself the night before. She just drove her car off an embankment outside of town. We didn't know what happened, and to this day many pieces are missing from the puzzle. Relatives told us she didn't want to live anymore. My brother had a fight with her two nights before and he was sure that it was his fault. I was too young to even understand."

"I'm sure it isn't anyone's fault." Callie patted Blaine's hand. "What a horrible thing to have to go through."

"My family has never been right. We struggle with so many issues. My brother is now an alcoholic and has been in prison for the past two years. And look at me," Blaine stumbled. "I've hooked up with one of the biggest jerks to grace Chicago."

"He can't be all that bad," Callie commented.

"I'm dating this." Blaine wanted to call him every name in the book but stopped herself. It was as though she knew if she said the words, Callie's face would turn red with shame. "He's also a real loser, after hearing about Miles."

"Didn't you children have any other relatives?"

Blaine nodded. "An aunt. She took us all in. We were now part of a family of seven and, being the outsiders," Blaine sighed again, "we were often overlooked. I don't blame her. She had enough children to worry about; she didn't need us in the mix."

Callie nodded. "That must have been hard for all of you."

"She wasn't horrible to us. We were never beaten, and we didn't starve to death. She fed us, but we noticed the difference between her kids and us. They always got better gifts at Christmas. We got gifts probably donated to a local shelter. We struggled in school. Aunt Denise would mend our clothes; as her children got new clothes, we got hand-me-downs.

"I don't blame her really. It wasn't her fault that my mother killed herself and left her to take care of us. She did the best she could."

"And your father?"

"I have no clue where he even is."

Callie now sighed. "I'm sorry, Blaine. That's a hard thing to have to handle as a little one. How old were you when your mother died?"

"Four. Old enough to remember the day the police came. Whenever we'd talk about Mom, it was that day that we remembered the most. The day she left us." Blaine twisted her hands in her lap, the tears now subsiding. "And we have no clue why."

"Perhaps your mother felt threatened," Callie added.

"By what?"

"That sounds like she really had her hands full raising you. All alone. Without your father."

Blaine nodded. "But that isn't any reason to ditch your kids like she did."

"Have you forgiven her?"

Blaine looked at Callie as if she'd lost her mind, "Forgiven her? Are you kidding me?"

"I'm sure she had it in her mind that there was no other way."

"What kind of mother ditches her kids like that?"

"Perhaps she felt desperate."

"Or someone who has no heart." Blaine leaned forward. "If you love your kids, you'd never do anything like what she did."

"Sometimes loving someone means doing many things you never thought you'd do." Callie shook her head. "There were days when I might have left Miles if I didn't know any better. I thought of doing it more times than I care to admit."

"Leave Miles?" Blaine was taken aback. "But why? He was so kind and good."

"That, my dear, was before the war took that Miles away from me."

Chapter 29

"I'm sorry you had to go through that." And Callie was. She couldn't imagine having a childhood filled with turmoil and the feeling of abandonment. All she knew were the trials of a new marriage with a man stricken with a mental illness. It paled in comparison to Blaine's life.

She then turned back to Blaine. "I'm not proud of the fact that I thought Miles would be too much for me to handle in the beginning. The first year was the hardest. From the horrible, middle-of-the-night screams to other things. That first year was one of the hardest in our marriage.

"And then," Callie looked out the window of the train once again, for fear her tears would threaten to spill again, "the children failed to come. We didn't want to wait too long, but soon we began to wonder why. Would it ever happen."

Callie looked back. "As you told me the story of your father, and your mother abandoning you, it made me think back to how much I wanted children and couldn't have them. As weeks turned into months, we soon realized that Miles' treatments had probably left him sterile."

* * *

Callie knew that the lack of sleep wasn't helping her be a good wife. If she wasn't being awakened by a blood-curdling scream, she was lying awake waiting for it. Lack of sleep and the fact that month after month she was disappointed began to wear on her.

Miles still didn't remember his nightmares. Until Callie would tell him about them in the morning. At first, he'd laugh them off, but as they would continue he soon became agitated about them. Callie didn't want to worry him further, so soon she stopped telling him.

Their new little home was small, with holes in the plaster and rough boards on the front porch needed fixing. Callie knew Miles was capable of handling the work and, sure enough, most days she'd return home from work to find him replacing the split boards on the front porch with new ones.

He plastered over many of the old walls and patched the holes left from the previous owner. Their wedding gifts now made the quaint little house a home. All the work got done, but there were moments when Miles would cut a board too short for the second time or the patching paste would be too runny, which made Miles livid.

During the outbursts, Callie would shrink into a corner or stay outside until Miles' temper calmed. She hadn't realized before they were married that he had a bad temper. They'd never been predicaments for her to see it.

She was weeding a bed of petunias close to the house and heard Miles either nail his finger with a hammer or drop it on a toe. The words coming from within the house scared her. She leaned back on her heels as she listened to his rants, even through the walls.

Soon other poundings on the wall didn't sound much like repairs, but further damage being done to the wall. She stood and listened some more as the wall from within her house seemed to be bursting apart by his hammer blows.

Heading to a nearby window, she stood on tiptoes to peer in just over the windowsill to see Miles slamming away at the wall with a hammer. As each blow hit, a swear word accompanied it. She'd rarely encountered such anger from a man, and it frightened her.

As she watched, a beautiful clock, given to her from an aunt as a shower gift fell to the floor and shattered.

Despite her fear, she wasn't going to stand outside and watch Miles destroy her home. She marched into the house, almost as mad as the man attempting to put more holes into her wall. She screamed at Miles, "What are you doing?"

Shattered glass and tiny clock arms now were strewn across her living room floor. "Miles, stop it." She attempted to grab the hammer out of his hand, but the look he gave her made her shrink to the far side of the room. He appeared as though, if she walked any closer, he'd hit her with the hammer he held now in the air over his head.

"Are you going to hurt me?"

Miles' face took on a new look. He gazed at her for a few minutes and gradually lowered the hammer to his side. Giving her another glare stare, he dropped the hammer, smashing the remaining pieces of the clock at his feet. Callie went to her knees on the floor and began picking up the pieces, placing them into the palm of her hand. "What is wrong with you? This was from Aunt Doris, and now look at it." The words she said now came from inside the depths of her tired, worn-out heart. She looked up and said, "Get out of my house."

Miles didn't hesitate. He picked up his car key on a side table and left. Soon she heard the tires screech out the driveway and down their road. Callie began to cry.

Who was this man? She had no clue. Who had she married? Where was her beloved, kind-hearted Miles? As she picked up the shattered pieces of her clock, it made her feel as though she was also picking up the shards of her life. Piece by piece, she sobbed away her heartache. She'd married this man for better and for worse, but she had no idea that he had changed so much from the Miles she'd loved for so many years before.

She knew war changed people, and there were stories of other men now battling issues like Miles, but this was her home. How would she ever cope if this continued? Where would they find further help? Did he need additional treatments? And as she picked up the little arm of the clock, now bent, she thought of what additional treatments would do to Miles. All she could envision was further damage to his reproductive organs.

As she went for a broom to sweep up the other slices of glass littering her floor, she thought about her life. Would there be no more happiness? Would they forever have to live with the horrible effects of war?

She bent to sweep up the rest of the mess. Holding the dust pan, Callie stood gazing at the fresh holes in her walls. They appeared to be too large to patch.

Going into the kitchen, Callie went to a trash can and slowly dumped the remaining pieces of the shattered clock into it. She felt as if her life were being dumped into the trash as well. She knelt on the floor beside the trash can and sobbed.

* * *

Callie ate alone that night. She'd made a dinner for both her and Miles, but he never returned home. She waited and waited on the porch as mosquitoes buzzing forced her inside. Shutting the windows against the cool night air, she sat on the couch and hugged herself. Rubbing her arms for warmth she thought what she'd do if Miles failed to return home. Would he leave her? More tears followed the thoughts.

Despite his actions and the broken clock, she wondered what she'd tell everyone if he never returned home. She loved Miles. She was sure of it, or did she just love the Miles she used to know? This new Miles made her even question whether someone had switched her soldier on the battlefield for someone else. But as she gazed up at their wedding photo now hanging on a good wall in their dining room, she saw the smile. The dimples. The familiar eyes that could look at her with deep love. He was in there. In this shell of a body she now called her husband.

As the evening wore on, Callie grew tired. Her head hurt from crying. She wondered where Miles could be. Her anger was now replaced with sorrow. She wanted Miles. Her Miles. Despite his illness, she wanted him to come home. She didn't want to live alone or without him.

As she lay in bed that night, the only sounds she heard were the crickets chirping from their yard and the frogs croaking from the nearby pond just down the road. She'd left her window open just a crack so she could hear when Miles returned home. The sounds gave her some comfort. They sounded peaceful and familiar. She curled up into a ball under the covers. It was a particularly cool night for August. They'd had a storm rumble through the night before, which had cooled off the previous humidity-filled day.

The cars on their road were minimal at this time of night. Most everyone was home, listening to the radio or settling into bed. But Callie layed there, tight in a ball, waiting to hear the car pulling into their driveway.

She'd rarely been alone at night and she hated it. Her anger over the broken clock and the fear of the night started to make her wish Miles would return sooner than later. She picked up her watch from the nightstand and read the time as four minutes past midnight. Since their wedding night, they'd never been without each other.

As a car pulled into the driveway Callie pulled back the covers, crawled to her knees, and peered out the window above her bed. She felt amazing relief as a car door slammed and she watched Miles approach the house. His shoulders slumped, his hands stuffed in his pockets.

He walked onto the porch and stopped for a few minutes. She realized he'd probably not taken his house key. They rarely locked the door, but she'd done it that night because she was scared and alone. She picked up her bathrobe, wrapping it around her, tying on the belt as she rushed into the living room. She got to the door as Miles was peering through the front window of the room. As she unbolted the lock, he approached the door from the other side.

She opened it up and there he stood. Tall and as handsome as ever, despite the fact that his hair stood on end and he looked cold standing in just a short-sleeved shirt. He pulled his hands out of his pockets, opened them to welcome her into his arms with a "Callie, I'm so sorry."

Callie was tired. She was so thankful he was home. She went into his arms. He caressed her hair as she leaned against his chest. "I'm sorry, too." He pulled her back from him and then picked her up and carried across the threshold. His warmth made her melt into him.

"Callie, you have nothing to be sorry for. You didn't lose your temper, I did. You didn't break that beautiful clock from your aunt, I did. I'm the one who should be the sorriest."

"Why did you take so long to come home?" Callie asked as she looked into his face.

"I'm so embarrassed. I don't know what makes me lose my temper so badly. Please forgive me."

Callie kissed his mouth. Soon the passion she'd had by being angry melted into a deeper, new-wife desire. The forgiveness was given and accepted.

* * *

A new day dawned and the couple found themselves entwined in bed. Callie inched as close as she could get to the calm, giant man lying next to her. They'd both slept soundly. There were no nightmares. Only blissful, relaxing sleep.

Callie turned her head to look at Miles, who was sleeping with his mouth open. It was as if he hadn't slept that peacefully in a long time. Maybe their frustrations would end soon. Perhaps the nightmares would cease and the temper flares would diminish. She only wished for one more thing as she lay tucked close against this man she loved. She wished, more than anything, that she could give him a baby.

Somehow Callie knew that a baby couldn't take away the fear or frustrations of Miles' illness and injuries, but it could help Callie cope better. She'd wanted to have Miles' baby ever since she saw that poor pitiful right ear of his.

She'd learned he'd acquired the injury after a drunk doctor had delivered him via forceps. He was embarrassed by his deformity, but for Callie it was a part of him she loved the most. That crooked ear which drooped a little away from his head. She'd placed many a kiss on that ear.

If only the heartache left from war could be replaced with new life. That would solve things. Perhaps it would get Miles' mind off the horrors he'd experienced overseas. It would give them a distraction and hope for the future. Perhaps even the habit of smoking that Miles had taken up overseas would be stopped once they had a baby.

Callie reached down and caressed her stomach. If only. Callie closed her eyes hard and asked for the blessing, one more time.

Chapter 30

Callie smiled as she placed the wrapping paper left over from a wrapped present into her lap, folding it corner to corner. The presents were adorable, from baby bonnets to rattles. Most of the clothes were for either sex, but pink dresses predominately reigned at her sister's baby shower.

They'd decided to have the shower in April, just a month before her sister was to give birth. One of the guests leaned over to Callie. "This is the third baby shower I've had to attend this year."

Callie agreed. "This is my fifth one."

"They're saying on the radio that it will be called a 'baby boom,'" the woman giggled. "It's nice to see so much life after so many years of heartache and losing so many of our boys."

Callie glanced over at her sister, who held up another baby t-shirt and rattle for the guests.

The woman next to her patted her knee. "You'll be next, Callie."

Callie smiled, but didn't say anything. Last June she'd been preparing for her wedding; this June she was awaiting the arrival of her first niece or nephew. Gasps in the room brought her out of her thoughts as another mint-green dress appeared out of the opened box on her sister's limited lap space.

Laughter erupted from the doorway of the kitchen as another woman patted her mother on the shoulder. "Hey, Granny!" The announcement of the baby's arrival last fall had brought joy. The men all placed bets that it would be a boy.

Callie overheard her mother. "Not sure I'm ready to be a granny," she told the women around her, "but you should hear Wilbur. He can't wait to become a grandfather. He insists on his name being an option. But the girls aren't thrilled with the name Wilbur." Laughter filled the room.

Callie stood and began folding clothes now out on display for the women crowding her mother's living room. As she fingered each one, she loved how soft and small everything was. A few she held to her cheek, smelling powder. The ache in her heart grew, tightening her chest as tears threatened to spill. She stepped away from the table.

She couldn't be jealous of her sister. She was so excited to be having this new baby. Callie didn't want to take away her joy. It had been almost a year. Every month a little bit of her hope died. She'd hide her tears as best as she could. Her prayers only resulting in resounding 'no' answers each month.

A friend from high school came up, hugging her from behind. "Isn't this exciting? Hard to believe Mary got pregnant so soon after she got married."

Callie swallowed hard to keep from crying. "Yes. Last summer it was wedding dresses; this year, baby clothes."

"Have you and Miles decided to start a family yet?"

Thankfully, before Callie could answer, another woman approached Mary and hugged her. "You lucky girl you. A bride last August and a new mother in June. Let me count the months." Everyone laughed.

Esther entered with another tray of small sandwiches for the luncheon table. "I'm still talking wedding dresses. Did you get your invitation yet, Anna?"

Callie's friend nodded. "Yes, can't wait to see you walk down the aisle. Isn't life grand?"

Everyone agreed. One family neighbor added, "Anything beats a war; only blessings to follow."

Callie sighed. For some. She needed to concentrate on the blessings. If only her heart would allow her.

* * *

Later that evening, Miles and she went for a walk down the gravel road by their house. They enjoyed doing this, as the winter weather had given way to spring once again.

"I love spring. I love going on walks with you." Miles squeezed her hand tight. They walked silently for a little while and Miles picked up her hand and kissed it. "Are you okay? You're awfully quiet tonight."

Callie nodded. She couldn't tell him how her heart ached. How she wanted to be the first in the family to bring a baby into the world. She'd repented so many times today for the jealously in her heart. It embarrassed her to think about it.

"I'm fine."

"The shower was good, right?"

"She got so many adorable clothes. Lots of dresses. I think we might get a girl."

"Mary will be happy with a girl, won't she?"

"Oh, I don't know. We have lots of girls, so it would be nice to start off the grandchildren with a boy for Bert and Daddy." Callie laughed. "We'll see."

"I hope this child bribes her for quarters like Mary used to do to me while courting you."

They both laughed.

"It's hard to believe Mary is a wife, let alone a mother, too."

"More kids to work on the farm for your dad." Miles smiled. "He'll like that."

Callie nodded. "I'm not sure who's more excited, Daddy or Bert."

"Yeah, Bert's pretty happy."

"What did you boys do today while we were at the party?" Callie asked as Miles opened their front door.

"We went out and saw your dad's fields. He's getting ready to plant. He showed us the seeds he's planning on putting in just as soon as the frost is gone."

Callie nodded. "Farming is such a guessing game sometimes."

"That it is."

"Callie, I've been thinking." Miles said as he pulled out a chair, scraping it across the linoleum floor, and sat down to remove his shoes.

Callie was afraid of what he would say. She'd kept her tears hidden all day long. If he were to say something about them having a baby today, she'd probably gush and weep all over him. She held her breath.

"Why don't we get a puppy?"

Callie relaxed. Miles was oblivious to her pain. Her heartache of not having children. She shook her head. "Are you going to pick up after it?"

Chapter 31

Her sister did give birth to a daughter shortly after the baby shower. They weren't shocked to acquire another girl. Even Callie's father didn't seem too disappointed.

The baby took up all their time. Callie often went to Mary's house to help her with her laundry, bathe the child, or even babysit so Mary could head to the store for groceries. It seemed Baby Janie consumed everyone's attention that summer. It'd been a long time since a baby that wasn't a calf, chick, or duckling had an introduction to the farm household.

Despite the joy, Callie's heart grew even more hardened. She noticed one night as Esther recalled how she'd just been to her boyfriend's high school graduation. As Esther recalled the event, and old friends who had attended, she asked Callie if she remembered one of their old girlfriends. All Callie heard her say was, "It was so sad to see her there. We all knew she would have wanted to be anywhere but at a graduation which would have included her brother, John."

The comment caught Callie off guard. She hadn't really been listening to her sister, now feeling her face contort as she tried to recall the name of the girl she'd been talking about.

Esther stopped. "Callie? Have you been listening to me?"

Embarrassed, Callie shook her head, "I'm sorry. Who did you say?"

"Thelma. Remember her?"

Callie nodded. "Oh yes. That's sad to think of her being there without John. I wonder why she attended."

"Perhaps for just her other friends. Who knows?" Esther lay on her stomach, propping her head up with her hands. "I can't wait to be happily married like you." Callie knew her sister was ready for marriage. They'd been planning her wedding since her boyfriend, Bill, had returned from the South Pacific.

Callie had never told her sisters about Miles' nightmares. Or about his sudden outbursts and even about the fear she had when he would break things due to his temper. She feared what her sisters, or even her parents, would think of Miles. She again nodded a half-hearted agreement. Whispering a silent prayer, she asked God to not bring Bill home with the trauma that had followed Miles.

As the girls grew silent, they heard a car pull into the driveway outside. Callie glanced down from her sister's upstairs bedroom to see her sister, Mary, with Baby Janie get out of the car. Both sisters raced downstairs to the car to see who could grab the baby first. Hanging outside the back window of the car was a white diaper, flapping in the breeze.

Callie pointed to the diaper. "Hanging out your dirty laundry again, Mary?"

They all laughed and Mary announced she'd found a new, more economical way to dry Janie's diapers. "If I'm headed out somewhere, I'll just throw it up into the top of the car window. By the time I arrive, I throw the clean diaper in Janie's diaper bag. It actually works out quite well."

Callie shook her head. Only Mary would think of something like this.

Callie had reached Janie before Esther and was soon coddling and cooing to her. She could now sit on her hip quite easily and she often recognized her aunts quite readily. The smiles brought warmth to Callie's heart. If God didn't allow her to have a baby yet, at least He'd provided Janie to love.

"You know what I just realized today," Mary announced as she threw a baby blanket over one shoulder and a diaper bag over the other to head into the farmhouse.

"What's that, dear?"

Before she could answer, their mother flew out of the kitchen door, wiping her hands on her apron hanging at her waist. "Janie, come see Grandma." The baby soon left Callie's arms for another.

As her mother moved the baby to her hip, Callie laughed. "Hey, it was my turn."

"Not with Grandma around," her mother announced.

As the woman took the baby inside, all three girls watched and commented how wonderful a grandmother their mother was turning out to be.

"I can't wait to be a mother myself," announced Esther.

Mary put her hand on her shoulder. "You gotta get married first there, little sister." They all laughed again. "Besides, it's Callie's turn first."

Callie shook her head and then lied. "We're not quite ready for a baby yet."

"Oh, come on, Callie. You've wanted a baby since we were kids."

Callie looked down. "Yeah, someday."

At that moment, their father came up from behind them, scaring them into screams just like he did when they were little. They all reacted with a slap on his back as he passed them for the door, "Is my granddaughter here?"

"That's what I was going to tell you guys. I just realized it last night. Janie is the first for both Bert's and my family. And then I began to count all of her grandparents. Greats included." Mary smiled.

"How many are there?"

"This child has nine grandparents."

Callie laughed. "Good grief, she'll be spoiled rotten."

"That's crazy," Esther commented. "I think we need to get busy and add to that. As soon as Bill gets home."

"Again," Callie took her little sister's hand and led her into the kitchen, "after the wedding."

Her sister answered her with a stuck-out tongue.

* * *

Their new puppy was awaiting Callie as she drove up the driveway just before dinner that night. She was home just in time to fix Miles a meal after his day at work. Greetings from the puppy were long jumps against her legs and licks when she picked him up to cuddle. He was going to be a big dog. Miles had insisted on a lab-mix.

As she dropped the puppy on the front porch, Callie headed into the kitchen. Before messing it up with her cooking concoctions, Callie gazed around at the clean, orderly little room.

She'd chosen flowered wallpaper for one of the walls mixed with red geraniums and green variegated leaves in terra cotta pots. A new potholder hung on a hook just over her stove. She loved her kitchen. It brought her joy and satisfaction to have it not only clean, but adorned with many of her wedding gifts. She'd dreamed of claiming a kitchen such as this one, her entire life.

She picked up a cookbook, handwritten from her grandmother. Turning to page six, she looked over the recipe of chicken and dumplings she'd wanted to make for Miles' dinner. She washed her hands in the sink and then reached for the flour canister on the shelf above her head.

As she mixed up the dough for the dumplings, she couldn't get over the look on her father's face each time he picked up Janie or sat with her on the floor. This baby had brought out the best in her father. A part she'd never seen before. He'd kiss the top of her head while she sat on a blanket in the middle of the kitchen floor.

She wondered what Miles would be like with a child. Would it bring out the best in him as well? Would he adore the child just as he'd done with the new puppy now barking at his arrival as he pulled into the driveway? She heard the car door slam, as she plopped dumplings onto the chicken mixture of the eight by eight glass casserole dish. She slipped it into the oven just as Miles came through the door.

She wiped her hands on her apron and smiled as she thought about their night. After dinner, perhaps they could take a walk. Enjoy the cool air of fall approaching. Sadly, the summer had gone by so quickly after Janie's arrival in early June. As she headed into the living room, she found Miles looking back out onto the porch. She wondered what he was doing. "Miles?"

He turned to her. His face ashen and his hair tousled from the wind. He wasn't smiling.

"Everything okay?"

"Not really."

Miles pushed past her, plopping down on the couch.

Panic grew in her heart. She wasn't quite sure what to do. Ask Miles or just let him tell her? Before she could ask, he told her.

"I got fired today."

Callie put the dish towel in her hand to her mouth. "What?"

"Yeah, your deadbeat husband got fired."

Callie lowered the dish towel, now wringing it in her hands. "What happened?"

"Guess."

"Isn't there enough work?"

"There's plenty of work."

"Well, then, what, Miles? What happened?"

"It was that stupid, cotton-pickin' Jay." Miles motioned flippantly with his hand. "He's such a..."

"Stop it. Don't swear in my house."

"Sheesh, Callie. Lighten up."

Silence penetrated the room. Callie wasn't sure what to do. Add to the silence or ask a question. "What did Jay do?"

"He made me mad. That's what he did."

Callie sighed. "Well, you'll find something else. Jobs are a dime a dozen now that the war is over."

"I hope so."

Callie sat down beside him. She had feared this day for a long time. When would his abrupt temper interrupt regular life? Today, she was getting her answer.

"Are you hungry?"

"I don't deserve to eat."

"I made chicken and dumplings."

"I'm going outside to smoke."

Why did the frustrating moments seem to be coming longer and more furiously? How much more could she handle? She got up and headed to the kitchen as she heard the timer ding over her new stove.

* * *

Miles had made a small chicken coop in their backyard into a makeshift amateur radio station. He'd been a radio man in the war and wanted to continue using his skills with his ham radio. He was able to communicate with many other ham radio operators around the world. A restriction had been put on ham radio operators during World War I and again during the past war. Miles had used surplus war radios, called ARC-5s, to fill his new little space in the now enclosed coop.

He'd often spend many a night out in the coop, contacting other friends around the world and even in the States. It was a hobby that he loved to do, especially after the war. Callie would often find him there, trying to connect with other operators late into the night.

The only way she could convince him to come inside was to wear something slinky to the chicken coop. It got his attention almost every time.

That night, it's where she took his dinner. She'd waited in the house for an hour. Giving him time to cool off again in his own space. Somehow the only thing to cool off was his dinner. She'd done her best to warm it up in the stove before heading out to him.

He was busy flipping switches and fumbling with the knobs on his machine when she came through the door with his dinner in hand. "Aren't you hungry?"

He shook his head and mumbled something into the microphone sitting near his mouth.

"Well," she placed the plate beside him on the table and then backed off, "I think you should have something to eat."

"Don't tell me what to do," Miles muttered.

She nodded. "I'm sorry. I'm going to go back in the house now."

Miles didn't answer her.

She wrapped her sweater around herself tighter and left the coop. As she went toward the house, she thought about the tiny savings they now had in the bank. It would last a while, but how long before it would go dry? She also wondered if she should seek help for Miles. Clearly, his issues from the war were still visible. Perhaps another treatment? Then she thought of her own infertility. She wondered if she should contact a doctor.

* * *

"Callie, can I ask you something?"

Callie wasn't sure where this question would take her at this moment, but she hoped it would result in the essence of telling her story, so she nodded.

"When Miles was so mean, as he began literally tearing down the walls of your home, and when he would keep you awake late at night with his nightmares, in the midst of all of that did you ever consider leaving him?"

Callie looked down at her feet, ashamed of her answer. "Why, yes, Blaine. I did. At times."

"Did you ever want to go through with it?"

Callie didn't look up, but nodded again. "I imagined a moment when I could. On those nights he would leave me alone. I pleaded to God many times that He would allow me to leave this nightmare of a marriage. But then..." Callie couldn't finish. She knew what she would need to say to this young woman and, unfortunately, it always shamed her to have to say it.

Blaine seemed perturbed by the Callie's sudden silence for a moment. "But then, what? I wouldn't put up with his crap. Yeah, he was sick and all and had been through horrible times. He hadn't caused his disease. His pain. But after a while, why would you have to deal with it all? Why didn't you just get a divorce?"

That's when Callie looked up. "I never gave myself that kind of option." The answer came from the deepest recesses of Callie's heart.

Blaine sat back in her seat and folded her arms. The walls were going up. Callie knew she had to shame herself to get her back.

"An escape isn't always the answer." The response from Blaine was exactly as Callie expected, but she continued. "I soon realized that my life's goal shouldn't be to figure out how to make myself happy."

Blaine shot her a glance right out of *Women's Independence Weekly*, if there were a magazine called that.

"Right around that time in our marriage, I found something that would always fulfill me. Keep my life centered, despite how Miles, or anyone else for that matter, treated me."

Blaine's look softened a bit, "Seriously? Does anyone or anything like that exist? 'Cause I haven't been able to find anything that can do that."

Now it was time. Callie felt the push, she just had to finally open her mouth for good. She smiled. "Yes it does. Through those early years of my marriage, I was like any other newlywed. I wanted to be happy. I longed for my marriage to be the best one on the block. The one everyone looked to as a model for happiness. Pride set in, as it always does. My pride. I mean, look at what I'd done. I deserved it for accepting Miles as my husband, knowing full well that he was imperfect, now flawed. The war had changed that sweet, innocent boy I fell in love with into a bit of a hardened soul.

"I truly believe that Miles wanted to protect me from what he'd had to endure. I slowly began to see how that, when he'd leave me, it was for my own good. Deep down, he wanted to hide the war and the experiences he had gone through so that his nightmares wouldn't go into my head." Callie stopped for a moment to gather her thoughts.

"Those coming out of the war had seen atrocities that left them with a fear and lack of human spirit that probably would never go away. Their biggest fear, I believe, was that people could be so evil. I think many, like Miles, had even seen an evil in themselves that disturbed them. And, for some reason, that truth began to seep into my soul.

"God tells us that we are all born evil. None of us is good. I think war and the need to defend ourselves brings that out greater than many ordinary life experiences can. If we believe what God says is true, we all have evil thoughts. None of us seeks God. We like ourselves. Our pride always gets in the way to think that He would know us better than we know ourselves. A real lie is that only weak people or sick people need God. We want to handle all that life dishes out. That's what even Miles thought for a time.

"Seeing Miles so afraid and his entire being not as it used to be made me see just how good God really is. I think there comes a time in everyone's life when things just get out of control. You've sought happiness in so many other ways and things whether it be money, travel, or fame, and none of them have given the least bit of satisfaction. Often, it has encouraged them to want and seek more. To keep discovering what will make them truly happy.

"At the moment when our marriage was at its weakest, when I felt that there was no hope of ever being with the Miles previous to the war, that's when I realized my greatest need. I was seeking to find it in a happy marriage and in having a child.

"I always love telling little children about God. You know why?"

Blaine shook her head.

"They just get Him. Their little minds just get it. They don't need lofty, knowledgeable answers. They just take His love and ask Him to be a part of their lives so easily. God isn't something they have to figure out. They just take Him as He is. They know He loves them, they know He would do anything for them, and they accept that. They only change when the world begins telling them differently.

"When we are weak, He is strong. When we are sad, He tells us that He is enough to make us happy. When we fear, it is only He who truly comforts us. The best part for me is that only He can satisfy our deep desires. He created us. He knows us better than we know ourselves." Tears began to fill Callie's eyes. They always came when she talked about her best friend.

"God? God can do all of that?" Blaine's arms did not unfold. The look on her face remained the same.

Callie then knew she'd said enough, yet she knew she had to add just one more thing. "A real, intimate relationship with God does all that and more."

Chapter 32

Blaine couldn't help but hang on every word of Callie's story. Callie didn't deserve a man like Miles. What had Callie done, but love him?

Callie seemed even more tired after telling her the last few bits of the story. "I hate talking about our first few years of marriage. Many people have no clue what I went through," Callie murmured, as if even now someone nearby would hear it. "I didn't want others to see him in a bad light." Callie sighed.

"Did it ever come out what had happened during the war? Did something scare him? Did he see things? What made him have a nervous breakdown?" Blaine asked with the intent of an investigative reporter.

"I never knew." Callie shook her head. "Miles had his major episode he believes in New Guinea, but he never really knew for sure. That frustrated him the most. He remembers nothing from the days prior or following his episode, attack, whatever it was that happened to him. His buddies were left fighting, and once he returned to the States, he lost all contact with anyone who might be able to tell him what happened."

"Couldn't the doctors even figure it out?"

"They didn't know either. They just treated him once he returned home. The only information that came with him is that he was deemed incompetent to keep fighting. That was all. The last thing Miles remembered was fighting with his buddies. The next thing he knew, he was waking up in a hospital in Indiana."

"He was wounded. Why wouldn't anyone tell him what had happened?"

"Maybe they tried." Callie twisted a tissue in her hand. "But Miles could never remember. He struggled with that the most. He tried to contact other soldiers from his unit once many would have returned home, but he never kept home addresses for any of them. Names were all he had, and perhaps hometowns. I offered once to go to one of the cities and look. Find someone, but Miles always shrugged it off. He'd say, 'Callie, how are you ever supposed to find a man named Joe in Columbus or Howard from New Jersey?' And he was right. There wasn't the Internet back then."

"How sad."

"There was one time though."

"What happened?"

"Miles heard about a reunion for his unit. But he was say sixty or even seventy years old by that time," Callie added. "We almost decided not to go to it, because it was miles away from our home, but we went. While at the reunion, Miles sought out anyone who he might have known in the war. He learned many in his unit had passed away during the heavy fighting in New Guinea. Somehow, that made me feel better. If many passed away, that meant the battle must have been harsh."

Blaine nodded.

"But there was one man. He was of Mexican heritage. He approached Miles from across the room and Miles immediately recognized him as he approached. They hugged. He couldn't answer all of Miles' questions, but he did answer quite a few. He did remember Miles, and they had been best buddies in the war. Gradually, the man began to tell Miles of the heavy fighting just before he left his division."

"Did he know what happened?" Blaine anticipated the answer.

"Unfortunately, he hadn't been fighting next to Miles when it happened. He only heard through comrades a story of Miles freezing while fighting. They told Miguel that he'd been sent home." Callie sighed. "That's all we've ever been able to piece together about the whole ordeal.

"Any other attempts at finding out the truth, just resulted in hearsay or rumors. No one knew what happened. I often wondered if someone had rescued Miles from some terrible fighting. Perhaps even God intervened in his life to bring him home early so he wasn't injured or killed liked the rest of his friends."

"Did you ever mention that to Miles?"

"Why, yes, all the time. I'd often tell him how blessed he was to be alive. Able to marry. Live a life that not many of his friends had the privilege to do. But nothing helped his spirits. He'd have a few months of being himself, and then one episode of sadness or shock would send him into another hermit-like state. My Miles was never the same."

* * *

Callie couldn't bear to be without a child for much longer. She'd been married almost two years now. Janie was toddling around her parents' house on her sister's visits. Her sister was expecting a second child, due the next spring. Esther had finally married Bill.

Callie and her mother were playing on the floor with Baby Janie as Esther strode into the house. She had a grin on her face like she had a secret bursting to be told.

Callie knew. She didn't have to hear the announcement from her baby sister. Looking down at Janie, her heart felt as though it would burst from the pain setting in. As Esther told them the news, she closed her eyes and prayed. She prayed she could offer the congratulations her sister deserved. She prayed she could hold back the tears now filling her eyes. As she did, she felt Mary grab her hand and give it a squeeze. She looked up into her other sister's eyes. She knew Callie's thoughts. Callie felt comfort to know someone sensed her pain.

Callie looked into the sweet face of her niece and pushed a strand of her brown hair behind one of her ears. No, she couldn't have children of her own, but she could enjoy the blessings of her sisters. She knew without a doubt they would welcome her doing that, and would encourage her to grow to love them as her own.

With that thought, she was able to stand up and hug her baby sister. She grew excited to think that maybe this baby would be a boy. A boy to fill a family now filled with girls.

Sure enough, Esther gave birth to the first boy in the family. Her father was ecstatic. He finally had his boy and he couldn't be more excited. Three grandchildren now filled out the family. Mary had another girl just after the baby boy arrived.

Their parents' home was a gathering place each Sunday afternoon. With three grandchildren, the house soon filled with play time, kisses, and hugs. Food was plentiful at her mother's home. Cakes, pies, roasts, the war rations now just a faint memory of the struggles of war.

Yet Callie's war was far from over. Miles secluded himself even more in his makeshift ham radio station in the tiny building behind their house. Often, she'd eat dinner alone. Or sit by the radio at night, mending socks or knitting a new sweater for one of the babies, alone. She tried hard to not let it bother her, but one night she was particularly lonely and decided to ask Miles about it as he came in from the backyard.

"Who did you reach tonight?"

"Not far. I've been talking to someone in England the past few weeks, but my attempts to reach him tonight were unsuccessful." Miles went into the kitchen. "Anything to eat?"

Callie fussed over a lost loop in her knitting and exasperatingly let Miles have the brunt of her frustrations. "I fixed dinner almost two hours ago. I made you a plate. It's in the fridge."

"Can you warm it up for me?"

Callie sighed and re-looped the lost piece of her yarn, "Turn on the oven. It will only take a few minutes."

Miles came to the doorway. "I'm not sure I know how to turn the stove on."

Callie placed the mint-green sweater on her lap and looked up. "Well, if you're going to wait until two hours after supper to come in and eat, I guess you're gonna have to learn how." She knew as the words came out of her mouth that it wasn't going to be a favorable response.

And it wasn't. Miles came toward her from the doorway. She looked up into his angry face. "Why don't you put down what you're working on and do it for me? Like a good wife."

Callie sighed again, but bravery filled her heart instead of fear. Although looking back to her knitting, she spoke, "A good wife does fix dinner for her husband. But a husband who cares nothing for his wife makes her eat alone, not even giving her the courtesy of coming into the house to eat after she's slaved in the kitchen for hours fixing it for him." Pride now filled her heart. Why should she be the one to be scolded for what she knew to be true?

Miles stopped in front of her. Callie looked up at him. He folded his arms. "So, this is how it's going to be?"

Callie shrugged. "Seems like that's how you want it to be."

Miles turned on his heel and headed back into the kitchen. She heard the plate being tossed back into the refrigerator. Miles spoke from the kitchen, "I'm going to bed."

Callie didn't like standing up for herself, but this kind of treatment wasn't okay with her. She hated being ignored. She worked hard to provide nice meals for Miles. It was time for him to stop wallowing in the backyard for hours at a time.

She went back to her knitting.

Miles was snoring when she got into bed, but instantly woke up as she carefully slid under the covers next to him. She hated scolding him, but she knew he needed to be aware of how hurtful his actions were in neglecting her. There had to be a balance between helping him cope with his issues and letting him take advantage of her.

He had his back to her, but as she got into bed he reached back and fumbled for her hand. "I'm sorry, Callie. You're right."

She leaned toward him and snuggled up against him. She couldn't be mad at him for long. He reached back around and patted her. "I love you, Callie."

"I love you, too," she responded. As they both settled into sleep, she heard herself add, "But don't be late for supper again."

* * *

One afternoon, Callie found herself babysitting her sister's daughters. Play blocks were scattered across her living room floor. The youngest baby, Kathy, was just beginning to sit up by herself, so Callie was sitting behind her for security. She heard a car door slam and her younger sister call from outside, "It's just me," she yelled loud enough for Callie to hear.

Callie picked up the small child and headed to the window. "Glad you're here. The girls are beginning to get bored with just me."

In walked her younger sister, with Baby Billy in her arms. "Oh what a morning. This child won't stop fussing until I pick him up." Esther appeared frazzled and tired.

"Here," Callie lifted the baby off her hip and said, "let's switch. Maybe all he needs is his Aunt Callie."

Esther laughed and handed over the child while taking the other baby, landing a kiss on the top of her head. "You have your hands full this morning, too."

"No." Callie smiled and unwrapped the baby in the blankets in her arms. "Never. I love watching the babies."

"Hard to believe we have three now," Esther laughed, "Isn't it?"

"It is." Callie sat down on the couch. The only seat in the room. She started to coo and talk to the baby boy now gazing up at her with laughing blue eyes. He smiled at her. "He smiled."

"Yup, welcome to the world, Little Bill. He's finally understanding that we love him here," Esther commented, and sat down beside Janie on the floor.

"Where's Mary today?"

"She had to do some grocery shopping, and I can only imagine how hard it is to shop with two little ones to carry through the store." Callie snuggled the baby boy closer and began to bounce him. "What are you feeding this boy, Esther? I think he weighs more than he did Sunday afternoon."

Esther laughed. "He should. He's been eating non-stop for the past three days. I've been up at least three times a night to feed him. Do they get hungrier at six weeks?"

Callie shrugged. "I don't know. Why would you think that?"

"I thought Mary said something about it."

"Who knows? He's a boy. What do we know about boys?"

They both laughed loudly, making Billy reflect a frustrating face and start to whimper. "Oh baby, I'm sorry." Callie put him up against her shoulder and patted his back. "We scared him."

Both women grew quiet. Callie patted the baby while her sister began playing with Janie.

"Did you have other plans today, Callie? Or had you planned on babysitting for Mary today?"

"She called early this morning. I had a feeling she might be getting low on supplies again. I've been trying to help her by watching the girls on Thursdays. It's her shopping day."

Esther nodded. "Does it bother you?"

"Bother me?" Callie looked at her sister. "Heavens no, why would it bother me?"

"Well," Esther paused and looked down at Janie, stroking her brown hair. "Not having one of your own yet." She then looked up for Callie's reaction.

Callie snuggled the baby closer to her, looking across her shoulder at the sweet face now growing calm, his eyelids giving way to sleep. "To be honest, I'm just happy to help you two right now. But, yes there are some days when I just ache for my own."

"I'm sorry," Esther said. "I don't mean to bring up the fact that we have children and you don't yet."

"It's fine." She needed to gather firm courage to even say it. "Who knows what will happen?"

"Do you think, perhaps, Miles' treatments caused it?"

Callie looked at her sister. They'd been pretty quiet about the whole infertility issue, even though Callie was pretty sure they were talking about Miles and her in private.

"I never want to speculate his fault in this." Callie pulled the baby off her shoulder and down into her arms. "We need a rocking chair in this house," she added as Billy began to rub his eyes and yawn.

"I'm sorry." Esther shook her head. "I should have never mentioned anything about this."

“No, it’s okay. You’re my sister. You can tell or ask me anything.” Callie swayed back and forth on the couch. “You know that.”

“Did the doctor ever say anything about it?”

Callie shook her head. “No. But I do believe God will give us a baby when the time is right. It’s just not the right time yet.” Callie smiled at her sister, but inside she was fighting tears.

“Have you thought about adoption?”

“Adoption?” Callie stopped swaying and looked at her sister. “No, we haven’t.”

“There’re lots of children who need good homes, and you’d be an amazing mother.” Esther pointed to Billy. “Look at you.”

Callie looked down at the baby in her arms now drifting off to sleep.

“I’ve been trying to get him to take a nap all morning. Finally, I just gave up and we got in the car to come over here.”

“In God’s time, Esther. We trust Him for these amazing blessings.”

Esther nodded.

***

After a busy morning and lunch, Mary came back for the girls and rushed them off to get home. She announced that her husband was soon going to work and she wanted to pack his lunch before he went. “There’s nothing at home to do that with. It’s all in the back of my car.”

Esther left soon after.

Callie had a bit of gardening to do before starting supper for Miles. She went outside, crouching in the garden with her hand trowel and proceeded to pull weeds. She often would pray while working outside. The atmosphere always seemed conducive outside to let God know her thoughts, needs, and wishes.

She began with health for her nieces and nephew. She then went to her parents, who had a particular financial need. Then proceeded to pray for Miles. She prayed for his health and well being, and that she'd be a good wife to him.

Soon her thoughts were wandering about the comment from Esther. Adoption? Would she ever consider it? What would Miles think? It had been three years now since they were married. She was beginning to give up hope herself.

Another woman in her sewing group had just taken on the task of fostering a child from their neighborhood. The mother was sick and had four other children at home. This child was her youngest and she could barely manage the other four, let alone a tiny child to care for. So, the woman had offered to foster the child until she began to feel better.

What about doing something like that? Miles and she could foster a child and see how that worked out. If it did, perhaps they could offer a permanent home to a child themselves.

Callie stood up and wiped her blackened hands on her apron hanging from her waist. She looked over her garden. Peonies were in full bloom, as well as a few irises. Her mother had given her the sprigs to grow from her own garden. They were just now taking root and producing the flowers she desired for her yard.

Perhaps she'd talk to the woman tomorrow at her sewing club meeting. Get a few ideas on how to get started. Find things out before she presented the idea to Miles. As she gazed at her home and the flowers surrounding it, she thought of filling it with a child. This would put some life into the tiny house she shared with Miles. What could it hurt?

* * *

Callie made Miles' favorite meal, placing some of her wedding china on the table to announce to him her good news. She'd found out many facts about fostering this past week, and was sure Miles would go for it.

Not only would they finally have a child to love in their home, but fostering would give them a little extra money to care for him, or her, as well. So that wouldn't be a burden on Miles' already-tight salary from his new job.

She'd even spoken to a representative from the county who put her in touch with a social worker. They'd been eager to talk to her. The next step was a home inspection, but she'd told the worker that she needed to talk it over with her husband first. Callie didn't want to proceed without Miles' blessing. If she got her hopes up too much and then he rejected the idea, that would be harder than what she'd been going through the past years of not getting pregnant.

Miles came home in a particularly good mood that night and breathed in as he came into the kitchen. "Oh, Callie, what in the world did you make for your hubby tonight?"

"Your favorites. Meatloaf, potatoes, and green beans."

Miles put his lunch box on the kitchen counter and reached for her, pulling her into his arms. She fought a little because she had a dirty spoon in her hand and didn't want to get it on his clothes. He planted kisses on her neck and she slowly melted into his arms and gave him a full-on kiss. "Wow, I know what I want for dessert."

Callie hit him and pulled away. "Stop it. I gotta get these potatoes in a bowl." She reached for a large bowl from the shelf above her stove and then proceeded to spoon the potatoes into the bowl for the table.

"I'm starving." Miles sat down and picked up the mail on the table. "What'd we get today?"

"Not much. The electric bill and thankfully it wasn't as high as it was a month ago."

Miles opened an envelope and looked over the page. "No, it's not. We haven't been using the furnace this past month. Thank heavens."

Soon Callie had all the food dished out, placing them on the table in front of Miles.

"That smells delicious."

Callie sat down opposite him and they said a blessing.

"So, how was your day?" Callie asked as she lifted meatloaf slices to both of their plates.

Miles went into some technological terms that Callie couldn't even begin to recognize and then added, "But I do like my new job." Miles had landed a good job in radio technology at a local telephone company. "I'm excited to see so many changes coming to the company."

"Miles, I want to talk to you about something." Callie put green beans in her mouth before she should have.

"What's that?" Miles spoke while chewing, mumbling about the great food. "Mmm, Callie, this meatloaf is delicious."

Callie swallowed and wiped her mouth with a napkin. "You know that friend of your sister's?"

"The one with that odd husband?"

Callie forgot about her husband and his brothers perspective on the husband. "Yes, her."

"That man is so strange. I feel sorry for that girl. She could have married so much better."

"Miles, don't be unkind."

"You're right." Miles shoveled in more mashed potatoes. "Go on. What about Nancy's husband?"

"Not about her husband, about their situation."

Miles stopped eating and looked up from his plate. "Situation?"

Callie knew this is where the repetition of their conversation, which had gone through her head for hours while preparing dinner, was of upmost importance.

"I haven't tried anything to prevent us from having children, Miles."

"Of course, Callie, I've known that, but what has this to do with Nancy? Or her husband?" Miles looked back at his plate and pierced some green beans with his fork.

"They have issues. Like us."

Miles stopped chewing and looked up again. "What about like us? Callie, what are you getting at?"

"They've recently been fostering children in their home." Callie knew if she just didn't throw it out onto the table like the dessert soon to come, she'd lose her nerve.

"Fostering?"

"Yes, they've had this sweet little girl since..."

Miles stumbled over the word. "What are you saying?"

"I want us to consider it." Callie was ready to follow with her list of reasons, but before she could Miles interrupted her again.

"I don't think so." He stopped eating and reached for a napkin.

"But let me..." Callie tried to interject, but again she was interrupted.

"I said no." Miles pushed his plate away. "I've heard awful stories like this. People taking strange," he hung onto the word for a little while longer than the rest, "children into their homes and soon they learn of all the wicked things happening to the other neighbor kids or," Miles wiped his mouth again, "to the dog." At that moment he reached out and snapped his fingers for their dog lying in the corner of the room sleeping. The dog stood up, came to Miles, and licked his fingers.

"I'm sure that's just rumors, Miles."

"I just don't like the idea, Callie."

"Okay." Callie didn't know what else to say. All her reasons for trying it had now flown out the window like it appeared as if dinner would, too.

"Why, Callie?" Miles now picked at the rest of his meatloaf with his fork.

Tears sprang to Callie's eyes. He had to know. He had to know, because he loved her, that her heart ached for a child. He'd watched her holding her nieces and nephew. He knew how hard it was on her to see her younger sisters having children and they couldn't get pregnant. Why would she have to explain it?

Miles looked at her. "Callie, give it some more time. I'm sure it will happen for us. Just be patient."

She'd been patient. Through all the nightmare scares. Through all the temper blasts and even the ways he avoided her on some evenings. She'd grown tired of being patient.

Callie didn't know what else to say. She dropped her fork on her plate, stood up, and walked to the sink and placed her plate in it. She left the dishes, the food still on the table, she walked out of the kitchen and right out the front door.

* * *

The humidity of the day hadn't dissipated with the evening as Callie continued to walk down the road. This wasn't what she'd envisioned when she dreamed of being married to Miles when he was overseas. She couldn't help but keep walking. She needed space. Time to think.

The only thing plaguing her was whether Miles was against adoption as well as fostering. If he was, she felt the chance of becoming a mother slip right away, just like the sun now fading into the west. She felt betrayed. Lost.

As she walked, she grew determined. Each step forging her way into what she wanted in life. How could this man deny her what she could have? What about his love for her? Wouldn't he want her to have her desires? What had turned him into such a cynic? What could a little child possibly do to harm anyone? And why was he taking his frustrations out on her?

But most of all, why did she feel like she was married to a stranger? Callie stopped on the side of the road and began to sob. One more time, she asked God for a child which she now labeled as a miracle He'd have to perform.

* * *

"How selfish." Blaine couldn't help but think that if the story stopped right now, she'd be devastated. Like reading the last four chapters of a book and knowing that it was scary to continue, but if you didn't, the 'happily ever after' would never come. "What did you do?"

"I did something almost worse than what Miles had done."

Blaine couldn't imagine what that could be at this moment. "I didn't listen to my husband."

"The next morning," Callie sighed, "I went and sought out Nancy and had her direct me to the social services office right there in town. I made an appointment and soon I was filling out paperwork to foster a child. I read through each paper as if I'd find a note somewhere. That God might send me a message underneath the dotted lines or the innuendos.

"I told no one what I was doing for fear that it would get back to Miles. I wasn't sure what I would do when he found out. For the few nights after that, he took his supper to the coop to eat and often came into bed late. Way after the time he thought I would stay awake. But I was awake. I was planning my next step.

"I truly believed in my heart that he had no right to take this away from me. Husband or not. This was something I wanted to do." Callie slowly shook her head.

Blaine couldn't believe her ears. After all the stories of Callie following Miles and doing what he said until the end of time, she never believed she would be as strong as she was now leading Blaine to believe. "Good for you, Callie. I'm so proud of you."

Callie looked up, shocked. She shook her head and told Blaine, "It was one of the worst things I'd ever done in my whole life."

* * *

He had to sign the final papers. Callie had them folded under her arm as she returned home from the social service office one afternoon. She took them into the house and placed them on the table. What would Miles do? Would he sign them for her? All he had to do was sign them and they'd have a child within a week or two. She was so close to becoming a mother. He couldn't deny her this.

All Callie could do was stare at them. She sat down at the table with a hot cup of tea and just eyed them.

A knock at her front door interrupted her thoughts. The door opened before she got into the living room, to find her mother coming through the door. "Callie, dear. I just came over to bring you some of the cookies I just made." Her mother didn't take her eyes off Callie's face.

Callie reached out for the plate. "Thank you, Mother."

Her mother went to sit on the couch, "Do you want some tea, Mom?"

Her mother nodded, then came into the kitchen. "Yes, I'm so thirsty. It's been so hot out during the last few days. This August weather is killing me."

Callie glanced at the papers on the table, still folded neatly in the middle of the table. "Sugar?"

"Yes, thank you, dear." He mother sat down and placed her purse next to the papers.

Callie sighed a bit. No need bringing her mother into this situation.

"Callie, I'm worried about you. You didn't stop by last Sunday night like you always do, and then this week you haven't called either of the girls. Is everything okay?"

"Everything's fine, Mom." She'd never been good at lying to her mother, so she kept her back turned as she took a teacup out of her cupboard and put it on the counter, added a teabag, poured hot water from a kettle into the cup and over the bag. She took longer than necessary to make the drink for her mother, but she needed to gain resolve. Pretend like nothing important was happening in her life.

"Okay," her mother acknowledged, "but you would tell me if something were wrong, right?"

Her control turned into meanness before she had a chance to stop it. "I don't tell you everything you know, I'm a married woman now, and some things you just don't tell anyone. Even your own mother!" It was cold, mean, and heartless, just like Callie felt right now.

She stood at the counter for her mother to respond. She didn't turn and look at her. She knew the look she expected was likely to be burning into her back now anyway. She closed her eyes as tears filled them. It didn't stop them and her cheeks grew wet.

She heard her mother's chair scrape the floor and soon she felt her mother's hands on her shoulders. "Callie, sweetheart, what's wrong?"

The walls of Callie's hardened heart began to disintegrate like the walls of Jericho. Her mother turned her around to face her and she looked into her eyes. Callie couldn't hold it in any longer and she burst into sobs. Her mother pulled her close and hugged her through the next sad minutes.

She didn't ask questions. She didn't tell her to behave and never talk to her like that again. She just held her. Callie clung to her like it was all the hope she had left.

And for the first time in a long time, her mother cried with her.

* * *

Before she left the house, Callie's mother knew all the truth about what Callie had been up to. She didn't judge her, nor did she try and change Callie's mind. She did warn her that doing things behind a husband's back was never a good idea, but that if Callie had made her mind up, that it wouldn't be her to change her mind.

She did remind Callie of their conversation when Miles went off to war. Callie nodded when she remembered, but she added, "But, Mother, I never suspected this is what it would mean. I want a child more than life itself. Why can't he just understand that?"

Her mother only nodded and then told her she'd pray for her through the rest of the day.

* * *

Callie wasn't going to take no for an answer from Miles. She wasn't sure what he'd do when she forced his signature. But she was determined to not let this opportunity pass by. In fact, that morning after she knew again that another month had passed without being pregnant, her mind was made up.

Miles took it well. He sat and listened to her tell him she needed his signature and why. He didn't give her many issues as to why she couldn't try fostering a child. He even took the pen from her hand and signed. Then he left her alone to go his radio shop.

She should have been ecstatic, but for some reason she felt even more alone than ever. She finished up the dinner dishes and sat in the living room knitting, despite the temperature of the day being hotter than any other day that summer. She knew the child they were to receive would probably never fit into the tiny pink sweater she was knitting, but it kept her mind busy to go through the pattern and follow the stitch guideline.

The next week, the social worker called to tell her that they'd found a young boy needing foster care and wondered if she was ready to have the young boy move in with her and Miles. Without Miles' consent or knowledge, Callie told the woman to bring him that next Friday.

She was on pins and needles the whole next week. She prepared a room for the young boy in their spare bedroom, cleaning it from top to bottom. Washing walls, vacuuming the carpet, finding a twin bed to fit into the room. She even had enough time to sew up some blue curtains for the window. Soon the room sparkled and looked welcoming.

The social worker met with her the day before she was to bring over the young boy. She explained to Callie that he was coming from an abusive home and what she might expect during his stay. Callie cringed. For the first time since making her decision about having the boy come, she began to wonder how she'd handle him if Miles weren't home.

That night, after dinner, she wondered if she should talk to Miles about the young boy. He did know they were to get a child from the room change down the hall, but he hadn't heard about the difficult life the boy had before coming to their care. Callie thought perhaps it wouldn't be necessary to share that with Miles. He was so against it all anyway. He'd only tell her, he'd told her so.

Chapter 34

Joseph Martin Brewer came to stay with them on Friday, August 29 at four-forty-five in the afternoon. Callie knew this because she'd written it in their family Bible soon after she took the boy to his bedroom, where he sat on the bed admiring his room.

He was only five years old, and looked shabby in his oversized gray t-shirt and threadbare pull-on shorts. His hair was hacked off in places where it should have been growing. Dirt was caked under his fingernails and he stepped out of his overgrown shoes with each step he took.

He smiled at Callie and talked a mile a minute. He asked about the dog, which he instantly fell in love with. He talked about how his father had once promised him a dog, but never delivered. He went on and on about his neighborhood and the many kids who lived there. Then he voiced his concerns with how quiet Callie's house was. "It's so quiet here," he kept repeating over and over.

Callie did her best to assure him that quiet was a good thing and that soon he would adjust.

Then he announced that he wanted to be called 'Joe,' instead of Joey like everyone called him. Callie tried her best to call him that, but Joey seemed to fit him better. Whenever she called him, 'Joey,' Joe would remind her, as though calling him that made him appear older than he really was.

But her biggest worry was Miles. What would he do? How would he interact with the little boy?

When Miles came home after work that night, he was quiet but polite to the chattering little boy, seated at their dining room table. The child ate like he hadn't eaten in weeks. Callie smiled as he asked politely for the things he wanted, but other than that, his table manners needed work. He guzzled his milk, even spilling it as he talked through a milky moustache. She handed him a napkin, but he'd set it beside his plate and not even use it.

Miles just ate his food and smiled at her. He didn't seem upset at all. He even asked Joey if he wanted to play checkers after supper. When Joey announced he didn't know how, Miles suggested he teach him. The little boy nodded in agreement and stuffed more macaroni and cheese in his mouth. It overflowed when he then proceeded to tell Miles about the games he used to play with his own father. Miles only nodded.

After the supper dishes were done, Callie went into the front room and took up her knitting again. The little pink sweater was almost finished. She held it up in the light to see if it needed white or pearl buttons, while Miles continued to teach Joey how to play checkers.

The young boy wasn't too bright, as he kept asking Miles the same questions over and over. Miles was patient and kind, and did his best to give the boy the instructions he needed to play.

Soon it grew late. Miles hadn't left the house. Callie was pleased with his kind treatment of the child. But she continued to wonder if the little guy could keep quiet long enough to go to sleep.

The days turned into weeks, and little Joey brought the couple many memorable moments. Miles even brought him home a bike he'd found for sale from a nearby neighbor so they could all go on bike rides in the evening. But then, after about three weeks, the little boy started wetting his bed.

Callie didn't think anything of it at first, but night after night she had to wash bed sheets and the mattress pad. A few nights later, he began having nightmares. The first one shook Callie out of such a sound sleep that at first she thought it was Miles. Then she realized Miles was the one up and out of bed.

She went into Joey's room and Miles was sitting on the edge of the bed, holding the little boy on his lap. He was doing his best to comfort the crying child. She stood in the doorway until Miles shooed her away with his hand. Callie went back to their bed and lay still, listening to the cries of the small child and Miles' efforts to comfort him. Tears sprang to her eyes.

Soon Miles encouraged the little boy back into his bed. Callie could hear him tell him that he'd be in the next room and to call him if he needed him. She heard Joey tell him okay.

When Miles returned to bed, Callie nuzzled back into him and kissed him on the neck. She then told him thank you for taking care of the little boy.

Miles responded with, "I know what it's like to have nightmares." Callie sighed and thanked God for their blessings as she drifted off to sleep.

* * *

The bed-wetting episodes grew worse. Every single night this little boy, who had been in their care for almost two months, began having temper tantrums. At first Miles and Callie could control him, but the violence grew.

Callie was a bit worried that Miles would be sure to remind her of the issues he felt they'd have with a strange child needing foster care, but the past months had proved only one thing to Callie: Miles adored the little boy almost as much as she did.

One night, as Miles and Joey played their evening game of checkers, Callie stood up to close the door to the cool, autumn weather. As she did, she noticed a car at the end of the road. She motioned for Miles to come look.

As he looked out the door the car's driver seemed to sense they were looking at him, and soon the car sped off in the opposite direction.

Miles shrugged his shoulders. "Must have been out with his girlfriend," he laughed.

Another night, when the little family was out riding their bicycles, the same car pulled around them on the road at an exceptionally slow pace. Miles noticed it and had Joey stop as the car maneuvered around them on the dirt road. Once the car pulled around them, Joey stopped riding his bike and got off.

Miles told him to get back on so they could get back up to the house. Joey threw a tantrum right there in the road. Miles went to scold him, but then seemed to sense to do something different. He motioned for Callie to go ahead.

Callie could hear the two talking as she got on her bike and headed for home.

Once home, Miles had Joey take his bike to the garage. As he did, he got close to Callie and said. "You know that car? Joey said it was his father."

That night, not only did Joey wet his bed again but he also had two nightmares in the middle of the night.

In the morning, before leaving for work, Miles took Callie's hand and led her out to his car. He pulled her close and then said, "Callie, I know how much you love this little boy." Callie knew the next sentence out of his mouth wouldn't be good news, but he added, "But I'm worried. If that man has hurt Joey, he might be back to do something again and I'm beginning to worry for your safety. Do you understand?"

Callie nodded.

"Especially with you and Joey home alone all day. Can you do me a favor and call the social worker today? Find out what you can. Tell her my concerns. Would you do that?"

Callie knew Miles was right.

Miles got into his car. "One more thing," he added. "Stay inside today. Lock the doors."

Callie nodded. "I will."

That afternoon the social worker made a visit. She asked Joey to go to his room and shut the door. The little boy obeyed. Callie sat in the living room with the woman.

"He's been abused in the past, Callie. That's why he was removed from the home. We do worry about his safety, but now that his father has found out where he lives we will have to move Joey to another home." The woman took Callie's hand. "I'm sorry. He seems so happy here."

Callie's heart began to ache. Miles and she had grown so used to the little boy, she couldn't imagine what could be worse. Having him leave, or never having had him at all? She began to cry.

"This is what happens in a fostering situation. I know this is your first attempt at doing this, but this is how every single event will be. These children are often in danger; that's why they're removed from their homes. It's imperative that we keep the child's whereabouts secret. I'm not sure how this one has gotten out, but now that it has we have to take steps to keep Joey safe," the woman told Callie.

Callie knew that to be true. She would never want Joey in danger.

"But you have to do me a favor."

"What's that?" Callie asked through her tears.

"You can't let anyone else know what has happened. Does your extended family know Joey?"

Callie nodded and assured the worker that they did know Joey and they were falling in love with him, too.

"I'm so sorry, Callie, but we need to keep this child safe. The only way to do that is to keep the whole issue as quiet as possible. Please don't tell anyone that the father has found Joey. Or that he has moved somewhere else."

Callie nodded and said, "I understand."

"Please. It's for his safety."

Callie agreed and as she blew her nose in a tissue, she led the woman to the front door.

"I'll need you to meet me at the corner market tomorrow at noon. No one will probably follow you there, but if they do just give me a sign by ignoring me in the parking lot. If no one follows you and you're sure, just bring Joey to my car. Don't bring any of his things with him. We don't want to raise any suspicions."

"Not even his bicycle? He loves that."

The social worker shook her head. "I'm sorry. Especially that. Just have the clothes on his back."

Callie closed the door behind the woman and locked the dead bolt. She then went to get Joey from his room. They had only twenty-four hours to make memories before he'd be gone for good.

***

Miles was as shocked as Callie to hear that Joey would be leaving them so soon. They'd had three good long months with the boy. He did his best to convince Callie to allow him to take the things which they had purchased for him, but Callie told him why he couldn't take the things.

They played checkers that night, but Miles kept a good eye on the road for most of the evening. He even locked both doors just after he arrived home from work.

After putting Joey to bed for the last time, they both sat in the living room. Tears filled their eyes as they talked about the times they'd had with the boy. Callie began to sob.

"Why? Why does this have to happen? Couldn't we just run away with him? He's safe with us. We love him."

Miles did his best to comfort her. He held her while she cried. But then he did something she wasn't expecting; he pulled her close and talked to her quietly. "You know, when you suggested we do this, I wasn't in agreement with you."

Callie nodded.

"Do you know why?"

Callie wasn't even sure she wanted to know, but she shook her head. "Why?"

"This." Miles patted her hand under his. "Callie, I knew you would fall in love. Fall in love with a child you couldn't keep. I wanted to tell you that. I wanted to somehow explain that to you, but then you went ahead and didn't even give me a chance. You went out and did all the paperwork and then forced me to sign."

Callie pulled away. "I never forced you to sign."

"You didn't?" Miles asked. "When I arrived home one night, there they were. On the table. Papers and a pen ready for me to sign."

Callie cried harder. "I'm sorry."

"I knew that if we were to do this, we'd end up like we are tonight. But to be fair to the boy, this innocent child who has stayed at our house now for months, I knew I had to go along with it all, Callie." He picked up her chin. "More than anything I want you happy. More than anything I wish this infertility would stop and you could have the child you so desire but, honey, this isn't our option."

"But why not, Miles? Why can't we do this?"

"Because, just like Joey we'll have to say goodbye some day. These children are not our own."

Callie sobbed harder.

"And, sweetie." Miles kissed her forehead, "I'm not sure you're gonna be able to get through this."

* * *

Callie took Joey by the hand in the corner market parking lot. She took a deep breath, blinked back tears, and escorted him to the corner of the lot where the social worker was sitting in her car. She placed the little boy into the backseat, kissed his cheek, and walked away.

The social worker drove away. She'd told Callie to just walk back to her car and leave, but Callie wanted to be extra sure that no one was following her so she went into the store to purchase their dinner for the evening. She picked out a loaf of bread, a nice package of chicken, and then scooted to the produce section to look over some tomatoes. She didn't need any of this, even the garden at her parents' house was overflowing with tomatoes, but she thought if someone or Joey's father was watching her, she didn't want to appear suspicious or not going about normal daily activities.

She didn't see anyone as she loaded her things in the back seat of her car to drive out of the parking lot. She even took back roads and didn't even drive home. Instead, Callie did the only thing she could think of to control the awful feeling in her gut and the intense heartache in her heart. She headed for that familiar dirt road.

She reached her mother's kitchen doorway and immediately went to her mother, who was trying to boil tomatoes to can on the stove. As her mother turned, she went into her arms.

Her mother must have sensed something horrible was wrong and took her daughter into her arms. She hugged her hard, while Callie cried harder than she ever felt imaginable.

She heard the door open to the kitchen and her father stomp his boots on the rug by the door. She couldn't let go of her mother. But then she heard footsteps approaching her from behind. Her father hugged her from the other side. She stood between the embrace of her parents. Somehow, they knew. Somehow, they just understood.

* * *

"I'd never felt such unimaginable pain. Miles knew. He knew what I would go through when the child would have to leave. I hadn't thought of what it would be like to love a child so, and have him taken away in such a harsh way." Callie wiped her eyes. "I think I'm running out of tissues, Blaine." She blew her nose.

"Didn't you get to tell Joey goodbye?" Blaine asked.

"No. He never knew why he had to get into that woman's car. Although when I turned to go into that market, I did watch the car out of the corner of my eye. He was crying in the backseat as the car pulled out of the lot. I could see him." Callie sighed. "I don't know what was harder at that moment: Seeing him like that, or having to calmly pick out a soft loaf of bread with my heart ripping in two."

"I'm so sorry, Callie," Blaine told her.

"It was a long time ago, Blaine. And the story doesn't end there."

Chapter 35

"In my more than eighty years of life, I've learned two very important lessons." Callie looked over at Blaine to see any glimpse of recognition of her words. She wanted her to really hear her next few words, so she grabbed her hand.

Blaine answered, "What?"

"I've learned to always be thankful. In all circumstances." She placed her hand on top of Blaine's. "And I've also learned that when God takes something precious or important away from us, He often replaces it with something so much greater."

Blaine smiled and nodded. "You got pregnant."

Callie removed her hands from Blaine's. "Let's just say, not in my timetable." Callie laughed. "One more thing. Life never happens as we plan."

"We mourned for months over the loss of Joey. We worried about him." Callie leaned her head back. "Our lives went back to normal after that. But for some reason, it didn't feel like normal anymore. We'd grown to love that little boy, or so we thought." Callie closed her eyes and felt herself being drawn back to nearly sixty years before.

* * *

It was Thanksgiving and the snow had fallen a bit earlier than normal. Miles had been away on a hunting trip with Esther and Mary's husbands, as well as Callie's father. He returned home just a few days before the holiday.

They'd talked long into the night about how he'd seen so many deer, but was unable to take one down to put in their freezer that year. "I can go out again, on the farm soon." Miles cuddled her closer and kissed Callie on the neck. "I sure missed you, girl."

Callie snuggled closer to him. "Me, too. It got awful quiet around here the week you were gone."

"Did you watch the kids this week?" Miles often asked her about their nieces and nephew, whom she loved so much. They both got a kick out of the growing girls and little Billy who could now sit up on his own. She told Miles about it as they giggled about something Janie had said.

Silence penetrated the room for a bit and Callie thought that soon she'd hear the soft snore of Miles drifting off to sleep. Instead he asked her softly, "Do you still miss Joey as much as I do?"

Miles had taken the loss of the little boy almost as hard as Callie. Yet somehow, having the child in their home helped to draw them closer. Miles didn't have nightmares as often now. They were beginning to subside.

Callie sighed. "I have my moments, but it's getting easier, too." She turned her head to kiss Miles.

"I wish I could give you one of your own." Miles rarely talked about Callie's infertility. She looked into his face. The darkness in the room didn't allow her to really read his eyes, but she knew, by the tone of his voice, he felt responsible for her lack of children.

She whispered, "I love you," and turned her head away from him, but she could feel his arms wrap tighter around her.

Callie had gone through many thoughts over the past few months after losing Joey. Much of it was just a plain old struggle with God. Why was she singled out to not have children? Were the things Miles suffered in the war going to be permanent? She'd kept her bargain. She'd been faithful to this man who had only been doing his duty and fighting for their country. Why would God punish her?

Then she realized that it wasn't a punishment. It was just life. Sad things happened to good people all the time. Many wives didn't even get their husbands back from the war. She had Miles. No, he wasn't perfect, and his demeanor and ways were not what she fell in love with, but he was still Miles.

And soon, after two or three months had passed, she began to learn to stop feeling so sorry for herself and replace it with something different. Thankfulness. Thankful that her sisters had children she could love and enjoy. Thankful that Miles was getting a bit better. He still had an awful temper, but the nightmares grew farther apart. He was emerging, but ever so slowly.

But on other days, when one of the babies would do something new, she would have to excuse herself and go into another room. Once apart from the others, she'd gain enough composure to not burst into tears at every word spoken about having a child. Her sisters were careful not to bring it up.

Following a few months of that, Callie learned and gained strength from just being thankful. Thankful for Miles and his slow recovery. Thankfulness for a warm home, food to eat. Miles' job was going well, and since Joey had left, he didn't spend as much time in his radio room and always sat down for dinner.

They'd packed away Joey's things. Some items went into the shed, like Joey's bicycle. But books and certain toys Callie put into a box to keep, just in case. The rest of the things she gave away.

Soon Callie could feel Miles lean closer into her and his arms relaxed their grip around her. He had drifted off to sleep. She hoped this was a good night. She prayed that no nightmares awakened him back to reality.

She fell asleep content and thankful.

* * *

The family enjoyed another Thanksgiving together on the farm. The babies kept the old farmhouse from lapsing into a dull place to spend a holiday. The food was delicious as always, but Callie soon lost her appetite. She'd had an upset stomach for the past few days and thought perhaps she was coming down with the flu.

Miles played on the floor with Billy as she helped to place the plates on the table for dinner. She seemed to feel better when she wasn't standing over the food cooking on the stove. She watched from the dining room as her mother pulled the turkey out of the oven.

War had now begun to be a distant memory. Lives continued. Food was plentiful. A new normal had taken over the country. Homes were being built all around their area for all the growing families.

Callie went into the kitchen to help bring out the bowls of potatoes and stuffing now coming out of the especially warm kitchen. As she lifted a bowl, she looked down at the large mound of white, whipped potatoes. Her mother had plopped a dab of butter at the very top and it slowly drifted over the mound as if it were a bobsled on a winter hill.

As Callie watched it, her stomach began to churn. Before she could react, she placed the china bowl back on the counter and ran out the back door of the house. She reached the outhouse just in time as she lost her breakfast.

One of her sisters came out, opening the door to the tiny building. Callie felt a warm coat slip over her shoulders. "Callie, aren't you feeling well?"

Callie shook her head. "I think I might have the flu." The door slammed shut on the tiny building. "You don't have to stay in here with me. Go back in the house. Maybe Mother will pack us up some food to take home with us. I think we'd better head home." She turned now to her sister who had her hands on her hips.

"How long has this been going on?"

"I thought it would go away."

Mary laughed. "It'll go away all right."

"What?" Callie shook her head. "I'm sure it's just the flu. One of the neighbors said his wife had it just a few days before."

"Callie!"

Callie took a bit of paper and wiped off her mouth. "What?"

"You'll have this go away all right. But it might take a few months."

Callie stopped wiping and looked up at her sister.

Her sister winked at her.

"No." Callie then thought it through a bit more. "I can't be."

"Perhaps it is the flu, but by the way you looked at that bowl of potatoes I'd say you have more than just the flu."

Callie covered her mouth with her hands. "Do you think?"

"I'm no doctor, but that's how it started for me. Twice now."

Callie pulled her sister into her arms. "I can't believe it. I mean," she almost felt as if she could turn and be sick all over again, but swallowed hard, "I've felt this way for the past three days. It's mild but then as soon as I look at food..." Callie turned again for fear that by just talking about it would cause her to lose more of her breakfast.

As she turned around, Mary did an about-face and headed back to the house. "I won't say anything yet. But if you miss something this month, I won't be surprised."

Callie sat down for a moment and felt the wave of nausea pass. Could she be? For something she was pretty sure would never happen to her, she began to now have her own assumptions. She couldn't wait to tell Miles, but above all she wondered why she hadn't figured it out herself.

* * *

Callie had resigned herself to the fact that it would never happen. She went almost a week before saying anything to Miles. Sure enough, Mary was right. She'd missed a period. She picked up the phone that morning to call Esther and get the name of her doctor and phone extension.

Miles seemed a bit shaken at first by the news, but then that dimple began to glimmer and tears filled his eyes. "Are you sure?"

"Well, I've never been pregnant before, but by all the signs. I think it could be a very definite possibility." Callie put a hand to her belly. The child she'd longed for over four years may now be finally growing inside her.

That next week Callie went to the doctor, and sure enough he not only confirmed her suspicions but told her that he was pretty sure she'd have a baby of her own in July of that next year. Callie asked him how things like this could happen. He stared at her for a moment and then said, "You do know how this works, right?"

Callie laughed when she realized that what she was asking sounding a bit naïve. She then told him of her thoughts that Miles wouldn't be able to have children after all of his treatments in the hospital in Indiana.

The doctor folded his arms and listened to her tell him about the nightmares, the loss of sleep, the angry outbursts.

"I've never been trying to prevent us from getting pregnant, but why do you think it took so long?"

The doctor shook his head. "We may never know. Perhaps you were burdened by Miles and his symptoms were making you anxious and worried all the time. Now that things are a bit better, perhaps your body began to feel less stressed. It's hard to tell, but as of right now it no longer is a problem." He wrote her a prescription for some vitamins and handed her the small sheet of paper. "Looks like you may have a few uncomfortable months in the summer, but everything looks good." He stretched his hand to Callie. "Congratulations!"

Callie shook her doctor's hand and then thanked him. "I never thought I'd hear those words."

He smiled and opened the examining room door for her. "If you experience anything unusual or you start spotting, let me know."

Callie's heart dropped. She hadn't thought through the fact that she could still have a miscarriage. But then she remembered to still be thankful. This was a moment to cherish, not to be in fear. She nodded and thanked the doctor for his kind words.

***

The train stopped at a depot just a few miles from home. Callie recognized the town. She'd traveled through it many times to get to the mall in a larger town nearby. Passengers not only got off, but a few boarded. Blaine watched them as they filed past her seat. All seemed ready to board.

Soon the train began to inch closer to home. She felt relieved. She was tired.

Chapter 36

Callie smiled as she reminisced about the sweet memories of giving birth to Amy that next July. "We were so excited to add to the grandchildren for my parents. No one was happier or more thrilled than Miles. He got himself his own little girl. A playmate for Janie, Kathy, and Billy. Life just couldn't get any better."

Callie looked out the window of the train as it sped through now-familiar countryside. She now knew the towns she was visiting before the conductor announced it to the passengers.

Blaine interrupted her thoughts. "Did your sisters have any more children?"

Callie looked over at her friend. "Of course. My parents became grandparents of ten children."

"Ten?" Blaine's mouth opened in awe. "How many did you eventually have?"

"We had just Amy, but we loved her so much. She truly was a gift from God."

Blaine smiled. "I'm so glad," she added.

"Mostly all boys. My sister, Esther, had five of them." Callie smiled. "My father loved his grandchildren and whenever they came to the farm he loved watching them climb through the barns, play in the hay, and chase the chickens."

Callie looked out the window again. "Those were the days. We loved spending Sunday afternoons with my folks and all the babies." Callie felt so tired. She'd been fighting the fact that she couldn't keep her eyes open on the trip. Perhaps she'd said too much. She leaned her head again on the back of the head rest, closed her eyes, and sighed. "But he didn't get to meet the last two boys. My father passed away of a massive heart attack when he was only sixty-one."

"Wow, that's pretty young," Blaine exclaimed.

She opened her eyes and looked back at Blaine. "It was so hard on Mother. We all tried hard to pitch in and help, but soon the farm went into disarray. She couldn't get out in the fields to farm. She ended up selling many acres around her home. We bought some and moved in just down the street. We did our best to comfort her, help her move on, but she soon moved out of the farmhouse and rented it out. She just couldn't sell it."

Callie stopped talking. She knew she needed to get up and use the restroom, but she just couldn't get over how tired she felt.

"Sounds like your life turned out pretty well then." Blaine nodded.

Callie laughed. "We did have great times when the babies were small. Soon the older ones graduated from high school, found mates, got married, and moved away." The urge to use the restroom just wouldn't go away, so Callie started to shift in her seat. "You know, Blaine, I need to get up and use the restroom."

Blaine shifted and moved so her legs were now in the aisle. "Sure, do you need any help?"

"You know," Callie hated to ask, but she felt so weak. "I think I do. I think I've been sitting way too long."

"Sure." Blaine now stood up and held her hand out to her. "C'mon, let me help you."

Callie stood so slowly. "Thank you, I appreciate it." She eased her way out of the seat and made her way out into the aisle. Blaine held her elbow for support.

* * *

Blaine helped the elderly woman all the way to the bathroom. At that moment, she seemed so frail. She'd be happy to finally see her to her final destination. Her story had been a great one to pass the time. She watched the door of the restroom so she could stand up and help Callie back to her seat. Callie seemed much less talkative and animated than when the trip had started.

Within a few minutes, the door to the restroom slid open and Callie eased her cane out into the aisle. Blaine stood up and went to her aid. "Here, Callie, let me help you back."

The woman looked up at her and smiled. "Thank you." As the pair made their way down the aisle, Callie seemed to trip and went down to her knees. Blaine couldn't catch her, but soon other passengers stood up to help.

The man across the aisle from them stood up and helped Callie to her feet. Everyone asked her if she was okay. She said she was fine, but Blaine wasn't so sure. Once back at their seats, and the fuss of the stumble was over, Callie leaned her head back and closed her eyes.

"I'm sorry, Blaine."

"Callie, don't be sorry. It's fine. You stumbled, that's all. No worries."

As the woman seemed to just want to sit still and quiet for a while, Blaine saw her face lacked the color it had back in Chicago. She didn't look well.

Without opening her eyes or even lifting her head, Callie began again, "But that wasn't all the pain, Blaine. Startled awake from one of Miles' nightmares, dealing with his violent temper which never seemed to end, and then our infertility problems. It could have ended with all of that but," Callie sighed, "it didn't."

Blaine was pretty sure what Callie wanted to add was important to the story, but she hated to think the whole retelling of it was not helping the woman to feel well. "Callie, you don't need to tell me anymore."

Callie opened her eyes. Shifted forward a bit in her seat and leaned over. She picked up her purse from at her feet, and lifted it to her lap. Rummaging through it, she found another tissue. "But I do. The story isn't complete without this part."

Blaine knew to talk the woman out of telling the story wasn't going to happen. She seemed intent on finishing.

Callie leaned back into her chair, holding up the tissue. "I think I'm going to need this."

Blaine wasn't sure she wanted to hear the end, but Callie began again. "Amy was about ten, the first time he tried it."

* * *

Callie couldn't believe how old Amy was. They'd just celebrated her tenth birthday. Everyone had been over to their house, filling it with laughter and fun. The boys groaned every time she opened a Barbie doll. Soon the presents were open, the leftover cake sat on the kitchen counter, and the families had said their goodbyes and had headed home.

Amy played with her new toys in the corner of the room. Miles seemed preoccupied the whole morning. Callie had prepared all the party herself, while he seemed more intent on playing with his ham radio equipment in the basement. She didn't think anything of it, but as she began to pick up the dining room table and get the vacuum out to sweep cake crumbs off the floor, she realized she'd done almost everything to prepare the party and now she ended up cleaning it up as well.

Miles rarely helped with things like this. He often called the parties frivolous and unnecessary. He knew Amy enjoyed having her cousins visit, but so many children in the house at one time seemed to annoy him.

As Callie left dishes piled high in the sink, she went to find Miles. She needed help getting the table back into its place under the window, after placing it in the middle of the room for the party.

She went into the basement and called for him. There was no answer. She was sure she'd seen him leave the room after everyone sang 'Happy Birthday' to Amy and watch her blow out her candles.

She'd wondered where he had been when Amy opened her presents. As she looked through the basement and came back up, she was stumped as to where she was going to find him. Perhaps he'd gone out into the garage.

She grew more frustrated with him the longer she tried to find him. Almost stopping her search, she thought about just returning to her clean-up work but something made her continue to search for him.

The garage door was open. She entered the garage and called for him. "Miles?" There was no answer.

Now her frustration grew to anger. Where could he have gone? It was so rude of him to leave the party, but now to be gone when everyone else had left seemed odd, but also annoying. Callie was tired. She needed help. Where was that man?

She went back into the kitchen and asked Amy to help her with the table. The little girl didn't want to stop playing, but she got up and came over to the other end of the table. She couldn't completely pick up her end, but she pushed as best as she could to help Callie maneuver the table back to its original spot under a window.

Callie thanked her and then asked, "Amy, do you know where your dad is?"

"No." Amy sat back down by her toys now scattered on the floor.

"Can you pick up all the wrapping paper for me?"

Amy sighed, but began to wad up the paper to dispose of in the garbage can.

At least Callie had Amy's help.

* * *

It was after midnight when Miles crawled into bed beside her. Trying to be quiet seemed futile, as he had not only stubbed his toe while coming into the bedroom but the cussing, even under his breath, made it even worse. Sleep hadn't even fallen upon Callie yet, so him trying to be extra quiet only added to her frustrating day.

She rolled over and just looked at him. His hair was standing on end and he smelled of cigarette smoke. He hadn't had one in years. He just stared back at her.

"Where have you been?" She didn't want to sound upset, but the anger in her heart came out in her tone.

"Around," was his trivial response.

"What am I supposed to understand by that?"

He pulled the covers back farther, allowing the unusually cool July night to penetrate her side of the bed. She shivered.

She didn't stop gazing at him as he got into bed and covered himself. He looked at her. "What?"

She'd had enough. It was one thing to seclude himself in his radio shop above the garage, but to miss Amy's party? What kind of father did that to his little girl?

"What's going on, Miles? It's not like you to miss Amy's special moments. What's the matter?"

He put his hand behind his head and looked away from her. He muttered something.

Callie decided she wasn't about to go to sleep angry. She took his chin and turned it toward her. "Miles, talk to me." Callie watched tears fill his eyes.

"I'm a worthless father."

It took all Callie could do to not agree with him, but for some reason she knew this was much more serious than missing a birthday party, and she caught herself. "Why?"

He turned away again. "I can't do anything right."

Callie looked away from him. This wasn't Miles talking. He loved Amy. She also knew he loved her. What could be bothering him?

Then he added, "You should have married someone else." She could tell now that he was crying. "Someone whole. Someone not fighting off demons like mine."

Callie swallowed hard. "What demons?"

He turned his face back to her, and as he did a beam of light from the moon highlighted his tear-stained face. "They won't leave me alone. They haunt me through the night and even during the day. I try. I try hard to fight them off with every ounce of my being, but whenever I do the images of what I saw, what I heard, how I felt while fighting flash before my eyes."

Callie took a finger and rubbed it on his cheek. Her angry heart subsided a bit and she tried to wipe tears off his cheeks which now trickled onto his pillow.

"I'm sorry you had to marry someone like me."

Callie swallowed hard. She knew she needed to talk quick or she'd lose him, "I'm not sorry. I'm sad I can't take away your demons and allow you to live a normal life."

"What's normal anymore?" Miles turned away again.

Callie thought hard. She needed to make a difference in his thoughts. She needed to prove to him, once and for all, that she wasn't sorry for marrying him. "I'm not sorry."

He turned his face to her again. "But what about all the nightmares? The lonely moments of me trying to fill my thoughts with other things so that the torment would go away, for even just a moment?"

She shook her head. "Not even then."

"How can you say that?"

Callie then began to tell him her heart. "Do you remember those long letters we used to write each other? We begged and prayed for the war to be over. Over so we could start our lives together."

Miles nodded.

"Each one had the same frustrations of being apart and just not knowing if we'd have a future together at all. Every single day there wasn't a letter, I would imagine all the worst things I could think of so that if we did get word that you were never coming home, I would be prepared. Ready. When I finally learned that you were wounded, the only thought I could think of was that I would get you back. I wouldn't have to endure an empty future without you. You'd be coming home.

"On the train heading to Indiana I also imagined all the worst scenarios I could figure out, so that whatever state I found you in, wouldn't be a surprise. Wouldn't shock me more than my worst nightmares."

"And look what you found." Miles sighed.

"Yes, look what I found." Callie shook her head. "You had all of your limbs and you weren't crippled for life. You weren't blind."

"No," Miles almost shouted, "I was a vegetable. A chicken. Callie, you ended up marrying a coward." Miles shook his head. "I let down my fellow soldiers, and some of them were my personal friends. Even since then, I've let you down. Amy. My parents."

Callie didn't know what else to do. She cradled her husband's head now resting on her shoulder and just let him cry. Then she added all she could think of to say, "Miles, let us decide that."

"I don't think I'll ever get over it. I have no clue what happened. I may never know. Till the day I die, I may never know what put me on a ship for home. I don't remember anything."

He cried for a while and then as he started to gain his composure, Callie allowed him the only thing that could often bring him comfort. She kissed him.

***

The next morning, Callie got up before Miles. She made him a nice breakfast, and when Amy woke up she had her scramble some eggs. The smell of bacon cooking penetrated the kitchen. Miles soon stumbled into the kitchen. The tiny family enjoyed a good breakfast, wonderful conversation, and Callie prayed to bless and ask for thanksgiving for their food and their chance to be a family. As she opened her eyes, and Miles glanced at her with tears in his eyes, but that amazing, dimpled smile. She hadn't seen him happy like that in a long time.

***

"So, he got better after that?" Blaine asked as she smiled at Callie.

Callie looked over at Blaine. Pain seemed to come out of nowhere and began to penetrate her breastbone. It felt as though an elephant gradually eased himself down on her chest. Her breathing became shallow and she knew that if she gave up looking at Blaine, she'd faint. "Blaine?"

Blaine must have sensed something was wrong. She grabbed her hand. "Callie, is something wrong?"

She knew something was horribly wrong. She needed to talk and talk fast. She wanted Blaine to know the one thing she'd not told many. The one secret about Miles she'd kept to herself for nearly fifty years. "That night, after we were all in bed..." Callie breathed as deeply as she could, but as she did the pain worsened and she leaned her head on the backrest of her seat.

"Callie, don't talk. I'm going for the conductor."

Callie used every single ounce of strength in her body to hold tight to Blaine's hand. "Blaine, that night," again she tried to breathe, but then she added, "Miles tried to kill himself."

As soon as she got the words out, Callie felt everything grow dark. She drifted into unconsciousness. She watched Blaine gaze at her and call her name, but she couldn't answer. She tried, but nothing came out. The pain was so excruciating she couldn't even think straight. Where was Mason? Was he on the train with them? Then, before she could think anything else, she saw him. He seemed to be standing down a long corridor.

She could feel her eyes grow wide; she could even hear Blaine yelling for someone to help her. She felt someone come to her, feel her neck. Scream something to someone else. A man across the aisle came over and helped lift her out of her seat. She felt herself being placed on the floor of the aisle.

Blaine looked at her from above, calling her name. Then she saw him again. Closer this time. Motioning for her. Holding out his hand for her to take it. And Callie did the very thing she'd been missing for the past ten years. She grabbed Miles' hand.

* * *

Blaine couldn't believe what was happening. She'd just spent the entire day with this woman. A stranger. Someone she didn't know when she woke up that morning and now she watched as a man felt for Callie's pulse. Someone came behind her and wrapped their arm around her shoulders. "Miss, do you want to sit down?"

But Blaine couldn't. She couldn't take her eyes off Callie. She saw Callie's face grow dim. Lifeless. Her eyes wide open. Was she actually dying in front of her?

The commotion in the passenger car grew nervous. Everyone was watching Callie struggling to live. Blaine couldn't sit down. She couldn't even speak. Tears began to dampen the front of her shirt and she wiped her face with the back of her hand. What was happening?

The conductor turned to her and said, "Is this woman related to you?"

She shook her head. "No."

"Do you know who she is?"

Blaine nodded. "Her name is Callie and I probably know more about her than anyone else on this train."

Chapter 37

The train stopped at the next depot and soon a gurney was being wheeled down the aisle to take Callie off the train. Blaine reached down and picked up all her belongings. The least she could do was be sure that all of them went with Callie.

She scooped up her purse and found her overnight bag in the compartment above their seats. She handed them to the conductor. "She got on the train with these."

He nodded. "Aren't you going with her?"

"I told you. I don't know this woman."

"Did you see where she put her ticket? At least I can find out where she was going."

Blaine picked up Callie's wallet out of her purse. She felt like she was violating Callie's personal space, but she wanted to help as much as she could. She fumbled with it for a minute then found the ticket sticking out of a side pocket.

She handed it to the conductor.

"Thank you."

"Where are you taking her?" Blaine could possibly come back in a day or two. Perhaps find out which hospital they were taking her to.

"We'll let the ambulance decide that." The conductor followed the gurney carrying Callie off the train down the aisle, holding all of her belongings.

Blaine sat down. Relieved. It wasn't her problem anymore. She couldn't believe it had happened, yet she loved hearing Callie's story. Such a beautiful love story. Callie was so faithful. She adored this woman who just a few, short hours before was a total stranger.

Blaine looked around at the other passengers, who now were getting back into their seats. The train car was quiet, except for the shouts of the conductor at the back of the train. They were probably trying to maneuver Callie's gurney off the train.

Blaine's hands were shaking. She picked up her water bottle and took three long swigs. A nagging began in Blaine's heart. The same one that had haunted her waiting for Callie to board the train. What if this were her grandmother? What would she want a stranger to do for her?

She shifted in her seat. She sat up and looked behind her. The aisle now quiet, the train seemed almost ready to start again.

Without much more hesitation, Blaine began to gather all her belongings. She stood up. The train whistle interrupted her thoughts. It was about to leave.

Blaine could see the conductor at the end of the car now. He was filling out some paperwork. She called out, "Wait!"

He turned back to her in the aisle.

"Stop the train. I need to go with that woman. I need to be with her."

***

As Callie was being put in the back of a waiting ambulance, the train pulled away from the station. Blaine watched it from just behind the ambulance and thought to herself how crazy it was that she wasn't on it, yet the pull to be with Callie was stronger than anything she ever had felt before.

As they began to shut the doors of the ambulance she called out, "Can I go with her?"

One of the attendants looked up. "Are you a relative?"

Blaine lied, "Yes."

"You'll have to sit up front."

Blaine headed to the front of the ambulance. She wasn't sure why she lied, but she didn't want the hassles she might get with not being related. She knew only one thing, she didn't want Callie to suffer alone. Blaine knew what it was like to be alone.

* * *

As the ambulance turned down street after street in the town of Lansing, Blaine hoped the hospital they were heading to was a good one. Blaine turned once or twice to see the paramedics starting to perform CPR. They took turns. This couldn't be good.

Soon they unloaded Callie at the hospital's emergency room entrance. Blaine hopped out of the ambulance passenger seat and followed the gurney into the hospital. She did her best to handle all of their belongings, balancing two purses, and Callie's bags as well as her own.

Snow now fell heavily in large flakes. She felt her hair grow damp and cold as she stood outside the hospital waiting for them to unload Callie from the ambulance. Several doctors had met the ambulance as it pulled up to the emergency entrance. They were all talking.

Blaine followed the gurney into the hospital and as it was wheeled down a hallway. A nurse grabbed her arm before she could follow past the swinging doors. "I need you for paperwork. They won't let you back there anyway."

Blaine nodded, but kept her eyes on the doorway. The nurse pulled her to a chair close by the door, motioning to her. "Sit here. I'll be right back."

The enormity of the situation finally sank in. What would she tell this woman about Callie? She knew her whole life story, but she didn't even know her full name. How could she answer any questions about her? Blaine began to panic. Why had she gotten off the train?

She looked down at Callie's purse in her lap. Perhaps she had identification items in it. Feeling as though she was again violating the privacy of the old woman, she pulled out Callie's wallet and found her license. The nurse returned with a clipboard. Blaine stooped to pick up the pretty bag of nuts that had come out of the purse with the wallet and had fallen to the floor. Blaine reached down and looked at the bag now almost empty. Callie had been so open and honest with her. She'd even shared a bag of nuts which she might have been saving for something or someone special. Perhaps it was supposed to be a Christmas gift. At that moment, Blaine knew she was doing the right thing.

After Blaine gave the nurse as much information as she could glean from Callie's wallet, the nurse excused Blaine from the admitting office, telling her she could sit in the hospital's emergency waiting room.

Blaine fidgeted, regarding what to do next. Maybe she should leave now. Up running that morning with Kyle, she'd been on the train for almost the whole day and now this. She searched online for the closest car rental places, within a twenty-mile radius. She'd probably have to call a taxi.

She still had all of Callie's belongings. Even Callie's suitcases were piled around her, as the ambulance driver had delivered them all with Callie.

Blaine debated on whether to let the nurse know she was leaving, but as she looked around at all the bags the door to the waiting room opened and a doctor strode toward her. He stretched out his hand to shake hers. "Are you Callie's daughter?"

Blaine stood and shook her head. "No."

"I'm sorry." The doctor motioned for her to sit down. "You're not old enough to be her daughter. Her granddaughter then?"

Again, Blaine shook her head. "We're actually just friends."

"Oh." the doctor hesitated.

"But I'm all she has," Blaine lied, even though she knew that Callie's grandson also would probably want to know what was happening to his grandmother. She never thought of him until now.

"Well," the doctor looked around the room, "I'm required to find a relative, but under the circumstances..."

"Can you at least tell me if she's okay?" Blaine interrupted.

The doctor nodded. "She's not doing very well. I think she's had a major heart attack."

Blaine sighed. "Like her father."

"Her father had a heart attack?"

"Yes, he died when he was sixty-one."

"Thank you for sharing that with me."

Blaine nodded.

"We're monitoring her closely, but I'm really not sure yet if she'll wake up or survive this. It was severe." The doctor took a pen out of his pocket with a pad of paper. He began drawing a diagram of a heart and showed Blaine exactly where he was assuming the damage occurred. "She might wake up, but she'll be in critical condition for a few days. We'll start with a few tests, and will be closely monitoring her. In case there's another one to follow."

Blaine nodded. She needed to get a taxi soon, but something made her ask, "Can I see her?"

The doctor nodded. "Yes, but only for a few minutes. We need her to rest."

Then Blaine heard herself say, "Can I stay with her tonight? In her room?" For some reason, she hated to think of Callie waking up without anyone with her.

"We'll see what we can do. Give us an hour or so and we'll get her stable and in ICU. As soon as she's there, I'll have one of the nurses bring you up." The doctor stood to leave. "It's just gonna be a wait and see game for a while." He shook Blaine's hand. "She's in good hands."

Blaine didn't stand, but shook the doctor's hand. "Thank you."

He nodded and went back through the swinging doors. Blaine looked around. This wasn't the way she wanted to spend her night but, due to the circumstances, what could she do? Leaving Callie all alone seemed inhumane. Unethical. On top of that, what better thing did Blaine have to do?

***

Callie tried to wake up, but something was preventing her from taking a deep breath. Opening her eyes was a struggle. They felt so heavy. She thought she could smell formaldehyde. Clarence used to sell it in the store; Callie could smell it distinctly ever since. Her nose itched, but when she tried to raise her hand to scratch it she couldn't seem to move.

She heard someone calling her name, but she couldn't figure out who it was. Before she could wake up, she felt something warm course through her veins.

Chapter 38

Blaine pushed her phone button to check the time. It was five after eleven. She'd sat in the waiting room for six hours. Several times she'd scolded herself for staying. Why did she feel it so important?

She was tired. They'd escorted her to Callie's room and now she sat beside her bed like a relative should be doing.

Blaine glanced over at a padded bench just below the window in Callie's room. Perhaps Blaine could sleep there for the night. She stood up and went to the window. The room overlooked part of downtown Lansing, and in the distance she could see the capital building. How had she gotten herself into this mess?

She turned again to look at Callie who was hooked up to several machines which now pumped, gauged, and beeped Callie's statistics to the nurses outside the room. Her face was pale. Her hair matted.

Blaine couldn't help but feel sorry for the woman who had been so friendly to her the entire trip. Blaine sat down beside her bed and placed her hand on Callie's, and slowly used her thumb to stroke the back of Callie's hand. The pull to let Callie know someone was with her was so strong. Blaine couldn't explain it.

What did it matter? She had nowhere to be or to go. All she was doing was wanting to get away from Kyle. Blaine sat back and looked up at the light over Callie's bed. Perhaps if she turned it off, she could doze off right in the chair beside Callie's bed. That way, if Callie woke up, Blaine would hear her.

She lay her head back on the chair and pulled another chair up closer to rest her feet on. Soon another nurse came in and asked if she'd like a blanket. Blaine nodded.

Soon she had a warm, soft blanket to cover up with, and before she could think of much more Blaine drifted off to sleep.

* * *

During the night, Blaine stirred several times to adjust her position. She'd look over at Callie to check her, but the monitors were still beeping. Once she pressed her phone, but it had died a few hours before.

"No," Blaine could hear someone mumbling but she wasn't quite sure where she was for a minute, then she heard a loud beeping sound. Blaine's feet hit the floor as the chair she had them placed them on pushed away from her.

A group of nurses came storming into the room. Blaine then remembered where she was as the group starting swarming Callie in the bed. Soon two doctors entered the room. Blaine stood up to get out of everyone's way, but asked, "What's happening?"

A nurse looked over her shoulder. "We're not sure. Can you step outside the room for a moment?"

Blaine gathered the blanket up from the floor and went out into the hallway. She pulled the blanket around her shoulders. Should she stay longer or leave? Blaine saw a window at the opposite end of the hallway and made her way down the hallway to see the sunrise. It glowed pink on the horizon. The clouds had gone and now a blue sky reflected a cold, yet clear morning.

Blaine pulled the blanket around her shoulders tighter. She thought about the day before. Callie's story. Then she thought of Chicago. It was silly to stay here with a woman she hardly knew. She turned to watch a young man walk down the hallway. He seemed intent on finding someone. Blaine suddenly remembered. Looking down at her phone, she realized she did know Callie's grandson's phone number. She'd texted him on the train. She did have a way to reach him. But her phone was still dead. Why hadn't she charged it overnight?

Soon a doctor left Callie's room and was making his way to her down the hallway. Blaine met him halfway. "What's happening?"

"We thought she was having another attack, but it was a false alarm. We'll have to keep monitoring her, of course." The doctor turned on his heel and began to walk away. "You can go back into the room now."

Blaine wanted to tell him she knew the woman's grandson, but the doctor quickly rushed back down the hallway in the opposite direction.

Blaine made her way down to the nurses' station and found a nurse talking on the phone at the desk. She waited for her to be free. If Blaine could get back into the room now, she'd plug her phone into an outlet and soon she'd be able to get Mason's phone number.

The nurse talked and talked. It sounded important, but Blaine waited. As soon as she hung up the phone she began to stand and leave the desk, but Blaine stopped her, "Excuse me. I'm here with Callie." Blaine pointed to Callie's room. "I know she has a grandson in Chicago. Do you think you could somehow call him for Callie? She'd want him to know what's happening to her."

The nurse shook her head. "Not unless you have a number, but if you'll excuse me I have to answer a page. I'll be right back."

Blaine waited about ten minutes, but the nurse never returned. She made her way back into Callie's room. What was she going to do? She wanted to leave, but thinking of Callie all alone just made her too upset. She tried asking another nurse now putting more medicine in Callie's IV.

"Can you get Callie's grandson?"

"Do you have a number for him?"

"Well, you see," Blaine wasn't sure how to let this nurse know that she and Callie met on the train and really didn't know each other, "I just happened to be on the same train as Callie," she pointed to Callie in the bed, "and, we kinda became friends on the trip here into Michigan and well, I really don't know her all that well." Before Blaine could finish the nurse was called from the room by another nurse.

Blaine plopped down in the chair beside Callie's bed again. If Mason was going to be notified, it appeared to be up to her.

* * *

Blaine needed to leave. Rubbing her forehead, she tried to come up with a plan but knew she couldn't leave until her phone had charged a bit. She looked down at her phone which still displayed a blinking, charging light. She also needed to find a taxi here in Lansing.

Blaine glanced up at the clock in Callie's room. It read seven-twenty-six. She was starving now. A nurse came into the room and Blaine asked if she could get some breakfast. The nurse directed her to head down to the lobby; the cafeteria was just off that. Before she headed down, she knew she had to call Callie's grandson.

Standing up, Blaine went to Callie's bedside. The woman was shaking her head. Blaine leaned down, "Callie?" She patted her hand.

Callie opened her eyes and looked from one side to the other.

"You're in the hospital. They think you've had a heart attack." Blaine rubbed Callie's arm. "They're just watching you now."

Callie acted as though she wanted to speak, but with the tube down her throat she wasn't able to. Her eyes were wide. She seemed agitated and afraid.

Blaine rubbed her arm. "It's okay. I'll stay with you. Don't be afraid." She scolded herself for saying it, but she felt she needed to calm Callie.

As she spoke, Callie seemed to relax, and closed her eyes again.

Blaine watched her friend for a few minutes, and then sat back down when she realized Callie had gone back to sleep. She looked down at her phone, which now revealed a slight bar of charge. She should probably call a taxi first thing, but then she decided to use the charge for a more important call.

Blaine pushed the number on her phone and waited for a response on the other end of the phone. Soon a young man answered. Blaine stumbled with what to say for a few minutes but introduced herself, "Hello, my name is Blaine Taylor. You don't know me but I was a passenger on the train traveling back to Michigan with your grandmother."

Blaine couldn't remember Callie's grandson's name, but she needed to know. "I'm sorry, but you are Callie's grandson, right?" The man answered affirmatively. "And what's your name?"

He told her it was Mason. "Yes, she's here with me now." Blaine waited a minute for Mason to respond. He asked her if his grandmother was okay. Even though he couldn't see her, Blaine shook her head. "No, not really. I'm here in Lansing with her. She's in the hospital."

Mason groaned.

"She's had a heart attack. How soon can you get here?"

She nodded. "Okay."

Blaine wasn't sure what he would ask her, but soon he asked her what any normal, concerned relative would ask. Blaine knew in her heart how she needed to respond and added, "Yes, I'll stay with her until you arrive. No problem."

What was she saying? How did she get stuck in this situation? "What?" Blaine asked Mason to repeat himself. "Sure. As soon as she wakes up again, I'll tell her."

Blaine finished the conversation by giving him the whereabouts of the hospital and what room they were in. Again, she promised, "Yes, I'll stay." She smiled and added, "You're welcome."

She lowered her phone in her lap and hit the 'end call' button on her phone. She looked over at the woman breathing slower beside her. Standing, Blaine went over the window in the room and looked out on the city below. She shook her head at herself. What had possessed her to stay with Callie? Instead of trying to figure out an answer, she thought back to the conversation with Callie's grandson. One thought kept running through her mind. His voice was so kind. He thanked her over and over again for staying with his grandmother, and promised to make it up to her once he arrived.

Blaine knew only one thing to be true. Callie had been so kind to her. What possessed a woman to go out of her way to make friends? Share her story so vividly? And by the conversation she'd just had with her grandson, the same kindness spilled from his being, too.

It sounded crazy, but for the first time in her life she wanted to know what drove this family to be this kind to a stranger.

Chapter 39

Doctors visited throughout the morning. They checked Callie's vitals, attached more bags of fluids to her IV stand, took her pulse, and looked at her eyes.

One particular doctor entered the room and shook Blaine's hand, introducing himself as Dr. Park. He was tall and way too young to have a medical degree. His smile was genuine and he soon had the nurses laughing at his comments.

He tried to get Callie to wake up by calling her name. "Callie? Can you hear me? My name is Dr. Park. Can you open your eyes for me?"

After several requests, Callie did open her eyes. Dr. Park smiled at her. "Hello, my dear. How are you feeling? Can you squeeze my hand?"

He looked down at the woman's hand, "Good job. I felt that. You're at Sparrow Hospital and I'm the doctor assigned to your case. Can you stay awake and talk a little?"

Callie slowly shook her head. The doctor told her not to try and talk, but to try and nod or squeeze his hand if she understood. He told Callie that she'd indeed had a heart attack on the train. They were monitoring her closely and it seemed as though the danger had passed for now. Then he added, "We do have concern that you have a major blockage in your heart valves. Do you understand that?"

Callie closed her eyes a bit, but seemed to try and nod. Blaine watched over the shoulders of a nurse in front of her.

"Good, that's good." The doctor patted Callie's shoulder. "We'll have you back as good as new as soon as we run some tests and figure out what's going on."

The doctor turned to Blaine. "Is this your grandmother?"

Blaine shook her head. "Just a friend."

"Well, Callie," the doctor turned back to her, "you get some rest, and soon we'll take you down to the MRI room to get a scan." Callie closed her eyes again.

Dr. Park turned to Blaine and held out his hand, "Your name is?"

"Blaine."

"Blaine, your friend has had a major cardiac arrest. We believe she has blockage and will probably schedule surgery as soon as we know the extent." He turned back to Callie a bit, "Does Callie have any family members?"

Blaine told the doctor about Mason. "He should be coming in this evening."

"Good. We may not be able to wait for him. A few of the nurses say you can calm her when she's agitated. She needs to stay calm until we can get her into surgery."

Blaine shook her head. "But I barely know her." Blaine tried to explain, "We just met on the train."

The African American nurse added, "Yes, honey, you do have a way of calming her."

The doctor nodded. "I can't ethically ask you to do anything you don't want to do. I just hate for her to be all alone."

Blaine folded her arms and nodded.

The doctor pulled his stethoscope out and placed it on Callie's chest. "I'm sure she'll appreciate someone here with her."

Blaine thought she'd better ask, "I have my things here and the nurses have been wonderful, but is there somewhere I can freshen up a bit for the day?"

The doctor took his stethoscope off Callie's chest and hung it around his neck again. "Sure, the nurses can show you where. Do you have any questions?"

Blaine was sure she didn't seem interested or wanting to be informed of the issues, but who was she to even ask? So she just shook her head.

"Okay then." The doctor stuck his hand out to her. "Let one of the nurses know if you need anything."

Blaine shook the doctor's hand. "Thanks."

Everyone left the room except Blaine. She stood closer to Callie on the bed. There wasn't anyone in the room, but Blaine said out loud, "Next time, Callie, you should keep your treats to yourself."

* * *

Blaine went to a bathroom close by after getting directions from one of the nurses, taking her toothbrush, paste, and a brush from her carry-on bag. If she could just brush her teeth, she'd feel better.

The nurse also said she could have her lunch in the room with Callie. She ordered fish and fries. "You might as well have her lunch; she's not looking like she's gonna eat anytime soon," a large African American nurse told Blaine.

After eating, several nurses and an orderly came into the room, unhooked Callie, and wheeled her out of the room. They told her Callie needed some testing done.

Blaine collapsed into the chair beside the bed again. Maybe she'd go for a walk while they were gone. She picked up her purse and slung the handles over a shoulder. It would be good to at least head downstairs and outside for a few minutes.

As she went down the elevator to the lobby, her phone rang. It was Kyle. She wasn't sure why, but she needed to hear a familiar voice. "Hello?"

Kyle was winded at the other end. He told her he'd just gone on a run and how cold it was in Chicago. He never asked how she was or even where she was. He went on to say that the neighbor's music was totally out of control the night before and he hadn't slept very well. He then spouted off about the landlord not caring after he'd called him at eleven-fifteen last night. He told her how he'd had a horrible morning trying to get up because of being so disrupted the night before.

Blaine never said a word. She just kept listening to Kyle go on and on about his life. His ordeals. His problems. Without much hesitation, or much thought, Blaine hung up on him.

Soon her phone rang again. She picked it up again, knowing exactly who it was calling her. "What?"

"Did you hang up on me?" Kyle scolded. She pushed the button to disconnect him again.

As she made her way through the lobby she knew only one more thing to do. She opened up her contacts on her phone and deleted his number. She never wanted to talk or hear from this man again. Going a little farther she decided to not only remove him, but she blocked his number as well. She was through with him.

* * *

Callie opened her eyes to gaze around a totally unknown room. It appeared to have a television in the center, hanging down from the ceiling. Callie looked at it and then looked off to one side and then back to the other. Was she in a hospital room?

The last thing she remembered was pain. A crushing pain in her chest. It still hurt, but was more of a dull ache. A nurse came up beside her on one side. "Callie? Can you hear me?"

Callie did her best to nod. She tried to speak first, but something blocked her mouth from talking.

"No worries, honey." The tall woman smiled at her with beautiful, white teeth. "I'm just going to adjust this for you. Do you hurt anywhere?"

Callie tried to point to her chest.

"Yeah, I'm sure. You've had a myocardial infarction. But do you hurt anywhere else?"

Callie shook her head. If she could talk, she'd have had a list.

"Okay, honey; I'm sure your friend will be back soon."

Her friend? She wondered who the woman could be talking about. Callie felt so tired. She attempted to keep her eyes open for a while to just look around her, but they kept closing.

The she heard another voice. "Callie?"

She looked up into the face of the girl on the train. Callie tried hard to think of her name. Then she had a sudden thought. What had become of her luggage? Her things? Her purse?

The young girl patted her hand. "Mason is coming, Callie. I've called him. He should be here later tonight."

Mason! Callie shut her eyes. Poor Mason. What would he do now? Hopefully, he wouldn't lose his job to run home and care for her. Callie couldn't help it, but she grew afraid. She felt tears start to well up in her eyes. What had she done? She felt as though she had to take this one last trip to Chicago to see Mason, but now look what had happened.

She felt a tissue dabbing her eyes, and she opened them. The young girl stood over her and smiled. "It's okay. He'll be here soon."

Then Callie remembered. She tried to smile but the mouth tube prevented her from doing so. She wasn't sure if the girl could sense it but she suddenly remembered her name. Blaine.

* * *

Blaine asked the nurse just before dinner if there was a good place to eat close by the hospital. The food in the hospital cafeteria was horrible. The nurse said that there were, but it might be safer to have someone deliver her food to the lobby. She could wait there for it. She even suggested a few places that normally delivered to the hospital for some of the employees.

Blaine left the room and dialed a number she'd found on the internet and found a sandwich place close by that delivered to the hospital. She waited in the lobby, and sure enough, her food was delivered within a few minutes.

As she headed back up to Callie's room, a young man made his way onto the elevator with her. He appeared nervous. Wringing his hands and then brushing his hands through his thick, dark hair. He was a little taller than Blaine. Blaine probably wouldn't have even noticed him, but he was strikingly handsome. He carried a backpack over his right shoulder. They both got off at the same floor.

Blaine made her way to the left to head back to Callie's room. The young man looked lost and headed the other way.

Blaine found Callie sleeping again as she sat down and prepared to eat her dinner. She took the remote from Callie's bed stand and pushed a button to turn on the television in the room. Unwrapping her sandwich, she took an enormous bite. She was famished.

Just as she took another large bite, the young man from the elevator rushed into the room. He dropped his backpack on the chair and approached Callie on the bed. "Nana!"

Callie's eyes immediately shot open.

"Oh, Nana." The man picked up Callie's hand. "Are you okay?"

Blaine's mouth was full. She couldn't say anything, but she didn't need to. He wasn't here to see her. He didn't even know she existed and she suddenly felt very out of place.

Wrapping her sandwich, she placed it on the table in front of her and took a long sip of her drink.

Mason was pushing Callie's hair off her forehead. "I got here as soon as I could. I'm here, Nana. I'm here."

Blaine stood up and shoved her hands into her pants pockets.

Mason nodded a greeting to her, but continued to look at his grandmother. He reached down and picked up her hand and kissed it.

"Nana, what in the world did you do this for?"

Callie closed her eyes again.

Silence penetrated the room. All that could be heard was the sound of pumping IVs and the machine to help Callie breathe.

Blaine finished chewing the mouthful of sandwich. "She's been like that all day. She can't seem to keep her eyes open for long. Probably because of all the heavy pain meds they've been giving her."

Mason looked up at her. "Who are you again?"

Blaine shrugged. "I'm Blaine. I met your grandmother...Nana...on the train from Chicago. We became friends."

Mason kissed his grandmother's hand again. Then slowly placed it back on the bed. He went around the bed and held his hand out to Blaine. "Nice to meet you. I'm Mason."

Blaine touched his hand. "I'm Blaine." She'd said that already. Why was she repeating herself? She gave him a weak handshake, but his was strong and firm.

"Um." He shoved his hands into the pockets of his pants. "I don't know what to say. Thank you so much for staying with my grandmother. I don't know," he pulled one hand out and brushed the sweat off his forehead, "how to ever thank you for staying with her all this time."

Blaine shook her head. "It's okay. I was heading in the same direction on the train. I helped her get to the train and then we just had a long, long," Blaine laughed a bit, "conversation on the train."

Mason stuffed his hand back into his pocket. "I bet. Nana can be quite the talker."

Blaine laughed again. "Yes, yes she can."

Mason shrugged. "I'm sorry."

"No, please don't be. She's been through quite a lot. I enjoyed listening to her story."

Mason turned back to his grandmother and added. "She has a ton of them, which one did she tell you this time."

Blaine sat back down. "Her love story."

Mason turned quickly back to her. "Of course."

"Yes, her love story. About your grandfather, I'm assuming."

Mason nodded. "That one is her favorite. She loved my grandfather very much."

"Yes, she did. I can't believe he experienced so much in his life." Blaine picked up her pop and took another long drink.

"Experienced?"

"You know, his war issues and all." Blaine then added, "You know, I just had this delivered. I'd be more than happy to share it with you. I'll never eat all of this sandwich."

"Wait. Nana told you about Grandfather's war issues?"

Blaine nodded. "Yes, I got to hear the whole story."

"How far back did she go?"

"All the way."

"All the way?"

"Yeah, she started when they first met."

Mason then pulled up a chair from the other side of the room and sat down. "Really?"

Blaine nodded. "It's amazing how faithful she was to him. For all those years."

"That's insane." Mason looked at her with beautiful blue eyes. He had an amazing smile, and right outside the side of his left cheek was a perfect dimple. "I'd love to hear what she had to say." Mason coughed into his hand. "She's never told any of us about Granddad's war issues."

Blaine stopped chewing her sandwich and shook her head. "What?"

"No. In fact, neither did Grandfather. We often wondered what secrets she had about him. All we knew as a family was that he did have something that brought him home earlier than the others, but besides that, we didn't know what the issue was or why they both kept it such a secret."

"Why the heck would she tell me something so personal then?" Blaine sat back in her chair and looked over at Callie now sleeping again beside her.

Mason looked up at her. "I don't know but, for some reason, she must have thought it needed to be told. Would you do me a favor, Blaine?"

Blaine nodded. "Of course."

"Could you stay a while longer and tell me?"

"I guess." Blaine had thought she'd leave as soon as Mason came through the door. Her escape. Her way out of this difficult, almost embarrassing situation, but at this moment, she was so happy he'd asked her to spend more time with him.

"But first," Mason leaned over and tapped the wrapper on her sandwich, "give me the number to this shop?"

Blaine picked up the other half of her sandwich. "Really. Have this. I'm not lying when I say I won't eat it all."

Mason sat down and she also handed him the other half of her bag of chips. "You might as well have these, too."

As Mason took a bite of the sandwich he told Blaine how much he loved his grandparents. "Their stories of the war era have always fascinated me. I'd hate for those to die with them."

Chapter 40

Blaine and Mason talked long into the night. She did her best to retell the story of Mason's grandparents' love story. She probably left out many specific details, but told about how they met and details of how they had managed to stay in love during the war.

Around midnight she found she couldn't keep her eyes open any longer. Mason had been rubbing his eyes as well. Callie hadn't been awake at all during their talk.

"Why don't you pull up that chair for your feet? That's how I managed to sleep last night."

"Blaine, I'm so happy you're here. Seems to me Nana must have had a good reason to meet you on the train, and an even better reason why she told you all this stuff."

Blaine pulled her foot chair closer and wrapped the blanket she'd placed over her feet up closer to her neck. "Why hadn't she told you all of her story before this? You're her grandson."

"I don't know. Whenever we talked about Gramps it was usually just about what he'd done for a living. I only knew him for a few short years. He died when I was pretty small."

"But there are many things she told me on the train that are significant to your life. Your mother's life. Why wouldn't she share that with you?"

Mason shook his head. "I don't know. Perhaps she did. I may not have paid as much attention to her stories as you have in such a short time." He smiled and placed his head on the back of his chair. "You know our generation. We rarely listen to the things we should."

Blaine nodded. "Maybe that's it. Maybe my grandmother wanted to tell me more things, but I was always too busy to listen."

Mason grabbed his jacket and put it over him. "I'm exhausted. What a day." He looked over at her. "Maybe I should have asked before this, but do you have plans? Are we keeping you from something?"

Blaine shook her head. "No, I was just heading..." What would she say? She lied again. "Home for part of my Christmas break."

"Where are you from?"

Blaine responded slowly, "Um, Lapeer."

"Well, let's try to sleep. It's been nice getting to know you tonight," Mason added.

"Thanks. You, too. I'm sure the doctor will come in tomorrow and give us a report of Callie's tests from today."

Mason nodded.

"Goodnight." Blaine lay her head on the back of her chair.

Mason flashed another grin. "Good night, Blaine."

That's all Blaine needed to realize she was so glad she'd stayed.

* * *

It wasn't long before Blaine could hear the soft breathing and occasional snore come from Mason's direction. For some reason, she couldn't fall right to sleep.

She'd told Mason much of what Callie had told her. Except for the last thing Callie had told her. Somehow, she didn't feel it her responsibility to tell Mason that at one point in his grandfather's life, he'd wanted to kill himself. She wasn't even sure why Callie had told her.

Life was scary. She'd never felt sheltered through her young years. So many things she'd faced would never happen to a normal child, like Mason, growing up in a loving home. She never felt she belonged to any family. The desertion of her father, the death of her mother, she'd been left alone to manage the best she could.

Maybe that's why she'd always find men like Kyle. They'd tell her what to do. Boss her around. There wasn't a day she didn't long for a family like Mason's and Callie's. Someone to care whether she arrived home at night. Someone to give her money when she was running low.

Tears filled her eyes as she looked over at Mason. He was blessed. He belonged to someone. She glanced over at Callie. What she wouldn't give to have this old woman as her grandmother. They cared for one another. Sacrificed for each other.

At that moment, she felt content to be in their presence. For a second in time, she felt as if she belonged to them. They were caring for her. A stranger. They were truly genuine, caring people. She fell asleep feeling valued. Perhaps that was the real reason she'd decided to stay.

Chapter 41

Mason stirred in his chair. One of his arms had fallen asleep and he shifted to give it some relief. It started tingling, and he shook his hand to restore life into his fingers. He sat up when he realized he wasn't home, but in his grandmother's hospital room.

Looking over at her, he found her still asleep. Tubes attached, and steady breathing. He sat forward resting his elbows on his knees to rub the sleep out of his eyes. He stretched. Looking at the clock, he noticed it was just after five in the morning.

He glanced at the young girl now curled up in the chair beside his grandmother's bed, her head almost resting on the arm of the chair. The position brought him pain just to see her. He wondered why she had been so diligent to stay with his grandmother. Who did that anymore?

He stood and went out into the hallway to find a restroom. He wasn't sure what the day would bring, but he knew a break like this might not come too soon.

Upon returning to the room, Blaine had awakened and was now standing behind two doctors. A few nurses were on the other side of the bed. He'd only been gone a few minutes, but they seemed to be performing a morning check-up. As he entered, Blaine spoke to the doctor in front of her, "This is Callie's grandson."

The doctor held out his hand to him. "Nice to meet you, young man."

Mason took his hand and gave it a good shake. "Nice to meet you."

"I'm your grandmother's doctor. Dr. Park. I think we may have to do surgery today." The doctor backed up a bit, nearly bumping right into Blaine.

He folded his arms. "The MRI showed a major block in two of your grandmother's arteries. It needs to be fixed and soon or she'll probably have another attack."

Mason gulped. "Okay."

"I've done many of these in my career. I'm fairly confident that we can relieve the blockage and get her out of danger with the operation." The doctor looked over at Callie. "Yet, there are always dangers in heart operations like this. Do you know how old your grandmother is?"

Mason raised his palms to the ceiling and shrugged. "Eighty something?"

The doctor was handed a clipboard and he flipped a page. "Well, looks like her chart says eighty-four."

Mason folded his arms. "Sorry. She always hated anyone knowing her age."

Dr. Park laughed. "Yeah, they do that at this age. Well wait," he glanced over at the nurses across Callie's bed, "I guess it is at any age for a female."

The nurses smiled, but said nothing.

"C'mon, ladies, you know I'm right."

One nurse chimed in, laughing, "Always, Dr. Park."

He laughed. "I'm sorry. I think we'll prep her for surgery around 10 a.m. and have her in for most of the afternoon. Can you be here for her when she wakes up tonight?"

Mason nodded. "Yes, I'll be here."

"Okay, then. Any questions?"

Mason felt guilty to say nothing, but he was still trying to get the kinks of sleeping in a chair out of his neck.

He looked over at Blaine. "Do you have any questions, Blaine?"

Blaine shook her head, but then said, "Um, how long will it take her to recuperate from an operation like this?"

The doctor turned to Blaine. "She will probably be in the hospital most of the week. But if all goes well, she can go home in about four days or so. She'll need care once home, though."

Mason couldn't believe what he was hearing. He wasn't sure how long he could take off work. He'd tried so hard to get in good with this company. Calling them just days before Christmas to have more time off might not go so well, but he couldn't leave Nana in the hospital all alone.

"I hate to ask, but what's the worst that could happen?"

Mason looked at the girl who now stood bold, asking the difficult questions he was afraid to ask.

"I'm not worried about the operation, but Callie isn't young. Her age is against her." The doctor looked down at the woman still sleeping.

"My parents are in Africa. Should I call them home?"

"Africa?" The doctor turned to Mason. "That's quite a ways away." He paused for a moment and stroked his chin. "I don't think it's necessary for them to travel all the way home, but warning them of the possibilities should be imperative."

Mason nodded.

"Like I said before," the doctor shifted on his feet, "I've done many of these, but it's harder when I get in there and older arteries are fragile. Unfortunately, anything could go wrong." The doctor looked at Mason. "I'll do my best."

Mason sighed. "Thank you, doctor. She's a pretty special lady."

Dr. Park nodded and looked over at Callie. "I'm sure. She looks like a very sweet woman."

A voice from behind them added, "She really is." Everyone turned to Blaine.

* * *

"Nana?" Mason jiggled Callie's arm. "Nana?" She acted as though she was trying hard to wake up for him. She opened her eyes, but slowly they shut again.

"It's been so hard for her to wake up," Blaine said as she stood on the other side of Callie's bed.

"Must be the medicine." Mason tried once again. "I want to tell her what's happening. She needs to know."

Blaine nodded. "I agree."

"Nana!" Mason spoke louder in Callie's ear. That time it startled her eyes open and she looked right at Mason.

"Nana, listen to me." He knelt closer by her bed. "They have to do an operation." He grabbed her hand. "On your heart. You have a blockage."

Callie looked at Mason with frightened eyes.

Blaine approached the bed from the other side. "Callie, you'll be fine. You're in good hands." Callie turned her head toward Blaine, then nodded.

"Nana, do you want me to call Mom and have her head home?" Mason asked her.

Callie then looked back to Mason and then back to Blaine. Closing her eyes slightly, she shook her head.

Mason added. "Are you sure?"

Callie nodded.

"I think I'll call her and let her know what's happening."

Callie nodded at that and then she turned her head and looked at Blaine. Tears began to fill her eyes.

"Callie, it's okay; I'll stay right here with Mason. I promise."

It must have been just what Callie wanted because she shut her eyes and fell asleep again. Breathing steady, and Mason could see her relax.

"Blaine, I feel horrible." Mason stood up.

"Why?"

"You don't have to stay here with me. I'm a grown man. I'm sure you have much better things to do, places to go." He headed around the bed. "It's nearly Christmas time. I'm sure your family is anxious to see you."

Blaine folded her arms. "Do you want me to leave?"

Mason felt torn. Even though they'd only known each other a few hours, he felt comfortable with her there. He hated being alone, but it was time to stand up and be the man his grandmother believed him to be. "I'm fine. You go ahead and go."

Blaine let her arms drop to her sides. She looked down. "Okay, if that's what you want."

She pushed past him and made her way to her things on the other side of the room. She picked up her purse, slung it up on her shoulder, and pulled up the handle of her luggage. "I'll be going then."

The tug on Mason's heart was true. He didn't know this girl. They were strangers, but she did seem so interested in his grandmother. Was he doing the right thing? On top of that, she was so pretty. He would love to get to know her better.

She stepped toward the bed and bent down to kiss Callie on the cheek. "Goodbye, Callie. I hope your surgery goes well. You're the sweetest woman I have ever met."

Mason's grandmother's eyes fluttered a bit, but she didn't wake up.

Mason watched the girl meander around the end of the bed and head toward the door. Her luggage rumbled across the floor.

As she left the room, Mason turned back to his grandmother, whose eyes were now wide open. The pleading in her eyes made him believe something was horribly wrong. He leaned closer toward her. "Nana, what's wrong?"

His grandmother raised a shaky hand toward the door. Mason turned and looked at the door. Blaine was gone now.

He turned back, and the fear in his grandmother's eyes seemed to grow even more intense. She was trying hard to say something despite the tube in her mouth, yet he could make out one word, "No."

"No what, Nana?"

She shook her head as her shaky hand kept pointing at the door. Mason guessed, "You want Blaine to stay?" She closed her eyes and nodded.

"Okay, I'll go get her." Mason felt guilty as he left the room and headed out into the hallway to try and catch Blaine. This young woman must be very important to his grandmother.

As he headed down the hallway toward the elevator, he reached it just as the doors closed.

* * *

There was no one else in the elevator as Blaine headed down to the lobby. She looked at her phone and dialed the taxi service she'd tried to dial two days before. A woman answered the phone, "Dixie Taxi Service, how may I help you?"

Blaine told her the name of the hospital and asked if the taxi could meet her at the lobby doors.

"We have someone just passing the hospital now. How fast can you get to the lobby?"

"I'll be right there. Give me five minutes," Blaine told her.

As she pushed 'end call' on her phone, Blaine leaned back against the elevator wall. She hated leaving Callie, but Mason was right. She had no right to be there nor did Mason need her. But her last comment to Callie now haunted her. "I won't leave him."

Everything Callie had shared with her came flooding back to her as though it were a replayed movie. All the memories of meeting Miles. Their first few months together. How Callie had waited through the war for him to return, even though she never really knew what condition he would be in upon his return. The comment from Callie's mother about keeping her word. Then having a disabled man come back home. Callie never left him, no matter what others told her about his condition. She couldn't know all the dangers or how he would be, but she never left him.

The tug of war in Blaine's heart wouldn't go away. She thought back to how comfortable and valued she'd felt just the night before. The doors opened to the lobby and she glanced down a hallway toward the entrance. Her cab was waiting at the front door.

* * *

Mason wasn't sure what to do after getting back to Callie's room. It was just a few minutes from seeing his Nana go into surgery. Should he leave her to chase Blaine? He looked back at the doorway to her room. He put his hand on his head. He didn't know this girl, yet for some reason, his Nana felt it important that she stay with her.

He ran back to the nurses' station and motioned that he was going to head downstairs for a moment. The nurse nodded. "I'll be back before my grandmother heads to surgery," he told her.

He rushed back to the elevator and pushed the 'down' button. He pushed it again, thinking it may make the elevator door open more quickly. It didn't. Pacing back and forth in front of the closed door, he started murmuring, "C'mon. C'mon."

The door finally opened and he rushed in and pushed the lobby button just inside the elevator door.

The doors closed.

Once downstairs, Mason rushed into the lobby. All was quiet but the rustle of a newspaper being read by a man sitting in one of the lobby chairs. He looked around for Blaine. He didn't see her or even hear her suitcase rumbling down the hallway. He looked down one hallway, scooted to the next hallway, and looked down another.

He rushed to the front door and didn't see her leaving. He looked around again. Blaine was not to be found.

Mason hurried up to the lobby desk and an elderly woman looked up. "Can I help you?"

"Yes, did you see a young blonde woman come down here?"

The woman nodded. "Yes, she left the lobby a few minutes ago."

Mason sighed. She was gone. He'd missed her by just a few minutes. He patted the desk. "Okay, thank you." He slipped his hands into his pockets and headed back to the elevator to head back up to his grandmother's room.

Chapter 42

Mason wanted to hurry back to the room. He didn't want them taking Nana to the operating room without being with her first. He rushed down the hallway to her room and heard talking. As he came into the room, a nurse was adjusting Callie's tubes and preparing her for surgery. She was talking to someone, and it wasn't his grandmother.

As he made his way back into the room, he saw Blaine's suitcase at the very corner of the room again. She was standing beside his grandmother's bed. He breathed deeply and smiled at her.

"I'm sorry." She looked up nervously. "I just couldn't leave her. If you still want me to leave, I will."

Mason went to her and did something that even surprised him. He hugged her. "It's okay. I'm glad you came back."

He wanted to tell her he'd chased after her, but then the nurse interrupted them.

"Callie will be going to surgery in just a few minutes. If you have anything to say to her, I'd do it now." She turned to leave. "I'll be right back to get her."

Blaine went back to the bedside and picked up his nana's hand. Mason went to the other side of the bed. His nana was wide awake and looking at him. Her eyes now soft and relaxed again. He was so happy Blaine had come back. It was obvious, his grandmother needed her.

"Nana, looks like you'll be going to the operating room soon." Mason rubbed her shoulder. "Can I do anything for you before you go?"

His nana nodded, and put her hands together, as if she were praying.

Mason nodded. "Of course." He looked up at Blaine. "She wants me to pray."

Blaine appeared uncomfortable, but nodded. "Okay."

Mason closed his eyes. "Dear Lord. We'd like to pray for Nana right now. She's going into surgery and it could be pretty serious." Mason stopped a moment to get his shaky, breathless voice under control. "We pray that you will give the doctor's wisdom as they work. Give their hands skill. Guide their work. May everything be done according to Your will. We pray for her safety and care. Give her confidence to trust in You. We'd like to also pray that You'll bring comfort to Mom and Dad when they hear the news. Help me to be wise in making decisions for Nana. And thank You for sending Blaine to be with us today. We thank You for Nana and for all of this, in Jesus' name, Amen."

He looked up from praying to see tears streaming down Blaine's face. He also could see his grandmother smiling up at him with tears in her eyes. He patted her shoulder. "It'll be all right, Nana. As soon as you leave, I'll call Mom."

She nodded.

The nurse came back in and began to put shots into Callie's lines, "She'll be sound asleep soon."

"God's here." Mason added. "She's all set now." Mason added, "Hurry up and get this over with, Nana. Christmas is coming. You're gonna love what I got you."

Callie's eyes sparkled as she closed them, succumbing to the medicine.

* * *

A half hour later, Blaine and Mason were sitting in a waiting room down the hallway. The doctor assured them he'd be coming out to give them a report as soon as he was finished.

Blaine looked so tired beside him. Her blonde hair probably looked as if it needed a good comb. She hadn't had a shower in days. He felt horrible to keep her there.

"Blaine, I hate to think of how long you've been sitting here with Nana. Are you sure you want to stay here with me?"

Blaine shook her head. "I'm not leaving. Callie needs me. You saw her face when I returned. I can't leave."

Mason leaned forward and rested his elbows on his knees. "You impress me. I'm glad you stayed."

Blaine reached up and rubbed down her hair. "I must look horrible."

Mason shook his head. "Actually, I was just thinking you look pretty amazing for having sat here so long. You must be exhausted."

"I'm used to not much sleep. It's all good."

Mason smiled at her. "You have such a great attitude."

Blaine blushed. "No one has ever told me that."

"You do. And look at you."

She looked at him quizzically. "Let's not."

"Why not?" Should he say it? He decided to not wait until he felt more comfortable with her. "You're beautiful."

Blaine looked at him as if he'd said something horrible.

Mason stammered. "I mean. I thought that the moment I first saw you, but even after sleeping in a chair all night. Two nights in a row, I can't believe how beautiful you still look."

The girl began to look away. Had he hurt her feelings.

She stood up and walked over to a window, looking outside. Mason chided himself. He'd said too much too soon, but that's how he felt. She was beautiful. Her slim figure against the snowy outdoors was even more attractive than her face. He could only dream of loving a girl like her someday.

She saw Blaine reach up and appear to wipe her eyes. She was crying. He stood up quickly and went to the window and placed his hands on her shoulders. "Blaine, I'm sorry. I didn't mean to make you cry."

She stammered now among her tears, "No, it's fine." She sniffled loudly.

What would make a girl cry for a man to tell her she was beautiful? He rubbed her shoulders. "I surely didn't think a comment like that would make you cry. Most women love to hear you say that to them."

She wiped at her eyes with the back of her hand. "Most women do like it. I think."

Mason knew he needed to make it all clear right now. Not wait. He turned her to him and hugged her. "I meant every word. You're beautiful. Outside, but especially," he pulled her away and looked into her eyes, "on the inside."

The silent tears now turned into sobs, and the only thing he knew to do was to hug her while she cried. "Why are you crying? I was trying to say something nice."

"It is nice," she mumbled into his shirt.

"Then, what's wrong?"

"It's just that I have never had anyone tell me that before." Blaine pulled away from him again. "I mean, look at me." She motioned down at herself. "I look horrible." She picked up her hair. "I haven't had a shower in three days." She continued wiping her face. "I'm sure my makeup is completely gone. My clothes are wrinkled and stinky, and you tell me I'm beautiful."

Mason pushed his hands into his pockets. "There you go. You must really be."

Blaine started to laugh. "It's just..."

"What?"

"I'm not even trying to impress you, and I am." Blaine giggled.

"You really are."

Mason took her hand and pulled her back to the chairs. "Sit down. I'll go get us some coffee."

"Black?"

"Please."

For the next four hours, the couple got to know one another. She told him about her family and the loss of her parents. She told him about her grandmother and how she'd taken care of Blaine after she'd left her Aunt's house as a teenager.

Mason smiled. He'd never had time for a girlfriend, let alone trying to even find one.

They talked about Chicago and how much they loved the city. They talked about Callie and Miles. Many of the things she told him, Mason had never heard about his grandparents. He was mesmerized by the story just as Blaine had been on the train ride.

The reason they were waiting began to fade away. Hours passed and Mason didn't even notice, until the doctor came back through the doors of the operating room. He headed straight for them.

"Things are going well. I'm just about done. I was wondering if you could give me some information first. Can you tell me when Callie had her last heart attack?"

Mason looked up at the doctor and shook his head. "Her last heart attack?"

"Yes. She's had it fairly recently. It was minor, but I think it wasn't too long ago."

"She's spent the last two weeks with me in Chicago. There wasn't any time really that she appeared to be sick or hurting."

"Well, it's been fairly recent. I can tell there has been recent damage."

Blaine interrupted the doctor, "I was with her the past few days. The only time would have been when she was trying to get to the train in Chicago. She was pretty winded and complained of heartburn."

"That could be it. I'm heading back now. Should be over in just an hour or so."

Mason sat down. "How did you know that?"

Blaine told Mason how Callie and she had met and how she felt bad for Callie trying to get to the train alone, and how she'd gotten off the train to go back to help her.

"I should have never left her alone." Mason raked his fingers through his hair. He then looked over at Blaine. "You wanna hear something ironic?"

Blaine nodded.

"I prayed she'd find someone to help her. I had an important meeting that morning and there wasn't any way for me to stay with her. So, I prayed that someone would be there for her."

"Really?"

Mason nodded. "Really."

"Why did you go back and help her?" Mason reached up and gripped her hand. "That was so great of you to do that for her."

"You know what, Mason, it wasn't what I have done for her; it's really what she's done for me. I'm so thankful to have been a part of her life these last few days. I'm pretty sure it wasn't how much she needed me, but how much I needed her."

"And to think," Mason added, "it might never have happened if you hadn't found her at the train station and helped her. You were the answer to my prayer."

Blaine looked surprised. "Mason, can I ask you something?"

He smiled and nodded. "Sure."

"When you were praying in Callie's room, you finished praying by saying 'thank you for all of this.' That makes no sense to me. Why would you thank God for something so sad happening to your grandmother?"

Mason smiled. "I always thank Him for everything that happens in my life. For the good things and the bad. Because, often the bad things produce good things."

"Good things?"

"Of course. For instance, if I hadn't had that stupid meeting, I would have been at the train station. You would have probably never have sat down beside my grandmother because I would have been in the seat beside her."

Blaine was still suspicious. "Okay..."

"And," Mason continued, "you wouldn't have talked to her because I would have been there. Right?"

"Right, maybe not."

"And she wouldn't have even needed your help getting on the train, because I would have been there."

Blaine nodded. "What does that even mean?"

Mason sat back and shook his head. "Women are so dense sometimes."

Without thinking, Blaine slapped his shoulder. "Stop."

"Without all of this, Nana and I would have never met you. And by the looks of Nana and how she was so upset that you left her today, I think she really, really likes you."

"Okay."

"And above all." Mason got closer to her, like he was going to tell her a secret, "I would have never been able to sit here beside such an amazing girl, getting to know her, and being so happy that I am. All things work together for good. Even the bad things we go through."

"Do you really believe that?"

Mason smiled. "With my whole heart."

For once in her life, Blaine felt she had done something right, and instead of giving her pain, it had brought her great joy.

Chapter 43

Callie came out of surgery just a few minutes later. The doctor told Blaine and Mason that it had gone well. "She'll be sore for a few days, but she should be feeling better real soon." As he turned to leave, he called over his shoulder, "I'd suggest you guys head out and get some good sleep tonight. She'll be in the recovery room for a few more hours and then sleep through the night. You'll be able to see her in the morning."

As they went back to the room, Blaine got out her phone. "I wonder if there's a hotel close by. I gotta get a shower tonight."

Mason agreed. "Let's grab our stuff and we'll go find a place for tonight. I could use a good night's sleep, too."

While they headed upstairs in the elevator, they found a hotel close by the hospital. Mason made and paid for two reservations.

They both grabbed their backpacks, and suitcases, and headed back to the elevator.

"Let's get our rooms, check in, and then we can go out to dinner."

"After a shower, Mason. Please."

Mason nodded. "Okay. After a shower."

***

Blaine loved putting on clean clothes after her shower, she did her makeup, brushed her teeth, and blow-dried her hair. She dug into her purse for her lipstick and applied some before leaving her room to find Mason.

Mason was in the lounge waiting for her. He also appeared to have had a shower. His hair wasn't standing up on end, and he looked very handsome in nice clothes.

She strode toward him. He crossed his arms, and shook his head.

"What?" She must have blushed, because he laughed. Dimple and all.

"I was so right. You're even more beautiful than before."

They'd only really known each other for two days, but it felt as if they'd been friends for years. "Okay, Miles. Let's go for dinner."

"Can we have pizza?"

Mason laughed. "Pizza?"

Blaine grew worried. "Is that okay?"

"It's more than okay; I love pizza."

Blaine sighed. "Good."

* * *

The next morning, the couple left their rooms and met again in the lobby.

"Sleep well?" Mason asked her.

"Like a rock. You?"

"Yes, indeed."

It didn't take them long to get back to the hospital. As they passed the nurses' station, the nurses all looked up at them and smiled.

When they entered, they heard Callie's voice. It was weak, but she was chattering. She no longer had a tube down her throat.

They came in and Callie looked up.

"Well, hello, you two."

Blaine went to Callie's bedside. "You look better, Callie. How do you feel this morning?"

Callie smiled, gradually reaching up to pat Mason's cheek. "Where have you been my whole life?"

Mason laughed. "Right here, Nana. Right here. Now answer Blaine."

Callie rubbed her nose. "Other than feeling like my chest has been pried open and scraped clean, I can breathe so much better."

"But, where have you two been?"

"We got a motel close by, Nana."

"Separate rooms?" Callie's eyebrows rose.

"Yes, Nana. Of course."

Mason looked over at Blaine, who was blushing.

"I was just thinking." Callie looked from Mason and then to Blaine. "I'm rather weak. You'll have to go back home to Chicago for a couple of days to finish up at work, but then you can head home for Christmas. Right, Mason?"

Mason pushed his hands into his pockets. "I'm not sure yet. I haven't called my boss to find out my next step."

Callie's breathing slowed. "I'll need someone to care for me for a few weeks. That's what the doctor told me this morning. Where are we gonna get a care service agency this close to Christmas to come and take care of me?"

Mason nodded again. "Yeah, I'm not sure how we're gonna work that out."

"I do."

"You do, how?"

Callie looked over at Blaine. "I was wondering. Blaine, could you come live with me for a while? You could help me. I'll pay you. Then you could even spend Christmas with us."

Blaine was silent.

Callie spoke up. "Unless your other plans will keep you doing something else."

Blaine shook her head, and tears began to slip down her cheeks. "I need to tell you something." She looked up at Mason. "Both of you."

Mason nodded. "Now, Nana, Blaine might have somewhere else to be. It's Christmastime."

Blaine shook her head. "I have no family. My old boyfriend in Chicago was my only family. The photo I showed you on the train is my high school friend's baby. I'm all alone."

Callie raised a shaky hand and patted the young girl's hand that gripped the railing of her bed. "No you aren't, sweetie. Your family is right here. By the way, I need to finish my story."

Mason shook his head, "I don't think so, Nana. That will have to wait until later."

"Young man, don't tell your Nana what to do." Callie shook her finger at him. "It's just a short explanation."

"What about, Callie?" Blaine asked.

"Miles. Do you remember what the last thing I told you about?"

Blaine nodded.

"He changed. After that episode, Miles' life changed and for the good. But Blaine, I am kinda tired. As soon as I get home, we'll talk more about all that, okay?"

Mason nodded, "I think that's a good idea."

Blaine couldn't believe how her life had changed in just a few short days. Kyle was no longer in the picture, or a threat. Mason headed back to Chicago to finish up at his job. He'd soon be back for Christmas to spend a few days with Callie. And now Blaine, too.

Callie stayed in the hospital four more days and Blaine helped her by renting a car, then driving them the rest of the way to Callie's home.

Callie's home was big enough for both of her visitors. Mason arrived on Christmas Eve.

It was hard to imagine what would have happened if she hadn't helped Callie get to the train. The thought made her heart hurt.

It had all happened like a magical orchestration of sorts. She no longer felt all alone. Mason complimented her instead of chiding her for what she ate or how she looked.

She wished she hadn't spent the last two years allowing Kyle the opportunity to make her life so miserable. The only thing she could do was promise herself that it wouldn't happen again.

Callie was all smiles as she helped her. They made a few preparations for Christmas meals, and Blaine even took some time to run out and purchase some presents for under the tree. Callie's daughter, Amy, had called several times and had even talked to Blaine on the phone, too.

Blaine wasn't sure of her future plans or what she would do next, but at this moment, she felt loved for the first time in her life.

And to think, it all happened on just a train ride.

About the Author

Elizabeth's first book, entitled, **"Under the Windowsill"** is a coming-of-age story about a young woman named Kenna who runs away to Mackinac Island in search of a better life.

Elizabeth's second book, entitled **"Promise at Daybreak"** has a Durand, Michigan setting and is about two elderly sisters who are forced together due to illness. They meet again to fulfill a pact they made at their mother's grave.

For more information on where to find Wehman's books, check out her website at **www.elizabethwehman.com** or like her on Facebook at Elizabeth Wehman/Author for new and upcoming books.

Made in the USA
Lexington, KY
12 May 2019